Floaters

⇜ Floaters ⇝

Tish O'Dowd Ezekiel

New York **Atheneum** 1984

Lines from "Lullaby," "In Praise of Limestone," and "As
I Walked Out One Evening," by W. H. Auden, from
W. H. Auden: Collected Poems, edited by Edward
Mendelson, published by Random House, Inc., copy-
right © 1976 by Edward Mendelson, William Meredith,
and Monroe K. Spears, executors of the Estate of
W. H. Auden.

Library of Congress Cataloging in Publication Data

Ezekiel, Tish O'Dowd.
   Floaters.

   I. Title.
PS3555.Z44F58   1984   813'.54   83-45498
ISBN 0-689-11446-X

Copyright © 1984 by Tish O'Dowd Ezekiel
All rights reserved
Published simultaneously in Canada by McClelland and Steward Ltd.
Composition by Maryland Linotype Composition Co., Inc.,
Baltimore, Maryland
Manufactured by Haddon Craftsmen, Scranton, Pennsylvania
Designed by Mary Cregan
First Edition

With love, this book is dedicated to
JANE SWIGART
RAFE EZEKIEL
BERT G. HORNBACK

Floaters

Floaters are pieces of the retina that have broken off and drift like shadows across the sky. Floaters are the little lights that explode out of the corners of our eyes when we are looking somewhere else.

Floaters are bodies that bob to the surface, that won't stay buried down there in the muck of the riverbed.

~§ ONE §~

No! she said stubbornly and hung on by her teeth. You can't just hack away bits and pieces of me the way they did to my mother's right big toe, her gallstones, and her left breast and, so I hear, a long long time ago, her never-amounted-to-much-anyway sexual organ. Hanging on, my neck, mind, and back became ever so rigid and fatherlike.

He's the one who experienced a series (two) of internal explosions, one of which occurred in his brain, the final one in his heart, but who was carried to his grave one beautiful sunshining September day otherwise and to all appearances quite intact. He wasn't even circumcised, much less castrated. Merely dead. Really stiff and no longer simply metaphorically cold. This was the real thing.

Well, fuck him too and all other stiffs, both living and dead, she said, and fuck yardsticks and measuring worms. I wonder if he guards the inmates of hell. He's dead just like my old dog, Boots, is dead. The only difference is that they buried Dad's carcass in a dark blue suit, whereas the vet just burned Boots's carcass right up, collar and all, I suppose.

My dad was always trying to get me to side with him during the troubles against my mother, against my own sex, against my self. I often did, hoping to please him. Sometimes I tried to stay out of the middle but I don't think I ever took her side. What for?

In what way would two weak losers be any better off than one weak loser standing alone mumbling to herself and wondering how in the hell she had gotten where she was and what in God's name had become of her and the brave little girl who used to go up on the mountain at night with a shaded lantern and food for her older brothers who had to hide out from the English or maybe be shot. How did she become grey and fat and irritable and irrational and bubbling boiling with rage? And why is it happening to me now? What did we do?

She told me once, many times really, about having had to soap her arm up to the elbow when she was a little girl and reach high up into a sow's birth canal to turn a little pig that was caught crosswise, holding up its own birth as well as the births of its brothers and sisters. She had been chosen for the job because, being young, her arm was small and slender. She told me how afraid she had been but how proud she was too when she had done it and the maneuver had been successful.

She told me too that she herself had been delivered by a blind midwife, the same old woman who on earlier and subsequent occasions had delivered her twelve siblings. Relief for the grunting sows.

My birth, she told me frequently throughout my child-hood, had been dry—a hard dry birth—and, again, un-natural instruments had to be used. To hear her tell it, I was dragged screaming from her womb by the metal grip of Dr. Root's forceps about my head. I suffered a black eye in the fracas and she claimed that henceforth her uterus had been tipped, never having managed to right itself after the exertion of expelling me. She also claimed inexplicably to have sustained a considerable hearing loss in her right ear. She described the experience repeatedly as having gone to Death's door in order to give me birth, after having carried me for nine months under her heart. That may account for the confusion in my mind between the womb and Death's door.

This proud slender little girl grew up to become a crazy fat lady who raved wildly and sat on and killed the chickens for family Sunday dinners. She did it in the kitchen with no interruption in the endless stream of words that spilled out of her frequently vicious mouth. Being small then and on the eye level of the poor chicken that was slowly being crushed and smothered beneath my mother's fat ass, I often found myself staring with horror into its bulging eyes and open breathless beak. Usually at the very end a dribble of shit would issue from our soon-to-be dinner.

My Aunt Gerda, my mother's friend, who wasn't really my aunt at all, lived on a farm in Canada and just used to lay her chicken's head on a stump and whack it off with her hatchet. She would set it down then in the pen with the other chickens and let it run around among them until it fell over finally. Then she'd pluck it.

Gerda was more direct and, being German, favored this quicker, more efficient method of dispatching the chicken. My mother, a Celt, to whom time meant little or nothing, didn't care how long her chicken took to die. She had the whole afternoon to devote to it if necessary.

Besides the business with the pigs, my mother often shared another warm childhood memory with me. She told me, long before I was old enough to go to school, how much I reminded her of her favorite baby brother, Michael, who, being vain and the family pet, used to climb up on a chair in order to comb his hair in the mirror and to admire himself. I was so like him—the resemblance so strong—it was like you'd cut the head of him. She followed this account of the eerie similarities between me and my uncle with a lengthy description of him burning up with fever and gasping for breath as he died of whooping cough at seven, an age that I had yet to clear myself. Like the blue jay, he whooped and whooped 'til he whooped his head right off. The fat lady assured me that he had been allowed to receive the Holy Eucharist even though he had not yet been given the usual formal instruction. Oh, I said.

Shit and Death and Blood. No wonder I'm scared. Heaps of pheasants, squirrels, rabbits, their warm guts blown away with their brains by my father's gun, lying behind me on the floor of the car as we drove home in the cold gathering dark of the night. I could smell their blood in the clouds of our breath—the same smell that came from me years later when I started to bleed. Daddy had taken his little girl and his big gun out to the snowy woods to kill all the little furry, feathery warm animals. Daddy's little girl kept very quiet when the gun went off suddenly and blew the startled squirrel from its perch high up in the dark bare trees. Winter-brittle branches snapping as they fell, the squirrels would land in the snow with a soft plop, reddening the whiteness, steam ascending from their soft scattered guts.

I got him! How's that? he exulted. Oh, wow! I said.
But, oh, I thought, their eyes lose their shine so quickly—
before they're even cold. I'll bet his did too. I never got a
chance to look. The doctor, who came to the house that
afternoon where my mother was alone, lost now and
wailing, to say Yes, he's dead all right, had shut up those
cool blue eyes once and for all. That was when, like the
multitude of bunnies who had gone before him, he felt
the sudden final explosion of his heart slamming itself
against his ribs in a futile effort to escape its own pain.

I cried when my brother called to tell me that my
father was dead. He used to pick me up in the twilight
after those long cold afternoons in the woods and carry
me, along with the shotgun and the tattered animals, back
through the deep snow to the car. Boots, excited by the
snow and the blood, ran in wide arcs before us. One spring
he took me on a morning to the apple orchards where he
worked each day before his job at the prison and propped
me up in one of the blossoming trees amid sunny yellow
buzzing bees. To amuse me, he summoned a bobolink
from a nearby field—whistled to it, drawing it nearer
each time until we saw it fly to one of the neighboring
trees. He was magic and frightening and thunderous, full
of anger and lightning, like any jealous god. He seduced
me away from the suffocation of my mother's bloody
womb, claimed me, and named me his name. I was his.
I was like him, I knew him and he saw me and for years
clawed after my heart and, once he had it, carried it, forgotten, like a holy card in the back of a wallet, which is
how I carry his memory now.

My mother, the fat lady with the enormous breasts that
sagged and swung down around her belly button when

she climbed awkwardly over the edge of her Saturday night tub, died only seventeen months after he did. Only a day or two before they cut one of them off, she asked me to apply a Band-Aid to the old clothes-pole wound that had been reactivated by her rampaging cancer. Once, as she was chasing a chicken that she wanted to kill for dinner around the backyard, one of the heavy wooden clothes poles with the two nails on top had fallen and torn into her breast right through her clothing and everything. Now it had started seeping, staining her dress as if she had too much milk. She cried herself to sleep the night before she went into the hospital. I held her and I cried too.

She had nursed me for a few days when I was born but her milk was poison to me. It sickened me and, rather than lose me altogether, they fed me something called Imperial Granum that was very hard to come by during 1943 when the war was still going on, you know. No, I don't recall. It had to be driven miles for by my father, the one with the big gun, who was too busy already. God, I'm sorry. I do remember—yes. Two jobs—always two jobs. Yes, not a word of complaint. Yes, not a word, just the inner tube in his brain exploding finally and the relief, a flood of blood no longer clammed up but flowing luxuriantly everywhere it didn't belong, bathing the grey folds of his brain, soothing them in an action that spoke louder than any words.

One Saturday morning near St. Valentine's Day, he shoveled a new fall of snow out of the driveway. The task finished, he came in and lay down on his bed. Experiencing the nausea that results from the increase of pressure on the brain, he walked from his bedroom across the kitchen floor towards the bathroom. But he staggered and fell, cracking his head hard on the linoleum. Though still conscious, he couldn't get up and lay there with his eyes staring strangely up at me and my mother. I was terrified. The man who had never missed a step, who did indeed work two jobs year after year, who held the known universe together by the strength in his arms and his furious pride in himself as a man, a husband, father and provider, was lying sprawled, nearly insensible, on the cold flowered kitchen floor.

Jesus. I was fourteen and had not even worn out my first bra. I had, however, coolly menstruated a couple of times. It was even turning out that the nuns in my grammar school had been right—I was smart even in the big world of the Protestants and Pinkerink High School. A couple of boys liked me even though I was so tall and my parents had brogues. I had been doing all right and now my father was unable to pick himself up off the kitchen floor and my mother was going crazy. I had been in my room, reading a Modess Press publication that I had sent away for in order to find out all the wonderful things that were going to happen to me any day now that I was a woman and my hormones were on the march. My mother, the woman, my woman, by this time, was carrying on like a lunatic. She was pleading with my father to get up. In his bloody fog, he couldn't fathom what she wanted of him, much less do what she asked.

We pulled and tugged at him. Between the two of us, we finally managed to raise him and return him, like a large addled infant, to his bed. He was nearly unconscious from the pain in his head. When I described what had happened on the phone, the local doctor diagnosed it as flu and recommended lowering my father's feet into either hot or cold water. Even I knew better. A couple of hours later, after a series of complicated phone calls, an ambulance pulled up in front of the house. Two attendants came in with a white flannel blanket, covered him and strapped his body to the stretcher, and wheeled him away into the coma where he was to wander for well over a month before surfacing.

Before they came with all their noise and flashing lights, I was in his room alone with him and he asked me in all that haze whether he had been a good father to me.

◄§ T W O §►

Dig down and bring them out like clams hidden in mud—words, sunlit or grim, that we breathed in before we knew to watch out. Lifting the fine net, whispering down into the cradle, the mother urges, Though my song be cracked and addled, mind the glimmer and draw near.

One May morning a truck delivers dry ice to the dairy next-door. I stand on the gravel in the sun at the rear of the truck while the tall man wearing gloves and white coveralls unloads it and I watch it silent, fuming, its wrath spilling over the sides of its box, tumbling, pouring down, wordless. Though I've never seen it before, I recognize it but don't know what to call it.

Since then I've watched clouds cascading down the gullies of sharp mountains or glowering behind the tops of hills, and once I saw a fog bank so thick it covered over all the rocks and mountains that were all that was left of America from where I stood. The fog left me alone on a small piece of granite whose edges shifted with the tide and whose next neighbor over is Ireland whose edges shift in the selfsame tide.

Mabel did that to her children. She was big—much fatter even than my mother—and she waddled in plaid slippers from one stricken chair to another. Somewhere near the middle of her vast face sprouted a moustache, a black caterpillar that marched whenever she raised her upper lip, and she often did. Her husband was small, though his moustache was bigger and darker, bushy and grand, but still. He worked hard. His name was Tony but Mabel complained anyway. Babies were everywhere; crawling about and mewing like kittens, they ranged over Mabel but she brushed them away. When she stood up to switch chairs, they tumbled from her lap and spilled onto the floor. When Mabel stood up, she blocked the sunlight coming in through the curtains and her curses blocked the light coming in at the door. Mabel had babies like some of us kids had marbles.

The cows in the fields down by the bridge like it better and stand in the slanting evening light in water up to their knees with their black-and-white calves tucked up alongside. Up in the meadow when their calves butt headlong against them, I hear the cows laugh.

I fled to that meadow, to a rock at the edge, a boulder all warm with the sun. My mother, though not Mabel and no swollen river, was raging. It must have been flood tide but later I cried I'm no rock, damn you, though I've been as still maybe as stone.

One Halloween my brother tows me with a rope on a bike with no brakes right into a tree. I howl and blood flows from the gash on my knee. When Mick helps me inside, my mother complains and patches my knee with iodine and a handkerchief from my father's top drawer. A dozen years later, I limp through the door of my co-op with blood on my knee. What's wrong? asks my friend, drinking coffee at the window, the sun all tangled, blond in his hair. I lost my pedal. God, you've been deflowered? With his own clean white handkerchief and a tin basin of warm soapy water, he washes away the dirt and small stones from the road so I love him from then on.

They thickened themselves out against what pushed in on them, my mother and Mabel, padded themselves out with their rage and their fat, and shoved back at the world day after day. Let's squash her, laughed my mother to my father as I lay between them in bed one fine early morning and, damned water buffaloes, they both rolled over together. Their shoulders met above my face and I shoved them away hard. You're all we've got to live for, she assures me later.

You've got cornsilk on your arms, my father whispers in my ear one day, holding me on his lap before he goes off to work.

⊸§ THREE §⊷

What if rummaging around in the mind's dim closets turns up only odd small mittens or a moth-ridden maroon coat, long abandoned and shabby with waiting too long on the hook, out of fashion, embarrassing, demeaning and shapeless, still somehow absurdly jaunty, like a canary feather stuck in a beat-up hat? What if crouching way in the back, the other one is still there, the defiant little homunculus, the perennial fetus, way in under the stairs, glaring fiercely out of the gloom with tiny fiery eyes? What if, spitting and smoking, the wicked baby dragon is still there?

God knows what's there. For a long time I never even knew what was in the steamer trunk in the basement. Down there below the trap door with its steep stairs, it stood up on orange crates away from the wall, away from the damp. Nearby were the winter's potatoes from the summer garden and the spill of apples that glowed in the dim corner light, piled up against the season of cold and stillness when every living thing has been crushed by snow. There it was—the trunk that had crossed the ocean in the belly of the whale that had brought them here to Pinkerink, Michigan, years ago from that county called Kerry that she said was always green and always mild. Next to the trunk stood tall ceramic crocks they had filled with brine for salt pork; you had to fish for it—reach your arm down into the darkness, into the cold, dreading to feel it, dreading whatever else might be down there, slippery and horrible in the stinging sea water they had trapped.

The wooden shelves on the other side of the trunk were filled with row upon row of dusty Mason jars, pears and peach halves impaled by cloves, floating uneasily behind the glass, jars of angry red tomatoes, fizzy, acid, poison, endless bottles of catsup, and cardboard boxes of homemade lye soap, dull yellow like cheap candles, blocks of it, cut and stacked in jagged piles. But in the middle of it all stood that steamer trunk, black and solemn, like a coffin, like a master of ceremonies in a stiff tuxedo, like an evil glassed-in fish swaying through the water with her secret, cutting rhythmic scallops in the dark to pass the nights as she listens for the first invisible crack in the glass.

The fat lady called me downstairs once when she had to get something out of the trunk. I was scarcely tall enough to see over the top of it and the grey winter light, filtering through the dingy basement windows, was too weak to flush the shadows from the corners. When she unlocked the lid and raised it, the vapor of mothballs leapt upward to mingle with the dank cellar air. The blue-speckled paper that covered the removable tray and the inside of the lid was stained with mildew. I was startled. The tray held bars and bars of Camay soap and cheap thin Cannon washclothes, fifteen or twenty of them, no longer new but never used, lots of them and the towels that went with them. It looked just like the bathroom closet upstairs except that these things were musty.

Wrapped up in one of the towels, though, was a flat narrow-necked bottle. She unwrapped it carefully and handed it to me to look at. In the bottle was a beautiful little ship with sails of delicate tissue. Its spars and masts were perfect thin slivers of wood, breath-light as the bones of a butterfly. Against the airless blue sky painted on the inside of one wall of the bottle, the lovely little ship suspended there longed for a wind, and I ached to smash the stoppered bottle on the concrete floor. I couldn't. I couldn't even cry. I just stared at the ship caught in the thick glass. Smiling, she took the bottle from me and, rewrapping it carefully, returned it to the dark corner of the tray. She lifted out the whole tray then and rested it on an old table while I stood on tiptoe to peer into the bottom reaches of the trunk.

More mothballs and blankets. That one, she pointed

out, came from the old country, a white wool one with green stripes. She held it out to me, told me they had wrapped me in it when my father had carried me into the hospital. They wheeled me away on the rolling bed and covered my face and the stinking sweet air they gave me to breathe put me to sleep while they talked and laughed far away all around me.

I woke up in a strange white metal crib. The fat lady was there in the room too. My throat was raw and torn and it hurt when I swallowed. When I screamed it hurt worse but I couldn't stop. Something was awful and I could taste blood. A nurse came and they both smiled at me as I stood screaming behind the bars of the crib. The nurse left and returned carrying a bowl of vanilla ice cream. They came closer, smiling and making soft sounds at me. I took a spoonful of the cool mass, then roared with outrage as it tore, a glacier, down the walls of my throat. Grabbing the bowl, I flung it hard against the wall where it shattered, jagged glass scattering across the floor. Their soft treacherous sounds ceased and I subsided, miserable, into a corner of the white crib. I remembered the white wool blanket with the bars of green running through it.

My mother put it away and, drawing back several layers of ordinary blankets, showed me a package covered with thin shiny brown paper and bound tight with a cord. The package was the size of one of the bricks in the red-brown chimney on the roof. Why would she wrap up a brick and lock it away in this trunk, hidden down here in the base-ment? I wondered whether my father knew she had wrapped up a brick and hidden it down here in the dark beneath all those blankets.

Then she untied the cord and the old paper crackled as

tenderly she lifted out what looked like a chunk of hard-packed dirt. Smiling, she offered me the block of dirt the way the priest on Sunday holds out the wafer that is supposed to be Christ. Was I supposed to kiss it? I thought she had finally really gone crazy. She was always telling me how I got on her nerves, even when I wasn't making any noise at all, at least that I could hear, except my breathing.

She smiled again, urging me to take it, and told me it was peat. Pete and Repeat were walking down the street, I thought. Poor Pete. I wanted to laugh; I was beginning to be scared of her smiling down at me and I wanted to laugh because I was nervous but I couldn't, so I just stood there bewildered and stared at that thing in her hand that I had expected to be worth it, worth being buried there and hidden and quiet and crazy. I always thought she must have gotten something terrific to make up for the way she was with all those fizzy peaches staring out at her there in the basement through dirty glass jars. All she had, then, all that time, in the middle of it all, at the very heart of that damned house, was that crazy lump of dirt. Now I could see, even in that dingy light, that she wanted to cry too but she couldn't either but just said over and over again, It's peat—you can make fire with it, and kept holding it out for me to take. You can make fire with it. It's peat. There's fire in it, she insisted.

◄§ FOUR §►

My brother Mick was seven years older than I was. High-spirited, eager, and strong-willed, Mick often ran afoul of our parents. Whenever he talked back or fought in school or didn't come home for supper or dumped his papers into the creek below our house instead of delivering them or galloped the piebald mare over that idle field by the corner where we caught the bus in the morning, my father and mother would strip him and beat him with a belt. Their voices beat him too. They stood patiently while Mick took off all his clothes, even his underwear, and then they would pursue him through the house as he tried to flee the buckle of my father's belt. Taking turns with the belt and the litany of his sins, pounding him with them, they raised red welts on his narrow shoulders and buttocks. They didn't yell at him; they didn't really even raise their voices. I wanted to kill them but, being small and afraid, I was useless to Mick. My brother never wept but he did cry out whenever the belt hit him. They didn't stop until they were finished.

All those beatings made Mick mean sometimes, and sometimes he was mean to me, though mostly I think we loved each other. Down in the woods by the creek, Mick had dug a hideout; an old door with blistered pink paint that he'd found somewhere concealed its entrance. With all those weeds around it, nobody would ever imagine anything was under that old door, but the space inside was big enough to crawl into and Mick had stashed a few comics and part of an old car seat down there. Once Mick tricked me into climbing into the hole and then slammed down the door on top of me. When I tried to shove the door away over my head, I couldn't because he was standing on it. Mick hollered in through the door that spiders and snakes and worms were crawling around in there in the dark with me. I started to cry. Pushing as hard as I could, I couldn't budge that door. After a few minutes, Mick stopped talking. I figured that he'd rolled a rock onto the top of the door and run away.

I was going to die. No one would hear me scream. The fat lady wouldn't miss me until suppertime and by then I'd have suffocated. Things were crawling on me in the dark. I pushed and cried and called out to Mick but he didn't answer.

Later, when I tried to say an Act of Perfect Contrition, the way you're supposed to if you can't get to a priest for confession before you die, the words got all jumbled up and I cried harder still when I realized I was going to hell on top of everything else. I begged Mick to answer me but I knew he was gone.

After a while, I couldn't cry anymore. I arranged my body so that it would look nice when they found it, if they ever did, like the Little Flower's body and Saint Maria Goretti's, who was stabbed to death by the Italian farmer. Folding my hands on my chest, I stretched out my legs and lay very still, listening to the creek and trying to determine whether it was harder to breathe yet, but then I started to cry again. I didn't want to die. Suddenly branches snapped. I heard running and Mick's loud laughter and now I could shove the door away—he'd been sitting on top of it all that time, listening.

Another time down in the woods, Mick tied me between

two young trees, my right arm and foot tied to one and the left arm and left foot bound to the other. I couldn't twist free; he was much stronger. Gathering dry leaves and dead twigs, Mick heaped them up into a little pile on the ground between my feet and then drew a book of matches from his pants pocket and set fire to the twigs. The smoke choked me. I yelled and swore at him and begged him to let me go but he just added more twigs, one by one, carefully, as if he were roasting a chicken. He didn't look up at me or say a word. He never let the fire get big enough really to burn me though the cuff of my blue jeans was scorched. When he was finished, he laughed and cut me loose with his knife.

Mick wasn't always mean to me. Sometimes he let me keep him company on his paper route. Once when we were cutting through the woods, he asked me to hold up a wire while he tossed the heavy white bag with the papers to the other side. A jolt of current shot through my bare hand and up my arm. That made him laugh too but he explained that it was just an electric fence for cows. When we reached the creek, we stopped, even though his customers were waiting, and made boats out of the newspapers and floated them down the creek. Mick knew how to fold them into sailboats and he showed me how to do it. The phone rang all that evening. My mother was mad and told my father when he came home from work late that night.

When Mick was twelve or thirteen, my parents left us alone one Sunday night during the winter. For a while, we played pinochle at the dining-room table, but then Mick leaned across the cards and started telling me how much he hated me and how he was going to kill me now that our father and mother were gone. I knew from his voice that he wasn't just pretending, but I tried to ignore him and just kept shuffling the cards over and over.

Shoving his chair back so hard it tipped over, Mick brought out from his bedroom one of the heavy quilts my mother made from flannel and flour sacks and scraps of the flowered material she used for sewing aprons. Holding it out like a big net, Mick stalked me, talking softly about how this was his chance—he'd always wanted to do it and now he could because they were gone. He hated me and he'd feel good when I was dead.

I ran then through the house but Mick kept coming after me, cornering me finally in the living room by the green chair. Bringing the thick quilt down over my head and shoulders, he locked my arms against my sides. I couldn't get loose. When I screamed and tried to kick him, he just slid behind me. With my arms pinned so tightly, I could scarcely breathe. His laugh sounded so mean that I believed he really would smother me. Crying so hard made it harder to breathe and soon I stopped struggling. I pleaded with him to let me go but he just kept repeating in a low voice that he hated me.

When he finally lifted the quilt off my head, he knocked me down onto the rug and knelt on my arms and held my wrists and wouldn't let me up until I promised not to tell our father and mother. I swore I wouldn't tell, but I couldn't stop sobbing, and when the car pulled into the driveway I ran into my room and pretended to be asleep so that my parents wouldn't find out. I didn't tell on him because I loved him better than I loved them. I still think he loved me too. It was difficult in that house for anyone to love anybody.

Once after he'd been beaten, Mick ran away from home and was gone for five days. On the second or third night, he scratched on my window screen past midnight when he figured our parents would be asleep. He asked me to get him his black sweater, some food from the kitchen, and some blankets. Our neighbor next door had an old dog-house down at the foot of his property where the woods came up from the creek. The dog had died a long time ago and Mick whispered in through the screen that he was sleeping in Zar's house at night, but he said it was cold. I pulled down the extra blankets from the shelf in my closet and took another off my bed. As quietly as I could, I pushed out the screen at the bottom where it hooked and handed Mick's sweater and the blankets out to him. Skinny and crewcut, Mick looked frightened standing down there shivering in the middle of my mother's flower-bed with white hollyhocks and snow-on-the-mountain all around him.

I tiptoed into the kitchen and gathered together things my parents wouldn't miss in the morning. Their bedroom was just off the kitchen. I was afraid they would wake up and catch me and my brother both, but the fat lady snored away as I opened and closed the cupboards and refrigerator. My father made no sound at all. I put apples and cheese and graham crackers and some marshmallows and canned beans and canned pineapple and an opener into the paper bag that made such an awful racket each time I added something.

Back in my room, I shoved out the screen again and passed the food out to my brother. He made me swear not to tell where he was hiding. As he walked away, carrying the wool sweater and the blankets and the heavy sack,

Mick turned back once and waved, and I watched him until I wasn't able to make out his white T-shirt anymore. Thinking about Mick lying lonely down there in the dark by the creek in that damp smelly old doghouse with the low roof, I couldn't fall asleep again for a long time. My mother's snoring bored through the wall of my bedroom. I hated her and I hated them both because I knew what a dreadful beating Mick could expect when he gave in finally and came home.

So that he could practice more, my brother taught me to bat and catch and play football and basketball. I had to catch or hit whatever he threw, of course, or my face would have been broken, but I got good at it too after awhile and Mick liked that. When he started high school, I used to go and watch Mick play. With his keen eyes, strong cheekbones and fine long limbs, Mick was tall and handsome but, besides, he was better than all the others. He played left-end on Pinkerink's football team. His orange-and-black jersey said number seven and once Mick stayed in the game for an entire quarter after his leg broke below the knee when he was tackled. My parents were angry when the coach brought Mick home that night with pain in his blue eyes and a full cast on his leg; they thought it was all foolishness and never once went to see him play even though he started all four years on both the football and basketball teams. Mick played center on the basketball team and one night he scored forty-one points. I never missed his games and left the house early so I could walk to the gym with him. He made me walk on the inside and, in the winter, he'd turn up the collar of my coat against the wind. It was beautiful, splendid, and, along with the rest of the crowd, I yelled until my throat hurt whenever Mick leaped high into the air to catch a pass or to sink one of those long stupendous jump shots that never even touched the rim.

Mick also drank and smoked and chased fast girls all during high school and he frequently fought fiercely with my father. My mother set them at one another. She was jealous whenever either of us got along with my father; I suppose she felt shut out.

As soon as Mick finished high school, he joined the army and left me there alone with the two of them. After basic training, the army sent him to Germany and for two years he never wrote letters home, but once, when it was my birthday, a package came from him. He had sent a thick coloring book and a big box of forty-eight crayons. I was twelve and I never colored anymore but I was glad to get them because I missed Mick a lot. The house felt sad and bleak without him there.

⇜ FIVE ⇝

Frank Spumone was killed right in the middle of our Thanksgiving dinner. My mother had just carried the turkey in from the kitchen on the big blue platter so that my dad could carve it. Turkey was one of the few things my mother really knew how to cook, that and stuffing. This one looked wonderful with the skin all crisp and brown and it was huge and the rich warm smell of it basted the room and all our souls for once. After grace, my father started to dismember the bird, slipping me choice bits of skin on the blade of the big knife. He and I were the only ones who ate skin; no one else liked it.

My brother and I had set the table early that morning with the matching rose dishes from the back of the cupboard. Mick had put an extra leaf in the table and I had smoothed the white Irish linen cloth over it. My grandmother had sent over the tablecloth when my father and mother were married. My mother saved it for good. It was hard to iron because it had to be dampened the night before and wrapped in a towel and the iron had to be so hot that it was easy to scorch the raised figures of flowers and birds. My mother only used it two or three times a year because she'd had it so long and her mother was dead now. She didn't want anything to happen to it.

Mick and I were passing around the bowls of gravy and mashed potatoes and canned peas and the other dishes when the phone rang. My mother came back into the dining room with the skirt of her flowered apron caught up in her hands, half-covering her face the way I'd seen her play peek-a-boo with the little baby across the street. Only she was crying and kept sobbing Frankie, oh Frankie, over and over.

My father laid the carving knife down and asked what in the hell was the matter with her now, but I could see he was scared. She took the apron away from her face and held it out before her as if she were using it to carry vegetables in from the garden, but there wasn't anything in it. Tears were cutting vicious streaks down her soft cheeks and she screamed at my father, Frank Spumone is dead, Frankie is dead. That made my father angrier still. What the hell are you saying? You mean Paul—Paul is dead.

Paul Spumone was Frank's father. He was deaf and had beautiful white wavy hair. He also had cancer and had left the hospital a few weeks earlier so that he could die at home. He waited now, day after day, propped up in the rented hospital bed that stood in the middle of the living room. Often he was in a lot of pain. Sometimes he groaned out loud and his daughter Pat and I would stop playing to listen. We wondered whether he could hear himself or knew he was making noise.

But my father had heard her right the first time, just as we all had. My mother told him, weeping, and with the turkey getting cold and fat collecting on the top of the gravy, that Frank had gone out for a drive in the country before dinner and that somehow he'd been killed. That was all the sheriff who had come to the house had told Mrs. Spumone. My dad swore again but pulled on his overcoat and brought my mother's coat out of the closet for her. She put it on right over her apron and they walked out of the house to go to the Spumones.

Our two families were best friends. The Spumones were immigrants, too, and Catholics and Democrats like us here in this small Protestant Republican town of Pinkerink. Their family was all spread out, with nearly fifteen years between Frank and my friend. His little sister came at the tail end, way after the others and was named, like me, after my father. Her middle name was Ann for my mother. Being Catholic, our parents took what God sent whenever it struck Him to send one. My mother had had trouble getting pregnant—a doctor once told her that she was infantile-built—and she had miscarried twice before giving birth to Mick. As it was, Pat and I had been sent to old tired menopausal mothers who didn't always seem to remember what it was they were supposed to do with us.

Frank and his brother Vince had both been in the war.

Vince was very handsome and had his father's curly hair. He played basketball in high school and, after he came out of the navy, he went to college and became a coach. Vince always made jokes and everybody liked him but Frank was everybody's favorite. Frank's hair was just brown and straight and he had a big Wop-nose. He'd always been burly and a lot quieter than Vince, even before the war.

Every Sunday while they were gone, my mother and Mrs. Spumone had lit little candles that flickered inside the rubycolored glass before the Blessed Mother's altar. Mick, my mother's only son, was too young for this war so she said rosary after rosary to help Mrs. Spumone pray her two sons home and it worked because, one at a time, they did come home.

Still brash and dazzling in his white uniform, Vince came first and laughed and picked up his mother and kissed her, tears and all, and teased her until he made her laugh and then she cried some more but she was happy that her beauty was home again. But Frank got hurt. He lost an eye, which the government replaced with a glass one, and under his scalp there was a metal plate the army had issued him to compensate for the pieces of his skull that had been torn away. When he first came home, he had to walk with a cane for a while. His mother cried for real when she saw how battered Frank was.

Nobody ever saw Frank's uniform again. He dug out the old brown leather jacket he'd always worn in high school and started helping out in his family's confectionary store down on Main Street. They sold beer and wine and penny candy and ice cream and comics and trays full of chocolates in the big oak-and-glass cases. There were wooden booths at the rear of the store but in the summer Pat and I would move from the back booth into the big walk-in cooler and sit on cases of beer and look at comics. When his father wasn't watching, Frank would sneak us grape and orange popsicles under his shirt when he came to fill the orders for beer.

Frank had come home just in time for Christmas three or four years earlier. He had burst into our living room when we were opening presents after Midnight Mass. I was trying on a new pair of skates that had shiny little bells jingling on their toes when he came in. My mother cried and my father swore and they both hugged him a lot. His mother and Paul followed Frank into the room and everybody hugged everybody else some more. Frank shook hands with Mick and slapped his back, then scooped me up, skates and bells and everything, and glared at me with his new eye. Burying my face in his neck, I could smell the cold and snow he had brought in with him and the old cracked leather of his jacket. I had prayed more for him than for Vince, even though Vince was more handsome.

The next spring out near the pink crap apple tree on the playground, Mixie Hurlbut teased my friend Pat about her brother's glass eye and made her cry. I hated Mixie for it and swore at her and scratched her arm. She told the nuns, so I was sent over to the church alone to pray.

So they were both home but Frank's head still hurt him for a long time, even after he no longer needed the cane, and his mother told my mother that Frank often couldn't sleep at night. When his father got so sick, Frank took over the store altogether. Vince was away at college but Frank said he didn't want to go anywhere anyway, so he'd do it. Since he couldn't sleep much, he'd lie out in the living room on the couch to keep his father company. Frank and his father had always been close—maybe because neither of them counted much on language. His father didn't need Frank to be witty and quick like Vince. Paul loved him because Frank knew a lot about pain and about silence. Frank kept his father company now while he waited, just as he used to keep him company evenings out in the vegetable garden behind the house where Paul raised his eggplants and cucumbers and tomatoes, and through all those years of long days and nights down at the store.

My father loved Frank too but told him he was too serious, that he was still young and should go out and have a good time for himself—find himself a girlfriend and take her out dancing or to a movie like other young men his age.

Now Frank was dead. Frank had given a ride to the two Raymond boys who sometimes helped out at the store. The older one, Buddy, had begged Frank to let him drive the big Oldsmobile and Frank had given in even though the boy had no license. Skidding on a curve, the kid lost control of the car. The passenger side slammed into a tree and Frank was killed outright. Buddy and his brother were only shaken up. They managed to walk to a farmhouse and the sheriff was called. My mother said they all had a terrible time down at the house getting Paul to understand and that finally my dad had to write on a piece of paper that Frank was dead. Paul wept and kept asking why God hadn't taken him, a dying old man, and left Frankie. Nobody knew what to say to him.

After my parents left for the Spumones', my brother

and I stared at each other across the big table. I started to cry, imagining Frank cold and still and gone and in a hole in the ground where I'd never see him again. Mick swore at me and told me to shut up or he'd hit me. I couldn't stop and he threw a stalk of celery across the table at me. It hit me across the face and made me cry harder and soon I couldn't see or think right I was crying so hard, so frightened and angry that Frank could be dead. Then, like crazy people, my brother and I tore into the plates full of food and flung fistsful of potatoes and turkey and cranberry sauce at each other's heads. Before we stopped there was food all over our clothes and the floor and walls, and the Irish tablecloth was stained with gravy and cranberry juice.

⋘ S I X ⋙

I called Pat and Alice Clampitt, the two little old gnomes who lived down the street, Grandpa and Grandma when I was little but, of course, they weren't. Three of my real grandparents were dead; I'd never seen any of them except in photographs. My dad's father was still alive when I was young but, like my other grandparents, he'd always lived in Ireland.

My father and grandfather never wrote to each other. My grandfather had wanted my father to stay home to take care of the farm. My grandfather's oldest son, Joseph, had already been swallowed up by America and Michael, who had been studying for the priesthood against his father's wishes, was dead from typhoid. That left my father, but he walked away from the old man too—left him standing there at the end of the lane, his fists knotted, cursing this last son who caught the boat in Cork three days later and sailed for America to join Uncle Joe and their sister, my Aunt Julia. Sometimes my father sent money back to his other sister, Kitty, who did stay behind with her father but I don't think he ever sent a letter. He never got any response from the old man. My grandfather lived to be very old, but still he died before I managed to get there.

My grandfather was fierce and stubborn. He raised horses and traded them and, before he was even thirty, my grandmother died, leaving him with five babies. Four months after my father was born, my grandmother lay hemorrhaging from a miscarriage and nobody could make her stop. That was the end of her. She wasn't thirty yet either. She bled to death quietly, slowly, the way a pig does when its throat's been slit.

My Aunt Julia, who was eight when her mother died, told me that the priest came down to the house where the women had laid out my grandmother and led the rosary that night for the repose of her soul and, two days later, in the rain the priest buried her in the yard of his grey stone church. Then he mumbled something to my grandfather and the five children about the will of God and turned his black back on them and walked away through the wet morning to the rectory, where the old woman who kept house for him had his rasher waiting.

My grandfather gathered his children up out of the damp and started home. Carrying two of them, he led the others down that long lane to the low thatched cottage. The fire gone out, it stood, bleak and silent, grey too, like the waters of Dingle Bay that gnawed at the edge of my grandfather's pasture.

Men and women came, Aunt Julia said, and built up the fire again. Holding the children on their laps, they cut and buttered thick slices of bread for the older four, and sprinkled extra sugar into the strong milky tea so that the sweetness might make them forget for a minute to miss their mother.

In the evening, my father having been fed by the women and laid in his cradle, the snuff plate was passed among those drawn up to the fire. The friends sighed and sought to console my grandfather who said nothing at all, not even raising his head when they spoke. He held my Aunt Julia next to him all evening, long after she grew sleepy from the heat and from the day. When they all left him finally to walk back through the wet fields to their own houses, my grandfather carried Aunt Julia to her bed and covered her. She awoke the next morning to my father's hungry cries and stumbled out, still in her new black dress, to warm the milk her father brought in for the baby's thin porridge.

A week later, my grandfather drove the bay horse and the cart to Tralee and fetched home his aunt, a maiden lady who had been a schoolteacher. Toward nightfall Aunt Julia, hearing the wheels on the gravel, ran out just as the mare drew up before the door. There the spinster sat. All her belongings were piled up behind her in the cart, shrouded against the drizzle by an old tarp. The woman nodded grimly at my aunt. Her child's heart aching for the tall lovely woman who was dead, Aunt Julia began to weep, but my grandfather hushed her and handed her down a cardboard suitcase from the back of the cart to carry into the house.

For the next decade and a half, until she too died, this thin parched woman, with neither cruelty nor love, kept the house clean and the children clean and fed and clothed while my grandfather worked his fields and drove his horses to the neighboring fairs. The woman had come so that the children might not perish altogether and dourly she held them fast to life.

She taught my father his prayers and, when the time came, she taught him to read. She took no joy in any of it and, whenever my father spoke to me of the woman who raised him all those years, he said only that she was a good woman and had done her duty as she saw it, but the rosaries he fingered, day in and day out, up in that silent tower at the prison where he worked were not for her but for his own mother, and the Masses he bought three or four times a year were for the tender laughing young woman Aunt Julia remembered for him, not for the dutiful spinster who had set out to do God's work and had done it. He reached back instead somehow through all that blackness, just as I do now, for the warmth of that dead woman's hand.

My father's heart had been gashed and his father, himself bereft, was little use to him. My grandfather never remarried and, more and more, he relinquished his children and his home to the solitary woman who knew only to scour them. With his sons, he was often quick-tempered and harsh, though rarely with his daughters.

One afternoon years later, sitting alone outside in the quiet spring sunshine, his long back propped against the rough outside wall of the cottage, my grandfather drank his customary pint of porter. Wiping the foam from his moustache then with the back of his hand, he carried the empty tankard to the table inside, walked over to his bed and lay down easily and died. My Aunt Kitty wrote that my grandfather died so easily that afternoon that the priest wasn't able to hear his confession or to administer the Eucharist. The priest had to content himself with merely anointing my grandfather's body, which was stiffening already beneath the chrism as it cooled.

The letter from my aunt reached my father two days before his birthday. My father seemed startled that the old man had actually died. Digging into the box beneath his bed, he pulled out the creased snapshot of my grandfather that had been sent from Ireland years before. In a ramshackle jacket, Grandpa leaned his long body against a fence, his moustache bristling and his big fists still clenched. My father stuck the photograph into the lower left-hand corner of the picture frame that held my grandmother's formal portrait where it hung in our dining room. It had been taken in Australia where she had gone at eighteen to visit her uncle who was an archbishop in Sydney. My battered granddad seemed a poor match for the young woman with elegant cheekbones whose head was piled high with abundant auburn hair. The following Sunday, for ten dollars apiece, my dad bought High Masses from Father Himmel for the two of them.

My other grandfather's moustache was bushy too. In one of the pictures that my mother kept stuffed inside an old album in that same cardboard box, her father posed before the whitewashed wall of their cottage. Her mother's hair was drawn back from her soft round face and, in her dark apron, my other grandmother stood next to my grandfather's chair. His big hands were spread out on his knees and the thick moustache covered his broad upper lip. This other grandfather of mine wore a wool cap with a snapbrim and his clean white shirt was buttoned all the way up, though he wore no tie. They were like boulders, the two of them, that had rumbled down the side of the Slieve Mish Mountains one night and come to rest there in the morning sunlight before the door of the cottage. Like my other grandparents, these two stood over six feet tall, but they were lucky and not stricken like the other two.

I would search their faces for some sign that I belonged to them and, squinting, peered past my grandmother through the open door into the dusky interior where my mother and her multitude of siblings had been drawn shy and reluctant into the firelight by the blind midwife who, once every year or so, came and lay all night alongside my grandmother on a pallet beside the fire my grandfather fed with chunks of peat to drive off the chill and the damp that also reached for the babies as they tunneled out, fleeing the shuddering tumult of the womb.

These grandparents were fortunate. They lost only two boys to the clammy winters. A healthy infant of two weeks was carried one drizzling February to the stone church to be baptized. He returned in his damp christening robes, free finally from Original Sin, but incubating the pneumonia virus that killed him by the end of the following week. Four winters later, his older brother, Michael, then seven, succumbed to whooping cough. For the first and last time, Michael saw snow that winter and, telling me, my mother laughed, remembering his delight. The snow was so soft and thick falling, she said, it hid the mountain behind their house, and below them, the bay disappeared.

The others reached adulthood and beyond. Except George, the eldest, all had children of their own.

I missed the firelight. My great-grandmother O'Connor spoke only Gaelic and sat nearest the fire. She knitted stockings and sewed shirts from flannel for the babies and kept them from falling into the fire. She taught my mother to pray and to count and to curse in Gaelic and showed her how to knit. My mother showed me.

When I was young, if ever my mother had too much to drink, she would weep for her lucky father with his bushy laughter and loud morning whistling, and I'd turn away from those tears for that dead man, leave her there alone and go away to bed. Now it's my turn.

I've been trying for years now to tell someone my father is dead—my mother too—that it's all over now and they can never tell me. My father is dead. Desolation rolled him over on top of my mother one night and summoned me from blackness. What turned him away from his radio that night, rolled him over the way a child rolls a caterpillar over with one finger to watch the desperate wiggling of its millions of feet? Why did he shiver half of me into her? Did he hate her then because he was more lonely? Or did he love her for a minute because he forgot, forgot his own mother who'd had no chance to tell him? Did some kind of love send half of me swirling upward, seeking the other half that waited in the silence?

Nobody knows how uneasy it makes me that he's dead. Twice or three times he looked at me and I thought in a moment he'll tell me. Open your mouth and say ahh and, baby bird, anxious communicant, I'd open my mouth and he'd lay a pat of butter sweet upon my tongue and take away the knife so softly I hardly felt it as the butter melted in the heat of my mouth and trickled down my throat.

When my father came home between jobs to change his clothes and to clean up, I balanced on the edge of the bathtub to watch him shave and handed him the towel when he was finished. Then he held me on his knee while he ate his lunch, let me part his hair in the middle and laughed when I made him look like Hitler. Listening to the noon news, he stretched out on his back on their bed and I lay tucked in his arm, my ear against his chest listening, listening to his heart beat over and over, trying to hear what it said but I could never quite make it out and finally, one day it thrashed about madly, then stopped altogether as he lay stretched out on his back on that same bed.

But he held me back then and I kept very still so I wouldn't bother him and he wouldn't get up and go away again, so I held my breath, but he always did, but he always came back. He always did that.

Sometimes he would flip a fifty-cent piece for me up into the air and over and then back down again from the back of his wrist. There was a tendon that snapped when he twisted his fist just so and up it would go and the eagle would fly and come to rest again and we'd laugh because I thought he was so wonderful and he knew how much this child born of his damned sadness loved him. He was gentle with me sometimes when I was little because I was born so late and he was so old by then.

In the morning in their bed I slid down him and around him, down the heavy quilts, down the mountainside he made for me with his knees and I had no respect for him

and I fell down onto his chest and rested against him
before I knew better and couldn't hear so well what his
heart said to my ear as I listened, pretending to be dumb
and a child.

I can't tell people when I say my father is dead. His
long stride is gone and the blue eyes are closed away from
me. He smoked a lot and his voice was as rough and warm
as the red-and-black wool of his hunting jacket. The first
two fingers on his right hand were yellow from nicotine
and the nail of the first one was split in half and always
grew in that way. When he picked me up when he came
home at noon, he smelled of apples or like the cows on
the farm. For seventy-five cents an hour, he milked cows,
cleaned the barns and pruned trees, and picked and sorted
apples, then crushed the bruised ones into cider for someone rich.

On days he took me with him, I followed after him,
after the tall black rubber boots that landed so far apart
I had to jump from one hole in the snow to another, both
feet together, or I'd lose. On the way home at noon, when
we came to the top of the hill by the cemetery, he'd shift
the car into neutral so we'd coast and he held me on his
lap and really took his hands off the wheel and let me
steer the car as it rolled down the hill toward town.

I was company for him and I wouldn't cry while I was
with him. I think he liked me. A piece of bleakness broke
off from that void and wove itself back and forth like a
Christmas potholder in and out of my soul. He recognized
the breed and held me some when he could but he was
lonely too.

But I know I'll never see my father again, whereas
mostly my mother expected to see hers again in heaven.

One night though, after Christmas, a little more than a
month before she died, she asked me in the kitchen, after
everyone else had gone to bed, whether they ever really
know when they cut off your breast if they got all the
cancer, and then she asked me point-blank whether I
thought there was a heaven. I'd had quite a bit of beer and
thought I lied skillfully but she cried anyway because she
knew. She was terrified of the surgery before her and for
once I wasn't cruel and didn't leave her there. That night
her truculent pigheaded faith abandoned her; she knew
herself extinguishable.

I wanted to shield her the way you don't want a child
whose soul is so vulnerable to know how really bad it is,
and you wait until they've grown up a little before you let
on. You make sure they care first and you stand aside, a
bit at a time, to let them really see. I wanted so much to
lie so well she'd never dream I ever doubted, but she
wouldn't believe me because I wasn't good at lying to her
about anything when she just asked me right out. Since
I was little I'd wanted to tell the truth and to know right
from wrong. When you're six and reach the age of
reason, they say from then on it's all your fault, whenever
you do wrong. In the supermarket, my mother would hand
me grapes to eat and, whether I ate them or not, I was
always ashamed and wanted to die.

I add their lives up on two sides of the sheet—the good
things and all the rest that's just heartbreaking and stupid,
that makes you want to turn away your head. All these
accident victims. How did it happen? You don't say—
Jesus! You just keep moving the stakes, keep including
more and more possibilities so you won't be surprised
when it happens.

I drag their poor dead bodies after me. I try to reach down and shake them, make them tell me, make them save me. What did they do but die and leave me here? I never saw them get the middle part. They were old and worn by the time I came. It was already over for them. They were beaten and, even so, they let me be born knowing they were whipped. All I got is goddamned sadness.

I inherited exhaustion, this warp of desolation, the loneliness God poured over my head when He baptized me. Is that how He makes sure we love Him, or at least miss Him, or at least hate Him? Is that why He creates loss, why He kills people just when we find some way to love them?

It makes you a niggard. It makes you scared like that shell-shocked guy, Art Terry, who lived next to the Spumones. He was permanently rattled. It was all too much. Pop bottles opening and cap-guns terrified him just like the real thing and, if you startled him, he began to shake just like before when he had seen and heard things so bad it fried his brain and he was lost because it was too much and he couldn't take it. He was lucky. His mother lived to be an old lady and she took care of her frightened child-man nearly forever the way Doug Cronk's mother took care of him for fifty years after he came out of her with his brain mangled by whatever he'd seen there in the shadows of her womb. Doug used to come to the baseball field to watch practice and he'd turn his Panthers cap backwards and make loud noises and try to have opinions about the season. It was no good.

I got a lot of it second- and even third-hand, but I got it nonetheless. I flinch and hunch my shoulders waiting for it to happen. It makes me anxious to get it over with, to have done with it, to be told once and for all. It's hard. You can't ever seem to forget any of them for very long.

ᵉ⳹ SEVEN ⳼ᵉ

They splattered like acid on my soul and my courage was eroded by all those deaths, by the litany of the dead that you could start anywhere and never finish—my mother's oldest nephew, George, named after my grandfather and killed like my father's oldest nephew, Joey, in a war. In return for their sons, their parents received telegrams, medals with ribbons, and bronzed coffins and big American flags. The boys' photographs (8 x 10 and nicely framed) stood atop the closed caskets. Nobody really knew whether the right body or really any body was inside because nobody had the guts to open the damned things up to find out for sure because they didn't want to have to wonder where their kids really were.

George and Joey were first-born sons, full of promise, handsome, well-loved boys who should have had long good lives but instead were broken casually, like kindling against the knee. Aunt Dora and Aunt Mae, numb and moaning, stared in their living rooms at the ugly coffins shrouded in flags. What did they have to do with their soft babies, their boys, their shining young men?

The folding wooden chairs brought over from church halls for the rosaries and the wakes filled up with uncles and aunts and more cousins, some of them in new uniforms, with neighbors and friends who brought casseroles and cakes to feed the mourners. Joey's mother, Dora, though she had twelve more children, had only the one Joey and my Aunt Julia sat beside her and held onto her hand while my Uncle Joe, Julia's brother, drank whiskey with the men in the kitchen, away from his son's coffin.

Aunt Julia had already lost both of her children, a boy named Jack who was ten, and a girl, Sheila, who was eight, within a week of one another to influenza—she had returned home from the first funeral to find the second child feverish. Aunt Julia never had more children after that. She drank too, always; though she was never drunk, she was never sober either.

My father loved his sister and usually spent his day-off talking with her in the darkened living room where Venetian blinds closed out the sun and Julia sat in the plush maroon chair with her hair drawn back tight in a bun at the nape of her neck. She was tall and slender and wore beautiful dark dresses made of crepe that lay in folds upon her still body. Her features were sharp and her eyes watchful though she seldom said much, even to my father who loved her.

Her husband, my Uncle Dan, spoiled me when I came with my father, poured me glass after glass of Dr. Pepper, read me the funnies, tickled me until I laughed so much in that dusky room that my Aunt Julia would beg him to stop. Uncle Dan gave me money when I was going home, folded up into little squares that he would slip into my hand when no one was looking.

Aunt Julia twice or three times a year baked devil's food cakes with marshmallow icing for the kids at St. Francis' Orphanage and bought ice cream and took it all there and spent the day with the kids, looking at them and hearing them, but mostly she sat sunken into that chair and drank whiskey neat and didn't say much. She died quite young finally of pneumonia, but really she drank herself to death my father said.

Uncle Dan died ten or fifteen years later, all alone one day, of a heart attack. My mother never liked Aunt Julia, probably because she was so dark and scary and quiet. My mother always said my father's whole family was black and gloomy.

Many years later, I met my dad's other sister, Kitty, in Ireland. I visited her in a little cottage a few hundred yards from where my dad was born at the foot of the Slieve Mish Mountains where the water of Dingle Bay reaches up, almost to the doorstep. Sometimes the water reaches even farther. Aunt Kitty, who's old and crippled with arthritis now, told me that once, years ago, she had stepped out of bed during the night only to find herself in water up to her ankles. She said she screamed, thinking she was standing in the chamber pot, but it turned out only to be the ocean.

On top of the television set that her son Seamus had brought home from Tralee for her to watch, along with the framed photograph of our murdered President Kennedy, God rest his poor soul, stood several old photographs. My grandmother was there as a young girl of maybe fifteen, well before she had married my grandfather. She was so beautiful, suspended there forever in her youth, an apple blossom adrift in crystal. She was so beautiful; in my two aunts, even now in this old one, I could see traces of the fine bones and clear eyes of her open young face.

My aunt told me that, enjoying his pint and his shot each day right up to that bright April afternoon, and with no sickness or forgetfulness, my grandfather had reached ninety-six. A fine age, she nodded. The same picture that we'd had at home was there beside my grandmother's— the old man with boundless fury in his two fists, leaning lightly against the wooden rails of a fence.

Aunt Kitty's dead husband was there too and a seven- or eight-year-old little girl. My aunt asked me to hand her the picture of the little girl and she kissed it and wept and held it out to me to look at and told me it was little Mary who, like her childless sheepish brother and his quiet barren little wife, would probably have been almost fifty by now if she had lived, but she hadn't. God it was awful, and her, my aunt, rigid with her arthritis and with still more old tears running down her damned old cheeks like all the rest of them.

She spoke then about her younger brother, my Uncle Michael, whose keen eyes at nineteen had been a blazing blue, not at all like these poor faded things, she said, wiping her own with a corner of her dark apron. He was a great reader, but typhoid had killed him in my father's arms just before my father sailed for America. My brother is named for him.

My other uncle, Joseph, Joey's father who had twelve other children on Dora, was dead by the time I met his sister in Ireland. Uncle Joe died of a heart attack three or four years after taking a mistress for himself and moving out of the house he had shared so long and so unhappily with Dora, who became a nagging, whiny, shrewish woman as her children grew so numerous.

My dad was ashamed of this brother and never spoke

to him after my uncle took up with that woman. Dad brought bushels of potatoes and other vegetables from our garden to Aunt Dora and, in the wintertime, he paid for loads of coal to be delivered to her house.

Soon after Uncle Joe moved out of his house, he came to our house one Saturday to help my dad plaster the ceiling in our kitchen but my dad never came down off the ladder or acknowledged his presence and after a while Uncle Joe left, and he never came back. I used to see him sometimes as I was growing up if, by chance, I happened to go to Mass in Meckleton, where he lived. Several Sundays we stood together by the open doors in the vestibule of the church. Uncle Joe always inquired about my dad. One Sunday I was on my way to the lake with friends and was wearing only my bathing suit under my trench coat and he thought that was pretty funny.

Neither of us took communion on those Sundays. I didn't even when I could have because I knew he couldn't. Their mother had turned his own kids against him by that time—certainly all of his daughters—and, like my father, most of them never spoke to him anymore.

My dad wept a few years later when he knelt down at the side of Uncle Joe's casket to pray for the repose of his soul. I was scared. I'd never seen him cry and I was afraid he would die too if he cried. Aunt Julia as dead by then and now so was Joe, the poor boy-o.

God, how they piled up one after another. Finally, my father, his heart breaking, did die. He left us to go to them—his beautiful young mother, his rusty father, his brothers, the sinner and the burning uncorrupted youth, his sad, quietly soused sister and all his blighted nieces and nephews. He burrowed down into the quiet of the earth past their sorrows, past his own, burrowed through the sad darkness back into the blind litter warmth that knows and remembers not even a name.

⋙ EIGHT ⋘

After a particularly bitter quarrel of our own, I hadn't seen my brother for a long time, but he called sometime ago at one in the morning because he was drunk. He and Mary Baggett, a cousin newly arrived from Ireland, had been drinking champagne all night so Mick missed me and wanted to tell me that he loves me but that I am a whore but God bless me. This took him nearly three hours because he repeats himself a lot when he's drunk. Then too, when he's drunk, sparks of his own anger dazzle him and he follows them like a child pursuing fireflies until they fade into the black of his mind. Then he can't remember how he got there all alone, sad in the dark, and he gropes his way back by evoking a mythical sunlit past we supposedly shared. Often he lies.

When Mick called, I had been asleep for over an hour. My husband and everyone else in the house were sleeping too so I grabbed the phone quickly. Mick's voice snatched at me out of the darkness and dragged me back into the land of the wobblybears where I was raised. Until nearly daybreak, he took great swipes at my mind with those big paws of his, all the time drooling honey from his black jaws. I hung up on him once but the phone rang again right away so I let him finish, knowing I probably wouldn't hear from him again for more months. Besides, it was fascinating the way watching your head tumble into the bloody wicker basket must have been fascinating if you'd just been guillotined.

Like a witch in a dunking pond, I endured anathemizings and redemptions that night that left me breathless. Once while he was catching his own breath, Mick told me that my Aunt Gerda had died the previous winter. I thought about her as he resumed his examination of my conscience, ignoring and outraging, as was often the custom in that family, the delicate layers of tissue and experience that separate soul from soul in this world.

Aunt Gerda lived most of her life in Canada and was one of my mother's oldest friends. Born in the south of Germany, she had emigrated, like my mother, at nineteen or twenty. Gerda and my mother met soon after they arrived, when they went to work as maids in Buffalo for some rich people named Potter.

My mother went to Buffalo when she came out from Ireland because she had a couple of bachelor uncles there who ran a blind pig during Prohibition. Two of her brothers, my uncles Will and George, as well as her older sister, Philomena, had come out before my mother, but she stayed with her two uncles until she found work and moved into the small room under one of the many gables of the Potters' roof. Her Uncle Mike and his brother Tim regularly met the young nieces and nephews with their great hopes and black trunks that lean Ireland shipped out to America.

Some arrived sick from the long voyage but others, hardier like my mother, landed exhilarated from the giddy nights and days of fiddling and dancing down in steerage. When I was little, my mother told me that those ten or twelve days on that boat had been the time of her life.

They probably were. When the steamer docked, her uncles and brothers took over where my grandfather had left off and guarded her and her virginity until they handed her over some years later, intact, to my father who trundled her off to Michigan where she didn't know a soul.

In the meantime, the uncles watched her closely. Soon after she arrived, my mother was going out one evening to a dance with her cousins. She was wearing a new red dress, the first dress she ever bought in this country, and it had cost her almost all that remained of the money she had brought over with her. Catching sight of her, Uncle Tim summoned her back into the house. He shamed her, insisting that the dress was so skimpy it couldn't even have flagged down a train. Unmoved by her tears, he blocked the door and refused to let her pass until she had changed her outfit.

One August afternoon years later, my mother led me by the hand up a long narrow staircase to a dingy apartment above a Buffalo saloon that now belonged to my mother's cousin, Sis Ryan, and her husband, Johnny Behan, who was a cop. Upstairs in the kitchen, sitting at a chipped white enamel table, was my mother's Uncle Tim, a feeble old man now, with his big freckled fist wrapped around the head of a cane. His wrinkled face, like a dried-up sunflower, turned into the light filtering through the bleary window that the steel mills coated every day with fresh soot. The soot didn't matter. The old man was blind and was only after the warmth. My mother cried when she saw his milky eyes and she kissed him even though I'm not sure he remembered which of his flood of nieces she was. It's Nance from Michigan, George's Annie, Pat-o's wife, she said.

She made me kiss the blind old man too. Fumbling in his ghastly pocket, he drew out a quarter and held it trembling out to me, nearly upsetting the pint of Guinness at his elbow. I left him holding the quarter and fled downstairs to Sis where I drank bottle after bottle of the orange pop that floated, half-submerged like stricken ships amid huge blocks of ice in the big red cooler, and Johnny came home and laughing sailed his hat with its shiny badge down the length of the gleaming bar to me and then I felt all right again.

When my mother started work for the Potters, Aunt Gerda had already been there a couple of months. She helped my mother arrange her belongings in one of the narrow little rooms up under the eaves where the Potters stowed the people they brought in to do their work. My young mother and Aunt Gerda, proud funny women, rubbed tarnish from the Potters' silverware, washed and ironed the linens, dusted their somber furniture, diapered the Potters' only child and taught him how to walk and talk. They said Yes'm all day and at night, mocking their missus, they giggled together upstairs and longed for furniture and babies of their own.

They got what they wanted, after a fashion. Aunt Gerda married Gustave Klugman, the Potters' gardener. Eventually the two of them left the Potters and bought a farm in Canada with money they had saved and Aunt Gerda gave birth to Gus, her only child, who was twelve or thirteen when I first remember him. Very early on, when Gus was still only four or five, Gustave Klugman died of a heart attack out in a dusty stubbly field one hot summer day, leaving Aunt Gerda alone with her young son and a lot of cows and pigs and years of crops to be sown and harvested. She went at it.

When I first knew her, Aunt Gerda had been at it for a long time. She never remarried and we always spent my dad's two week vacation with her, late in August, so that he could help bring in her wheat and hay.

Aunt Gerda was tan and sturdy and strong. She chain-smoked Pall Malls and shoved her short curly brown hair up under an old blue denim cap to keep the dust off. Her boots always stank of the cowbarn and she wore pants and old patched sweaters and never flowered aprons like the ones my mother wore. She swore and laughed a thick laugh that often ended in a smoky cough that left her breathless and with tears standing in her shiny dark eyes. Her accent never faded and, squatting on the low three-legged stool with her cap turned backwards, she leaned her forehead against the black-and-white lady-cows and sang to them in German as alternating streams of milk hissed and rattled against the metal sides of the pail. Slopping the pigs, showing me where to hunt for eggs and how to avoid the pecking hens, hoisting heavy cans of milk to dump them into the separator that whirred and spun in the milkhouse, or guiding the grey Ford tractor down the rutted back lanes, she was always easy and sure.

Besides working in the fields and barns, Aunt Gerda washed and shined and polished the enormous farmhouse with its lovely oak floors and broad staircases and endless sunny rooms. As I wandered through it, summer after summer, it seemed that the house went on forever, that there was no end to the hooked rugs and breezy white curtains and featherbeds and carved chests and wardrobes. In your stocking feet, you could take great running slides across the waxed floors and land on the beds kerplunk and then drift slowly down through the foot-high feather ticking as if you were making an angel in the snow.

One afternoon, in a corner of the attic, I found a dusty leather case. I lifted out a violin that belonged to the dead man I never knew who had been my Aunt Gerda's husband. I liked him and his moustache and dark eyes and his arms that folded across his young chest where he stood smiling in the old sunlight of a photograph Aunt Gerda kept propped against the mirror of her dresser among her combs and brushes. I liked him and I was sorry he was dead so I took out his violin up there in the silence at the top of his house way up among the very tips of the tall pines that stood still in the heat outside on his front lawn, and I rested the violin under my chin and, drawing the stiff bow across dry old strings, I squawked out a lullaby for the dead man I'd never get to know.

Aunt Gerda's barns were as wonderful as her house. Every morning and evening, like nuns on their way to chapel, the cows filed in in solemn procession, each seeking her own stanchion where the day's portion of grain and meal waited. The breath from their nostrils raised little whirlwinds in the trough that ran along before them and their eyes grew soft and meditative as they chewed. Their hearts praised both Aunt Gerda and God who, in his bounty, had given her to them.

Calves being weaned were penned up inside the barn. They always grew restive when their fading memories were quickened by the milky presence of their big dim mothers. I felt sorry for the calves and would slip my hand inside the slats of the pen to let them suck on my fingers.

The barn had a pigpen too and I'd sit so still in a corner of it that the piglets would stop squealing after a while and come tiptoeing up, closer and closer, on their shiny little hooves, their tiny pink minds full of sniffing and curiousity. I loved it. I was St. Francis.

Grain was kept in huge bins and machinery was stored in another part of the barn. Beneath a high vaulted roof where generations of swallows sweated and toiled to raise their greedy young, on either side of an open space where the tractor could draw up the wagon from the fields, bales of hay and straw were brought in and stacked up almost to the ceiling. My brother and I would climb the wooden ladders, clutching the heavy rope that hung from one of the roofbeams, and we'd fly across the vast open aisle in the middle and then, like Lucifer suddenly falling from grace, let go and drop forever it seemed until the hay on the other side caught us.

Most summers several litters of kittens skittered underfoot in the barn. Aunt Gerda must have drowned some of them occasionally but I never saw her do it. As adults, the kittens would help guard the grain supply. As wobbly babies and jittery adolescents, they weren't much good for anything. Sometimes, Mick and I would each round up a battalion of them, climb the ladder with armful after armful. Once we had them assembled up there in the warmth under the roof, we lined them up, some with pigeon feathers tangled in their fur to distinguish the Indian kittens from the settler kittens, and we encouraged them to massacre one another. The kittens, it turned out, had not much feeling for history; they spent most of the afternoon imagining ways to escape down that ladder in time for the evening's milking when Aunt Gerda and my father would squirt their faces with milk warm from the cows' abundant udders.

Tagging after her around the farm, I always thought that Aunt Gerda never married again because she loved Gustave so much she didn't want to, and maybe because she knew how to do everything all by herself. She did have a friend Adolph, another German, who lived on the next farm. He walked over evenings to play cards out in the kitchen with Aunt Gerda and my parents. Adolph always lost the pots; he often raised a fuss and the other three made fun of him. Adolph was engaged for over twenty years to a woman named Rosie but he never married her.

Adolph owned a short-haired brown-and-white dog named Prince whom he had taught to sit up and raise his right paw over his ear when he said Heil Hitler to him. The dog also trotted out to the pasture in the morning without being told and gathered in the cows to the barn when it was time for Adolph to milk them. I heard my dad mutter once to Aunt Gerda that the dog was a damned sight smarter than Adolph and that someday Prince would be sending Adolph out to fetch in the cows. Aunt Gerda added under her breath that if Prince ever figured out the gears on the tractor it would be all over for Adolph.

I think Aunt Gerda wouldn't marry Adolph partly because she ran her farm better than he did his. She probably didn't want to get mixed up in the big machinery deals he was always boasting about or with his messy barns. Besides, Adolph was embarassing the way stupid people are when they think that they're being cunning.

My dad told me Adolph was a blowhard and I knew myself that he could never measure up to the lovely man in the picture who had made my Aunt Gerda so happy that after all these years she laughed when she spoke of him and her voice still grew warm with the pleasure of him.

My dad didn't make it any easier for Adolph either. I think my father and Aunt Gerda loved each other a lot. He liked how good she was at everything and they looked at the world pretty much the same. Every winter when things were slow on the farm, Aunt Gerda came to Michigan for a couple of weeks and she and my dad tramped through the snowy woods laughing and blowing squirrels out of the trees with their shotguns. Dad and Aunt Gerda both loved my mother and my mother knew it but it still must have hurt her some anyway to watch them going out together to the fields and woods while she put away the dishes and washed fingerprints off cupboard doors.

At night when he came home from the prison, Dad would get Aunt Gerda all riled up by pretending to cheat at cards. He'd roll his sleeves up and, laying his bare forearm on the board, stick pennies from the pots to the underside of his arm and then flick them off into his own pile. Aunt Gerda played for real, the way she did everything, and it maddened her that he wouldn't take the game seriously and play right and she'd curse him and storm away from the table in a huff. Years later though, when my dad had his stroke and spent six weeks lying unconscious and uninsured in the hospital, Aunt Gerda came from Canada to be with my mother, and brought six or seven thousand dollars with her to help pay his bill and bring him home again.

When she traveled on the train to see us, Aunt Gerda always arrived in a brown skirt and white blouse and matching brown jacket. Wrapped around that stocky body, the suit just looked like a lousy disguise. On top of her head, a dark old hat with a morose feather ornament would be riding queasily. Between Aunt Gerda and the feathery hat there existed only mutual contempt. After the long train ride, each appeared eager to be shut of the other.

While she had her at our house, my mother would persuade Aunt Gerda to let me put pincurls in her hair. When I combed them out, Aunt Gerda would make a nutty face at the mirror I held up for her, run her stubby fingers through the arrangement and mess it up again. Dad and I thought she was pretty funny.

My mother also tried unsuccessfully to convert her. Although she never, to my knowledge, darkened the door of any church, Aunt Gerda insisted she was Lutheran. Every Sunday my mother would go into Aunt Gerda's room to convince Martin, as she called her during their religious wars, to dress and come to Mass with us. Come on, you old pagan, and every Sunday Aunt Gerda would roll over and snore belligerently until my mother gave up and left her alone. Sometimes Aunt Gerda counterattacked with such blasphemy that my mother feared for the roof over our heads and threatened her with the holy water that she kept up in the cupboard for when there was lightning.

Early one Friday morning as my mother lay sleeping, Aunt Gerda tiptoed into her room carrying a hambone from the previous night's dinner. Softly crooning all the while of the juicy virtues of pig, she passed it back and forth under my mother's nose. My mother's face softened as the aroma seeped into her dreams. Suddenly she bolted up from the pillow. Blast you, you devil, and your old hambone. You'll both rot in hell. Aunt Gerda howled and, slavering and waving the hambone beneath her own nose, she mimicked my mother's beatific smile.

One morning, after I grew up, Aunt Gerda stood beside my mother in the warm September sunshine while Father Himmel, his own eyes wet with tears, sprinkled holy water from the hyssop over my father's coffin as the undertaker lowered it down. She came one more time on the train and watched with Mick and me on a black and frozen day not long after, as my mother, her other friend, whom she'd also loved with all her blunt and stubborn soul, was settled in beside my father.

The day after the funeral, Aunt Gerda and I went through my mother's closet. Aunt Gerda picked out a winter coat and some sweaters to take home with her. In a while, my brother and I would send the rest of my mother's clothes to aunts in Ireland. I wasn't ready to open the drawers of her dresser yet. On top of the dresser, I saw the hairbrush my father had given my mother when they married. Its back and the back of the matching hand-mirror were inlaid with shimmering mother-of-pearl whose silky colors I had loved to touch as a child. Grey hairs were tangled among the soft yellow bristles of the brush.

A couple of days later, Mick and I drove Aunt Gerda back to Canada. The day's drive was long and it was after midnight when we arrived. Taking the key from Aunt Gerda, Mick unlocked the door of the dark house and carried in the battered leather suitcase. I followed with Aunt Gerda, keeping a hand under her elbow because she was tired and I worried that she might fall on the ice.

Only ten or twelve years old, this house was small and built of cinderblock. Like all its dingy neighbors up and down the street, it was sided with sheets of fake fieldstone. Aunt Gerda had accepted the house in partial payment for her farm several years earlier. My mother had told me about the transaction once but I had never seen the place before. Always with her eye on a buck, Aunt Gerda lived in the basement and rented out the top to a young family I heard screaming at one another over breakfast the following morning.

Sitting in the chilly cramped kitchen after we arrived that night, we were surrounded by the heavy presence of chests and wardrobes and stuffed chairs from the farm that had all been jammed into the two other small rooms. The three of us smoked and drank coffee and ate the stale powdered-sugar doughnuts Aunt Gerda found in the back of a cupboard over the sink, and she told us that when it got so that she could no longer do the chores alone, she had sold the farm to a Frenchman with too many children and moved into town. Her own son, Gus, she said, didn't want the farm. He was married to an American named Lydia who had no use for either the farm or Aunt Gerda.

Aunt Gerda told us that, in the beginning, it had broken her heart when, driving out to the farm to collect her payment each month, she saw gates sagging on broken hinges, paint peeling away from windowsills and barn walls, and rain and snow rotting the wood below. Windows broke and were never replaced. Loose shingles flapped in the wind on the barn roof. Aunt Gerda said that after the first few months, she never entered either the house itself or the filthy barns again.

The Frenchman and his pregnant wife complained

about doctor bills and the high cost of feed and the repairs they needed to make on the machinery. Their payments were often both late and short until finally Aunt Gerda was called out one morning two winters before by an insurance claim-adjuster to view the smouldering remains of the barn of which she was still part-owner. The fire had started somehow during the night. The barn burned to the ground and all the livestock was lost.

Aunt Gerda stopped speaking then and stared into the empty cup she held in her hand. Mick and I lit fresh cigarettes and I passed one to her. When I dared, I looked up at Aunt Gerda across the wide oak table and saw her through the smoke, small and worn, and there on her lip a trace of powdered sugar trembled like Death deciding, like the dust I'd seen that morning gathering already on my mother's dresser, and I bit the sleeve of my sweater hard to keep from screaming Look out—run! to Aunt Gerda. In the morning when we were leaving, she held us to her for a long time.

When Mick told me during his phone call that Aunt Gerda had died that winter, he told me how he had flown down for her funeral and he boasted how much he'd loved her.

❧ NINE ☙

Recently at a meeting of university people who gather on alternate Wednesday evenings to defend elitism, I was told two happy-field-nigger stories by a smug, heavyset psychiatry professor who had taken his stand right next to a huge chunk of Cheddar cheese and a bowl of wheat crackers. As I listened, I breathed shallowly to keep the fumes of his after-shave lotion out of my lungs. Between cracker sandwiches, he told me about a cabdriver in Detroit who so loves his work that he even takes people from out of town who get stranded with him in traffic jams home to his own house to feed them dinner. Huh, I said. God's on his pumpkin, Eddy's in his cab, and you've got crumbs all over that expensive silk tie.

Then he told me that when he was a kid, a little illiterate Polish woman used to come in to help his mother with the laundry, and sometimes, when the cracker man's parents went out for the evening, the little illiterate Polish woman would stretch herself out just like a watchdog, he said, right across the bottom step there in the entrance hall, and she wouldn't budge until the parents came home.

Buffalo had an awful stench too. Sulphur from the steel mills, my father explained. The worst thing was that you stopped noticing it after a few days and by then it was all over your skin, in your clothes and hair like the fine layer of soot that settled everyday over the geraniums my aunt kept on the windowsill above her kitchen sink. Every few days, Aunt Mae would lift them down and rinse off their fuzzy leaves and soft red blossoms, making a light mist from the faucet with her thumb.

Aunt Mae was short and plump with shiny black eyes. Like my mother's, her grey hair was curly from home permanents. Every August, stretching up out of her plaid slippers to kiss my cheek, she'd cluck and marvel at how tall I'd grown during the year since she'd seen me.

Her husband, my mother's brother, was an immense man. In the evenings when my Uncle Will came home from the docks, where he loaded and unloaded the sunless bellies of ships, his sweaty T-shirt, streaked with grime and dust from the grainsacks he'd shouldered all day, billowed around him like a dismal banner. The screen door slammed shut behind him, his empty black metal lunchbox clattered against the pink flowered oilcloth of the kitchen table, and he sank silently into his chair, waiting for the bottle of cold beer my aunt would set before him. Beneath the shock of thick grey hair, his heavy face was red from the heat and the beer and his eyes would close. On top of the refrigerator an electric fan, a small listless cyclops, turning its one blind black little eye first this way, then that, barely stirred the pile of mail that lay beside it.

My mother loved her brother even though she knew that some days he grew sullen or fierce with drink and raged through the house like someone cornered, rattling the Sunday dishes and my aunt's china figurines. But with her chair next to his at the big round table, my mother stroked and patted my uncle's brawny arm through dinner. She saw him only once a year for a few days and she missed him.

Meat and potatoes and my father's dumb jokes revived my uncle. Come here to me, girl. Pulling me down onto his knee as I passed behind his chair to go outdoors, he scraped his rough chin against the top of my head and against my cheek.

My uncle's only daughter was dead and so was his oldest son, whose plane had been shot down somewhere over Korea. Georgie's face laughing up into the light was what I saw when I first woke up in the morning; his tie loosened and his pilot's hat with its wings and braid set at a jaunty angle, he stood in the picture frame on the wall above my head with his left arm flung around my Uncle Will's shoulders and with the bottle of beer in his right hand raised high in a goofy salute. When George died, someone's bones were shipped home and there was a funeral. That was the first blow of the ax and afterwards lots of evenings my Uncle Will grew silent and drank too much as dusk came on and my aunt in her slippers padded about absent-mindedly rearranging the china birds on their shelf beside the medal in its box that the government had sent.

The second blow fell when a wire shorted out somewhere and no red light flashed and no bells clanged to warn their daughter that a train coming would smash her car and kill her. Driving alone at night after work to a cottage on a lake in Canada where her fiancé and friends had arranged a party for her twenty-fifth birthday, my cousin didn't see the light. After she graduated from college, she'd taught third grade in the parish school and lived at home with her parents and the two brothers she had left, to put money aside for when she and her young man could be married. Her hair, black and shiny as patent leather, swung forward and tickled my grumpy uncle's cheek when, laughing, she grabbed him by both ears and kissed him good-night.

After that funeral, my uncle grew older but still worked his long days on the docks, staggering dumb beneath grief and those heavy bags of grain whose dust settled, a thick fog, in his lungs. My aunt, awake and forlorn in the nights beside him, was racked both by his coughing and the selfsame sorrow.

My other two cousins were lucky; they were spared.

Working full time at night, one as a stockboy in a ware-house somewhere downtown and the other as a city fire-man, both finished law school. Saturday nights Brady, brash and braying like a donkey, yelled out through the bathroom steam for his mother to bring him a clean white shirt. A towel wrapped around his waist, he hollered out at me next to come keep him company while he shaved. He was full of blather and chatter and gab and dabbed at my nose with the red brush full of lather and laughed when I sneezed. I adored him and, balancing on the slippery edge of the clawfooted tub, I watched while, making faces at me and at himself in the mirror, he shaved his dark whiskers. He whistled and sang in that house full of silence and sighs and, tormenting his mother, he chased the poor woman from room to room until she cried Oh, Brady, my Brady, flung up her hands to the sky and, giving way to his foolishness, danced round in his arms. You'll be the death of me, Brady-boy. Oh no, Ma, he replied. Martin the fireman, much quieter and shy, stood by, shook his head, grinned at his brother's antics, then bowed and asked me to dance.

Catastrophe swarmed through Buffalo like stripey spring snakes from beneath an overturned rock, but mostly I was too dumb to notice, or just forgot to think about it much, like the stink from the mills. The houses of my mother's other brother and sisters had all been struck or blighted too somehow.

Her oldest brother, George, an I.R.A. man, pale and thoughtful with round gold-rimmed glasses and thinning hair, never came in the evenings to the noisy gatherings where the grown-ups drank highballs and beer in kitchens rollicking with shouts and laughter, where giddy light from bare bulbs bounced off dishes and forks, off ice in the tall glasses, off enameled walls and the rungs of painted wooden chairs that the men tilted back against cupboards or the white stove. Boiled ham and cabbage and potatoes and onions mingled with their thick brogues and cigarette smoke and every year new cousins, greenhorns with frizzy hair and open faces, who had come over from the old country during the year, tumbled in during the evening to meet their Aunt Nance and Uncle Pat-o from Michigan, and my mother would clap her hands, then open them wide and cry out, Oh, Jesus—Maggie's little Kathleen, or Mainey's Willy or Sis or Danny or whichever one of my new cousins it was, and she'd hug them again and again and, with her eyes all teary, she'd pat them and make them sit down beside her there in the loud kitchen and tell her everything about their mothers and fathers and sisters and brothers still home on the small farms with their fields of black-and-white cows and the soft sheep on the green mountain and the bay shining bright below that they'd just left to come here to this reeking city where they'd sort mail or load ships or sell shoes.

As the night wore on and thick slice after thick slice from the big juicy ham on its platter in the middle of the table exposed more and more of the shiny white bone beneath, the voices grew soft remembering their dead beside the stone church at home in the parish of Keel and all the fiddlers and tinkers, the schoolmasters, the dancers and harsh priests, and finally with curses, they remembered the English soldiers who pounded house doors with the butts of their rifles.

There were always more people than chairs on those evenings, so I sat on my dad's or an uncle's or maybe a cousin's knee, drowsy, half-listening, making pictures with my finger on the oilcloth with the sweat from my ginger ale glass while the voices swirled around me, washed over me, soothing and salty.

These kitchens were rented—nobody in Buffalo owned the roof over his head—and the floors like the rest of the houses sagged and sloped so that the cracked linoleum rose up in places suddenly like the deck of a ship in a storm and the patterns, geometric sometimes with black rectangles laid over faded yellow circles or worn green triangles, disintegrated and were hard to make out. The low sinks full of dishes had two separate faucets with porcelain handles and were curtained below with a bit of bright cloth that matched aprons that matched covers of cushions for chairs. Long dim hallways with woolen runners led to small wallpapered bedrooms with crucifixes over the heads of the metal beds and pictures on the walls of saints and of my grandparents like those at home with holy cards stuck in the corners and dusty sheaves of palm tucked behind the frames.

Mostly nobody sat in the living rooms; ashtrays—souvenirs of Niagara Falls or the shrine of St. Anne de Beaupré—were never used, cellophane still covered the lampshades, and curtains, sheer white or flowered, hung at the windows. The man from the army who brought the flag and Georgie's medal had sat in a stiff green plush chair that had linen doilies pinned to the back and the arms and, with the heat of his coffee cup, he'd seared a light ring in the varnish of one of the endtables.

My Uncle George never joined us on those evenings because his wife would never come with him, and he wouldn't leave her at home. They were childless and she was thin and bitter and proud, with a tight mouth and dark scornful eyes. She sat like a dragon and smoked, ensconced in her chair in the living room with its drapes drawn shut where she and my uncle received us during the call that my mother insisted we make. My uncle said little but poured us all tea in matching cups and brought out sticky chocolate fudge cookies from packages for me and for Mick. Madge, his wife, had a voice like a hatchet and I was glad when we left that stiff still place. My uncle was like someone whose blood had been drained out one night into a basin while he lay asleep. He sat alone night after night and read by the lamp at his shoulder and grew older and finally died.

In another aunt's house sometimes there lived a small red-faced husband with a swollen nose and eyes squinty like a possum's that darted this way and that. Though he worked sometimes, he drank up the money and showed up at home only when it ran dry. He was ashamed before my father and always disappeared soon after we came. Years later, when Jimmy's liver gave way and he lay stretched out in a dark blue suit at the wake, my father muttered to my cousin Brady as they knelt down to pray before the coffin that this was the first time he'd ever yet gotten a good look at the son of a bitch.

Jimmy's wife, my mother's oldest sister, was called Judd though her name was Philomena. Stout and with a sizable jaw, she resembled my mother but her hair had never turned grey and she wore it braided in a coil at the back of her head. Her oldest son, a curly-headed baby who grinned with his four new teeth from the highchair that he pounded with his spoon in the picture propped up near the clock in our dining room at home, had died of meningitis at four and her daughter, full-grown but with not much of a chin, had fallen in love with a man already married and was lost in the sin, but God made it all up to my aunt with her other son, Jamie.

Until Jamie was eleven or twelve, he was perfectly ordinary, but then the pituitary gland at the base of his brain in a fit of adolescent frenzy ran amuck and he started to grow and grow and grow and no one could stop him, though my aunt prayed and the doctors all tried. When finally he stopped, Jamie was nearly eight feet. He almost filled the small apartment where he lived with his flustered, sporadic father, his scarlet sister, and the mother who loved him. His shoes and his clothes were all specially made, and his bed, and later his car.

When Jamie sat on the couch, those huge black leather shoes, resting one on the other, reached the center of the room. Stooping to pass beneath curtained doorways, when he straightened again it took forever and your eyes opened wider and wider to take him all in. But Jamie's heart had grown apace; he was warm and funny and outgoing and easy; he finished law school, became the Democratic councilman for his ward; maybe he even fell in love—who can say?—but what could he say? He brought home money, kept the house going, and with his giant hands reached up and kept the roof from caving in on all of them there.

One humid night Jamie stayed in from bingo to play pinochle in the kitchen with me, but before settling in, we walked down to the corner to the store with the Salada tea sign on its green wooden screen door. Though it was a short walk, it took us a long time; people outside on their stoops called out in soft voices through the heat and the dusk to my cousin, who held my hand somewhere in his. Jamie introduced me to old women sitting on cushions they'd carried outside. They shook my free hand and said how pleased they were to meet Jamie's little cousin. Grizzled old men, kids my age, and men like my father stepped out of the shadows to speak to Jamie, who shook his big head from side to side to condole with them over some new grief—a lay-off maybe, or an accident at the foundry—or leaned down to get a closer look at some wagon or trike a child pulled over for him to admire. Overhead, in the dark hush above the streetlights, above the talk, I could hear nighthawks like the ones I listened to at home from my bed after I'd turned out my light and was waiting to hear my father, coming home from work, pull into the driveway and fasten the garage doors before I fell asleep, and, suddenly, along with the neighbors' beer and the dust and the automobile exhaust, I could smell that smell hanging heavy in the air and I wanted to cry, but Jamie said, C'mon, cuz, and off we went to buy a devil's food cake and pineapple ice cream to split between us and comics for me and Delaware Punch.

We played pinochle and seven-up in the kitchen that night until the others came home. Since Jamie's legs wouldn't fit under the table, he kept them stretched out with his bare feet near the door, and whenever I reached into the refrigerator for more pop he shut it after me with a flick of his toes. Jamie played for blood. He razzed me to rattle me so I'd play the wrong card and, when I totaled our scores and told him I'd won, his long arm snaked behind his shoulder and he fished the sponge from the dishpan and sailed it all soggy and soapy at my head.

When he died at thirty-four from the strain on his heart,

like his shoes and his suits, Jamie's coffin was built special
for him, made-to-measure like the rest of his life, and his
mother, my aunt, by then no longer a new widow, was
left with her sad-eyed daughter who couldn't love where
she ought to.

I knew all about them—even my Uncle Tom, my
mother's youngest sister's husband, a postman, tall with
curly red hair, who'd whirl me and his two daughters high
in the air while we grabbed fistsful of that thick hair,
luxuriant and beautiful like a setter's. One evening, barely
forty, climbing up the long stairs, coming home from his
route, his heart dropped him down dead on the landing
where my aunt, frying pork chops and hearing the thud
and the cry, dried her hands on her apron and came
running with his two little daughters, pink and freckled
like new strawberries. I knew about them all, but I
couldn't think of it all at once or hear what it meant.

The son of the people who lived next door to Uncle
Will and Aunt Mae was nearly my age and a Mongolian
idiot. I watched him those summers, sitting day after day
on the green glider and staring through vague dopey eyes
at a car parked by the curb or at his own hand on the
porch railing. His hair stood up straight from low down
on his forehead the way Tom's did in the comics when the
mouse Jerry shoved the end of the cat's tail into a light
socket. My aunt said he was harmless—God help him—
couldn't even tie his own shoes, but he scared me anyway
with his full-moon face and those eyes like some calf's
who'd been slammed with a hammer. What was it like
inside the dim cave of his brain? Did it hurt? I peered over
the railing and into his face, but his dull eyes were murky
pools deep in the woods that didn't reflect.

Those same neighbors had some kind of collie that they kept penned up at the rear of the house, though I don't know why; though vicious, he'd proved himself no watchdog. His fur was tangled and dirty; thick mats stuck out behind his ears, along his belly and tail. Pacing back and forth in his pen, he'd worn away what little grass there had been and the path he'd worn was packed down and cracked in the summer heat. Though livelier by far than his young master's, the dog's eyes were crazy and red with dust and fury. Flattening out on his belly, he snarled and raged whenever I came near the pen.

But I figured I'd fix him and make him happy. I knew about wolves and about collies; I'd read Jack London and all of Albert Payson Terhune. I knew that it just took perseverance and kindness and in no time I'd teach him to trust, even if somebody'd kicked him before. So day after day I swiped scraps of ham, bits of beef, leftovers, bread soaked in milk and threw them over the fence to this foul-mouthed Cerberus who gobbled them down and bared his teeth if I dared come too close with my foolish crooning.

It didn't work. The morning we left late that August to drive home to Michigan, when I crossed the backyard to tell him good-bye and to give him two pieces of bacon I'd snitched from my breakfast, his teeth snapped the meat up out of the dust and his red eyes were as malevolent and wary as ever.

The phone rang one evening the following spring. My cousin Brady told us his father was dead. All that dust from the grainsacks, the stinking filth from the mills had settled in his lungs, a rich soil for tumors, and had choked him to death. Worn out from coughing up blood, he had turned his face to the white hospital wall, lay silent some hours, then died, Brady said, without saying a word.

You can't think all these things at once and they're too much to tell to some paunchy psychiatrist between bites of his cracker, but he's reckless and wrong.

ᴥ TEN ᴥ

It's often not easy to associate freely with yourself; you encounter armed guards at checkpoints and at the intersections of main roads, and you can suddenly come upon the blue-suited border patrol at the foot of a bridge arcing high above some deep long-flowing river.

Sunlight drifting in through the latticework of the grape arbor speckled the painted tin dishes and cups on the small red table and warmed the curly hair of our dolls propped up in their chairs. My cousin Ike and I poured orange pop for the four of us and then drank it all. Ike's hair was fine and swirly like our dolls'.

She had been baptized Eileen Theresa but people called her Ike because he was president then. Her parents had been killed in an automobile wreck soon after Ike was born, so she and her older sister Bridie, went to live in Detroit with my Aunt Tess and Uncle Dan because Aunt Tess and their mother were sisters. Aunt Tess drew the two of them up onto her lap, tucked them in close to her, and that was that.

Aunt Tess and Uncle Dan were each my dad's second cousin, but not one another's. Danny Mike Grogan was the only child of their own that Aunt Tess and Uncle Dan ever had. A few years older than Bridie, he was a shy, quiet kid who kept a gallon jar of steel buffalo nickels in his room. When he grew up, people were afraid he'd never marry, but he did finally when he was nearly thirty and he and his wife had a couple of babies, so people left him alone then.

I loved the warm speckling sunlight and the thick smell of the purple grapes that hung above us and all around us. Bees buzzed after their sweetness but didn't bother us at all. My bare knees came up high under the table because the chairs were short and I was a tall skinny child.

Sometimes in those days my mother washed out grey rags and hung them to dry on the bathroom doorknob so that it was hard not to touch them if you were coming in or going out. I didn't know then what she did with them, but I hated the sight of them just as I hated her patched old brassieres and the sprung orange girdle she wore on Sundays and kept flattened during the week between the mattress and box springs of her bed, right along with some old newspapers and a few coins wadded up in a handker-chief and her own and my father's naturalization papers, and her stockings still rolled down around her elastic garters and even the damned drawers of her dresser so stuffed you could scarcely tug them open, first the left side, then the right, then the left again till the whole thing let go at once and nearly knocked you over. She saved old letters and Christmas cards in red heart-shaped candy boxes in the drawers right with the clothes she never wore, sweaters all rolled up, stockings with runs in them, nylon slips with yellowy lace tops.

Nothing in that house was ever right or where it belonged. Often, it seemed, she didn't care and didn't try, but just let things happen. Fleas drove the dog mad in summer. Bugs crawled in the cornmeal. Vegetables rotted at the back of the refrigerator, milk soured, and she just bled and rinsed out the rags. Sometimes, for weeks at a time, she'd quit, let it all cave in, not even prop it up, and I do it too sometimes now and I'm not skinny anymore or a kid.

My red-haired Aunt Tess played the concertina instead, wore a bright blue hat with feathers to Mass on Sundays, and she laughed hard, even in church sometimes and then poked me in the ribs with her elbow to make me stop, and once when we were crossing the Ambassador Bridge from Windsor to Detroit, the two of us were in the back seat of my father's car after a long, August day's drive and I got her started just by repeating the name of the idiot who lived in their village back in Ireland. Thigeen Ham couldn't make O in the gutter with a stick, my father had said earlier that afternoon. Thigeen Ham, Thigeen Ham, Thigeen Ham, I said over and over just because it was so goofy on my tongue.

What's your name? inquired the gruff customs officer, his badge on his hat, reaching in through the open window for the folded black leather packet that held Aunt Tess's papers. Her name's Thigeen Ham, I smiled up at him, and Aunt Tess went off, choking with laughter and the smoke from her Chesterfield. Stop, you devil you, or I'll wet my pants. For the love of Christ, my father snarled from the front seat, straighten up and tell the man your name so I can get home. Border crossings made him nervous; originally he'd landed in Nova Scotia and had come across illegally from Windsor to Detroit on a bus taking people to a dance, and I guess he never got over it.

I loved Aunt Tess's wild laughter and I loved the nice

brawny way she wouldn't let the sky fall in or the soot settle over our limbs. Instead she shoved her striped orange cat off the counter and chopped up carrots and cabbages and potatoes and onions to throw in with the ham to boil in the big white pot on the back of the stove, and she turned fat bunches of grapes into purple jelly for me to carry home in jars on my lap for the winter.

After the dishes were dried and put away in the evenings, Aunt Tess brought her concertina out from under her bed and, seated on one of the white wooden kitchen chairs, she'd tug her apron taut over her knees, cross her ankles, and off she'd go. The concertina was old —she'd brought it over from home on the boat with her— and its buttons were yellowed and the leather straps Aunt Tess slipped over her hands were frayed, but as she sang and played, the room spun around her and I, sleepy near her, spun with it and watched her fingers nimble like Jack on the buttons and saw her head tilted back slightly and swaying, her blue eyes closed, her freckled arms dancing the concertina alive on her knees. Her voice was sweet and filled like the grapes with sunlight.

Another evening, in a strange room in a small Irish town, I awake from dreams to the far-off sound of a calliope and there, out across the tops of summer trees, a carousel outlined with colored lights starts up, its elegant riderless horses rising and falling with the same music, lovely forever, going around and around and the sweet dusky air carries her voice over the trees to me too and I see her once more there in the kitchen swaying like kelp in the tide and I search her face over again and again like the face on a holy card to know how she did it because my unborn son, though still tucked inside and with room to grow, listens too as he drifts through mild waters that we'll spill at his birth.

⤳ ELEVEN ⤶

Days in the woods I scarcely stopped at all. Warm summers I trotted up and down paths that followed the creek; the dark moist dirt was soft to my feet. Before our creek joined the other and turned right, the bank rose and the path rose with it and, shoving off with my toes and the pads of my feet, I rose too and sailed, flew up glad with the rocky creek below. And I knew when the trees asked who was I who I was, and I told them I'm the girl who always runs. See me. I'm green too. The sun dapples my arm.

I straddled bright limbs, bounced high. Bark carved my fingers and I listened, a blind person, to what it said. I laid my ear against the chaos of starlings before that sudden startling hush at twilight. My mother, my real mother, not my false mother, nursed me, dandled me, hugged me close and showed me bright things those long days down there in the woods. I built dams with dry twigs and moved stones and laughed when they washed downstream. It didn't stop for my foot or the dry twigs—just went around—sensible water, on its way, no bother at all.

My woods held me; I hid sometimes at midday when the sun scalded and nobody moved who wasn't inside or underneath and I listened when the cicadas sang and tumbled and sang again and I crouched under dark leaves and peered out damp and musty-sweet into sunlight where no one stirred. You can see through a dragonfly's wings and the chicory brushed my arm with the same sky blue as the Virgin's robes but I was a pagan baby suckled by warm mounds of dark earth.

I fled that other woman, the grey witch with her rags who might turn me to stone, stop my heart, beat me cold as she cursed me, poisoned me, bade me die and I ran down, tore my leg and it bled on barbed wire, and I hid, said no so loud to her mourning, cried no, go away, dead lady, don't bury me deep, skidded down the bank, wet feet in the creek, waded out to be safe. Don't let her get me, no, water, don't let her get me with her pilfering fingers, don't let her get me, I cried and the woods heard me and hid me so deep.

⤳ TWELVE ⤵

Climbing the tall ladder in the dark, I grip the cool metal bar, flip once, twice, slam! then slip down the long slide to where she waits, arms outstretched, in the darkness. Did you see? Twice? Yes, and around and around in the night on the merry-go-round, with her laughing each time I come round to her again, then her hands on my shoulders shoving me away.

The park is empty but the fountain runs all night anyway. We have lots of water. I hear the water even though in the dark I can't see the fountain over next to the honor roll. The honor roll is supposed to look like a big, yellow-brick book. On one page, behind the glass, the names of young dead men are written out with movable letters; on the other are those of boys like Frank Spumone who only got wounded. Sitting at the picnic table with my mother before starting home, I swing my legs and, pretending to be blind, trace the initials of some of them, gouged deep some long summer ago; moving in the dark, my finger makes out hearts, varnished and revarnished by the county.

Across from me my mother, singing softly, wordlessly, to herself, has forgotten me. I stop banging my sandal against the thick leg of the picnic table and watch her face emerging from the darkness, kindled for a moment in the low beams of a car swinging wide around the curve in front of the Halls' house; she's somewhere else and likes it better. Her songs don't begin anywhere and head nowhere. We walk home through the dark slowly, leisurely, even past the cemetery where I touch her freckled forearm and ask, Does it scare you at night like this? No, what harm can the dead do you?

Other nights I play hide-and-seek, scrambling, a young nude, for cover. Shy. In among lilacs, hiding in the dusk between backyards where tips of pines finger the evening sky. Hoping the others will come find me, I remember in the dusk that the woman in the small blue house is a Spiritualist, consorts with demons, lifts tables, is divorced. Jesus. Save me too from fat Lois, her heavy-voiced daughter whose Superman collection exceeds my own. I'll grow potatoes, raise chickens; I am my mommy's girl. Honest, I am.

She washes fingerprints off cupboards. She sits in my father's red chair while he's out at work, rests her cracked white teacup on his smoking-stand with its two little doors, watches Groucho Marx and answers the questions out loud to nobody, watches Jack Webb like a hungry lady-spider.

She stays at home, is always there when I come home, a dread sour ghost to haunt the dumb child. I pound with a cold black implacable fist for the damned tortoise to creep to the door, check the serial number on my lunch pail, and let me in. Am I home already? For supper there's thin grim gruel to grow on.

Sleepy brooding slug, she cut me right behind the neck the way they do to frogs—you're a woman now—left me dead below and dreadful from the neck up. Have a potato, baby, sofa, cupboard, silver salt and pepper shaker. Oh, I couldn't. You be the lady, smelly bitch, grey-haired witch, stinking of death, reaching in somehow to the exact right spot for the potato, pulling it out. Eat it. Oh, I couldn't. Now I reach in, Potato Lady, pull you out; I know just where you are.

Inside it was always winter, always dusk and no one ever came looking. The couch was red and burned your skin; gold metal flecks tore like fingernails at the backs of legs and from the wall Baby Jesus thundered disappointment down at me.

When Ronnie Spillett, sitting beside me one day on a log down in the woods, told me it goes in and out and asked would I ever do it, I laughed. His younger brother Herman did it, he said, with Phyllis down by the bridge. I saw the other fat woman with all those children across the street, yodelling morosely along with the radio, her hair cut in bangs and her bare breast swollen as big as her baby's head and I got up off that log and ran.

Later, for a while, I loved Pal Oakley, the bus driver with curly hair and bright plaid shirts but a Mexican who only said WHAT? replaced Pal and, for a while, I hated Mexicans, or at least the ones who made a million babies but mostly Mary Mañana's little sister who stood wet in the mud by the cockeyed mailbox when the bus pulled Mary and Lorenzo and Lupe away and left her, thin girl in a thin dress in the light rain by the snail-slick tracks, her nose dripping, tears dropping.

I could hardly breathe as she turned on small bare feet to go back inside the damned tar-paper home God had made for her and her drunken, stupid father whose teeth had all been knocked away by this time and for her mother who waxed and waned with babies like a crazy moon; I pressed my forehead against the lousy glass as the bus bumped across the slippery tracks of a train I heard at night like the miserable cry of a death-dealing owl. Beautiful dark rain and her tears perplex, a sacramental, along with the dripping nose, but what harm can the dead do?

Yesterday, nearly ten years since pain blinded the Potato Lady and shut her down, sent her mind wandering off somewhere, mumbling names until Death shriveled her and spaded up the ground and plunked her in, I, taking pleasure walking, looking down at the toes of my boots in the snow, grew ashamed suddenly and frightened that I could forget and glance down and admire my boots with her waiting still below unwept, unwatered in the dark.

THIRTEEN

There must ever have been days when she loved me some, I suppose. One July morning right around my birthday, she and Mrs. Spumone packed me and Pat, a couple of quilts, the wicker picnic basket, and two bamboo poles into our wagons and pulled us behind them out into the country to Raccoon Lake. Neither of our mothers drove, so we never went anywhere alone with them except downtown or maybe to each other's houses. I knew the road because my dad drove it back and forth to Mass every Sunday. Our mothers pulled us up the long hill to where the pavement stopped and the gravel began and, rounding the dusty bend at the top of our road, we passed Old Man Cleaver's shack.

Cleaver was matted and dirty. I used to hide in the bushes out near the porch and watch him swing past our house on his crutches on his way downtown. His face was mean and Boots hated him. She'd run at him, growling and snapping. She never bit him but she wanted to. He'd curse her and try to smack her head with his crutch. I never believed Old Man Cleaver needed crutches. Lots of times I'd seen him look around and then just carry them across the railroad tracks at the end of our block.

Cleaver lived alone in a tar-paper shack that was just a big room with two or three windows and a haphazard door. A metal chimney on the roof smoked in the wintertime but nothing was coming out of it now. My dad told my mother once that Cleaver was so filthy neither of the two barbers downtown would shave him or cut his hair. Cleaver's shack had no running water or electricity; he used kerosene lamps for light and a tipsy outhouse stood out in the deep weeds that grew up all around his place.

Dad also told my mother that Phil Burpee, the man who owned the Shell station, had come home one night after closing up and found Cleaver standing on the outside cellar door, peering in through the window of the living room where Lizzie Burpee was lying on the couch, drinking

Pepsi and watching TV. Phil sicked their dog on Cleaver and offered to kill him if he ever caught him around there again. Mike Burpee was a Springer Spaniel and my dog's father.

Our dog really did hate Cleaver but I figured it was probably because he must have connected hard sometime with his crutch. I wasn't sure it meant much otherwise because Boots hated Father Himmel too, and that was because the priest used to sit in her chair in the living room whenever he came to visit and my mother never had the nerve to tell him to get up out of the way of the dog.

My mother said Cleaver had a daughter somewhere who was a schoolteacher and that she should be ashamed of herself for letting her father live like a rotten old hermit. My mother said he probably hoped he'd get a letter from his daughter and that was why he walked down to the post office everday. Even so, my mother didn't want him peeping in our windows at night with my dad out at work, so she never called Boots off. Boots never got a tooth into the smelly old man anyway.

Around the bend at the very top of the hill, looking out over the town, stood a large white farmhouse with a broad porch running along the front of it. Mrs. Opal was small and tidy and gave voice and piano lessons after school. On the ledge of the porch, she kept pots of red and pink geraniums that bloomed all summer. She had three boys; the oldest was named Orson after his burly red-faced father but everyone called him Sonny so they wouldn't mix the two of them up. Their collies ran out to the road when we rolled past to bark once or twice and wag their tails at us. My mother knew them because she babysat sometimes when Mrs. Opal had to go out at night for a recital.

At the foot of the hill, set way back off the road, was the slaughterhouse where the farmers' cows and pigs came in the backs of trucks to be killed. This morning two cows gazed drowsily out through the wooden slats as a red pickup rattled over the ruts toward the slapped-together shed waiting in the middle of the field. I'd never looked inside the slaughterhouse windows, though they weren't covered up with gunnysacks like Cleaver's; Mick told me that heads and tails and guts were scattered all over inside.

The wagons turned onto the paved road and we headed out toward the church. It was a blue shiny morning. Drivers waved as they swung out wide around us. Pat and I got out and ran ahead along the ditches thick with chicory and dandelions, up and down the steep sides until we grew hot and dizzy and giddy and falling, laughing, all over each other. Our mothers walked behind us close together by the side of the road, solid and thick in their flowered aprons and sleeveless cotton housedresses. They were stout and grey and probably always had been, but this morning their faces and souls were warm from the sun and their talk lingered in the air, drifting out easy behind them like the tails of kites.

Like Pat, Mrs. Spumone was much darker than my mother and I. Whenever she yelled at us, Mrs. Spumone's brown eyes grew ferocious; while her rage flamed into blazing Italian, Pat and I sucked in small hot breaths and held them far too long. With a final splendid dragon blast of contempt for the two of us, Mrs. Spumone would turn away. In a few minutes, if we only kept still, she'd speak English again.

Like my mother, Mrs. Spumone was stunned to find herself in the midst of Protestants and the D.A.R. She'd grown up in a sunlit village south of Naples and now, with bowls full of apples and bananas and her refrigerator spilling over with fat lusty grapes and huge oranges, Mrs. Spumone resisted the hardtack Michigan winters but, like my mother, she never knew what to make of either the pale, tidy members of our community or the trash who drank too much and divorced one another like animals. Mrs. Spumone didn't have much to do with any of them. My mother was her friend. Sometimes, in the evening, Mrs. Spumone walked down to the store to keep her husband company, but Paul never permitted her to wait on a customer. She cared for her children, kept the house clean, and cooked the meals, except Sunday's spaghetti, which Paul himself made with magnificent drama.

Being deaf, Paul never bothered about going to Mass, and when we came home on Sundays, still fasting from the night before, his thick red sauce simmered on the stove and a vat of boiling water stood ready for the moment when Paul solemnly, delicately slid in the slender pasta, never disturbing the rolling boil. When we were all seated around the mahogany table in the dining room, Paul carried in the spaghetti on a platter the size of my sled. He was Herod, presenting the Baptist's head to Salome.

The hike was long for me and Pat, and the sun turned hot. We rode the final couple of miles in the wagons, our feet in their red buckled sandals dangling out over the back. Clucking and grunting and mooing at the tops of our lungs, we greeted all the horses and cows and pigs and chickens we passed along the way.

When we reached the lane leading back through the fields to Raccoon Lake, our mothers hid the wagons in the weeds. Handing us the quilts, they shouldered the two poles and started off down the lane with the picnic basket between them. On either side of the lane the fields were tall with ripening corn and timothy and wheat. As Pat and I followed after the red-and-white bobbers, huge brown grasshoppers flew up suddenly from the dust under our feet, whirring and buzzing, distraught helicopters. It was nearly noon by now, and the whine of invisible cicadas rose and fell around us in great arcs.

We were some distance from the road, having walked the length of four or five fields, when my mother spotted the cluster of willows that edged the lake. She thrust the fishing poles through the fence and separated the strands of barbed wire, stepping on the lower one so we might crawl through into the high grass on the other side. Pat and I could scarcely see over the top of the dense grass. My mother and Mrs. Spumone struck out across the field to-ward the lake. Our eyes on the bobbers, we ran to keep up. We were itchy from the dust and heat, and when a covey of grey partridge startled up, having held their cover until we'd nearly trampled their tailfeathers, we howled until the women turned and waited for us to catch up.

A spring fed the lake and my mother told me the creek that ran through the woods below our house flowed out of it. I'd never been back here. You couldn't see barns or houses or anything at all much that had to do with people. Pulled up on the shore, though, in among the pussy wil-lows, an old rowboat lay upside-down.

Away from the edge of the lake, where the ground wasn't quite so damp, my mother and Mrs. Spumone spread out the quilts, flattening the grass beneath them. Pat and I flopped down and watched as our mothers flung off their shoes and waded out into the water to cool off. Cupping their hands, they splashed the dust and sweat from their faces and bare arms and then stood, peaceful like the cows in the creek near our house. They talked in low voices, heedless of the water creeping up the hems of their dresses. The water was blue like the sky above and the two of us watched as all around red-winged blackbirds called out to one another and teetered on the slender rushes that grew along the rim of the lake. Bright shoulder patches flashed as the birds flew from perch to quivering perch.

The women forgot all about us until we complained miserably that we were starving. They waded up onto the low bank, their broad feet black with muck from the lake bottom. Sandwiches, hard-boiled eggs, and a jar of lemonade emerged from the hamper, and Mrs. Spumone broke off bunches of cool green grapes for me. Pat and I tore into the food like wolves; then, our bellies full, we moaned and rolled off into the thick grass.

I parted the grass and watched as my mother drew from the pocket of her apron two old spoons that she and Mrs. Spumone used to dig in the soft mud for worms. Then she pulled fishhooks from where she'd stuck them in the bib of her apron and, tying them to the lines of the bamboo poles, she threaded the hooks through the writhing worms. Mrs. Spumone righted the boat and fitted the oars into the oarlocks and together they shoved the old grey boat into the water. Flinging our sandals behind us onto the quilt, Pat and I slid down the squishy bank into the cool water and clambered over the sides.

My mother, warning us to mind the sharp hooks, rowed out into the middle and then let the boat drift. Bright bobbers hit the water with a soft plunk. Except for the blackbirds, the air was utterly still and I stretched out along the bottom of the boat and laid my head back on the narrow seat in the bow. I leaned far back until blue sky was all I saw no matter where I looked. The sun, God's one good eye my mother called it, gazed down into my eyes. Shadows from my brain drifted in small dark clouds against the blue. When our mothers spoke, murmuring softly so as not to frighten the fish, their voices, warm and sleepy like the rocking of the boat, lulled me.

Suddenly, with great commotion, my mother's bobber began plunging violently up and down in the water like an enthusiastic convert. Deftly my mother swung the bamboo pole high into the air and hauled in a strange spiny creature that looked as if it had grown up out of the muck at the bottom of the lake. The slimy color of mud, it had no scales like other fish I'd seen. I was afraid of it—Pat was too. Thready bits of flesh dangled near its jaws and its eyes bulged horribly. My mother laughed when I shied away from it. It's just an old fish. She drew the barbed hook from its angry bloody mouth. An old bullhead, she said, and threw it back, explaining that they weren't much for eating. I was glad to see it disappear back into the murk. My mother baited her hook again from the pile of worms that wiggled in waxed paper near her bare feet. Then she rinsed the fish's blood and the worm's guts off her hands and we all settled back down.

More of the ugly things were pulled out and tossed back as the afternoon wore on, but the bullheads were the only offers the women got that day. Pat and I grew crabby after a while and started kicking one another, so my mother told us a story I liked about a tinker queen and the young fox she'd found in a meadow one day, its hind leg caught by an iron trap.

My mother told me and Pat how the queen wrenched open the dreadful rusty jaws and carried the cub back to her painted wagon and her piebald mare. The red-headed queen cleaned and bandaged the torn paw, made a nest for the black-eared baby from a calico skirt that had been her mother's before the old queen died. Each day she talked to the cub as it curled in its box under the seat while she and the mare traveled up and down the mountain roads. Often she sang to the wounded cub and reached down her freckled hand to stroke its head. As the wound closed and the paw began to heal, the little fox took more of an interest in things and sometimes, my mother said, the queen held it on her lap and pointed out nice sights as they trotted through the countryside. The queen's green eyes laughed down at the fox whenever she told it a joke and its shiny black ones blinked back at her. At night, when the stars came out and the fire died away, they were company for one another.

My mother asked did I remember what happened next. I nodded. One day the red-haired queen and her painted horse and the young fox were all drinking at a stream. The fox ran, teasing a dragonfly, and the queen saw that not even the memory of a limp remained. I always wanted to cry now. The queen knew the small fox was wild and didn't belong trotting after any wagon, not even a tinker queen's. They winked one last time, my mother said, in the meadow by the rocky stream. Then the red fox turned and started off across the meadow toward the foot of the mountain. There were caves and hollows there for dens. The calico queen threw back her head and laughed as the fox disappeared amid the silky blue cornflowers. My mother laughed too, winking across at Mrs. Spumone, and asked why was I so solemn when it came to foxes.

The sun dropped lower. Clouds of gnats appeared here and there over the surface of the lake. This was the best time to fish but my mother and Mrs. Spumone were anxious to get home with the light, so they rowed the boat to shore, overturning it again against the rain and stowing the grey oars underneath.

Mrs. Spumone told me and Pat to rinse our feet and to buckle on our sandals while she and my mother shook out the quilts and gathered up the remains of our picnic. Instead, Pat and I skidded down the muddy bank. Just as she fell, Pat caught hold of one of my braids and we both went in. We choked and spat and, pretending not to be able to climb the slippery bank, dragged one another over backwards again into the water. Before Mrs. Spumone reached in and hauled us out, we were covered with mud. She shot us one of her looks and curled her dark upper lip at us. My mother shook her head and predicted we would perish with pneumonia before they could get us home. Pat and I drew on our sandals, picked up the heavy quilts, and trudged off after the bobbers.

By the time we reached the road, the air had begun to cool. My mother noticed me shivering a little under my sunburn and wrapped the quilt around me and my wet clothes and propped me up against the picnic basket. My feet stuck out behind the wagon as we started out down the road. With the dark quilts pulled up around our ears, Pat and I looked like dirty little old nuns. We giggled and called each other Sister Mary Muddy over and over until our mothers made us stop.

Since it was the middle of summer, there was light enough for the walk home. The farmers we passed bringing in their black-and-white cows for the evening milking waved their sticks to us and inquired whether we'd caught anything.

When my mother and Mrs. Spumone ran out of talk on the way home, they sang songs to each other that they'd learned as kids. I was drowsy in the twilight, and the songs sounded alike to me, though I couldn't understand the Italian. My mother's were mostly about boys being killed and women weeping and how it never got any better. Her voice made me sad. She wasn't pretending. I thought how it must be to have a baby and then have somebody hang him or shoot him. I remembered when Mr. Miles, the old man who mended shoes, ran over Freckles, Boots's sister, and how she lay out in the road with the shine gone out of her eyes and blood oozing from her mouth.

When we reached the foot of the gravel road that led up the hill to the Opals' farm, the sun was setting behind that dark shed with its bloody windows out in the field. The women were tired from pulling us. Nodding in the wagon as it bounced along the ruts, I gazed out across the fields where lines of trees marched into night. We reached the top of our road finally and I turned around in the wagon, resting my chin on the hamper, as we rattled past Cleaver's shack. It was dark inside, though by now most of the houses below in the town were alight.

The rest of the way home was downhill. Our mothers were glad; their arms ached. Down the road where the pavement began again and the creek ran under the shadowy bridge, I heard dogs barking and, in the dusk, my eyes picked him out.

Coming up the road toward us, Cleaver leaned heavily into his crutches. He bared his teeth in a kind of smile and said good evening to my mother and Mrs. Spumone. They nodded to him. Stained and filthy, the man's clothes were a shambles. The ratty white shirt he wore had nearly turned black and half its collar was ripped away. One leg of his trousers was torn and beneath I could see his grey thigh.

He nearly brushed against me as he passed so close by the wagon and I sucked in my breath and shuddered deeper down into my quilt. Cleaver saw and shot me a vicious look over his shoulder, and I knew as he stumped up the murky road toward his shack why Boots hated him and I was glad she did. He was mean and he was dirty; wrapped around the handles of his crutches, his fingers were black claws and his grimy teeth wanted to tear your flesh.

When we reached the streetlight in front of our house, our mothers stopped the wagons to say good-night. Pat was asleep so Mrs. Spumone was going straight home. My clothes were damp and cold and bats swooped in and out of the light overhead. My mother and Mrs. Spumone arranged to meet the following day and then Mrs. Spumone handed my mother the fishing poles and started for home with Pat.

My mother thought I was asleep too, so she left me in the wagon by the front door while she walked around to the garage to put the poles away. The streetlight caught the fishhooks on her calico apron as she turned away from me. The house was dark. God knows where Mick was and my father wouldn't be home for hours yet. Seeing Cleaver's wicked hole of a mouth again, I shivered. What was taking my mother so long? A noise in the bushes made me cry out. Boots leapt out of the darkness and scrambled into the wagon all over the quilt and all over me and licked and licked my face, sunburn and mud and all. Lights flicked on inside the house. My mother took me and Boots indoors then and hooked the screen door against the night.

❧ FOURTEEN ☙

It was Josie Spumone's wedding. Pat and I must still have been in grade school. I don't recall the ceremony, only the reception where, at one of the long white tables, my father was carrying on, announcing to the other guests that the smiling, hard-of-hearing old woman seated next to him was his mother. The deaf old woman who smiled and nodded was Mary McFlaherty whose husband, Davy, had died in a farming accident long before I was born.

Aunt Mary was childless, although she and Davy had adopted a baby named Ethel who was by now an unmarried nurse. Over the years, virginity had reclaimed the old woman the way first weeds, then young saplings, will recover an abandoned clearing. She was prim in her navy blue, with only a brooch alleviating the severity, the stark fidelity she bore toward the dead Davy who, according to the fat lady, had been a prince, clean and decent and hardworking.

Mary McFlaherty was refined; her soul was spun out into a silver thread that disappeared into thin air at its extremities. She was tiny with a stiff, straight, old-lady back that never touched the cushion or wood of whatever chair she happened to light upon. When I was younger, and before her hearing went altogether, Mary would sit for hours in her parlor on Sundays talking with my mother. For years, once or twice a month, my father and mother and I drove the twenty-five miles to the town where Aunt Mary lived as a companion to a Mrs. Tansy, a woman older and stiffer still. We would spend the long Sunday afternoon with her, the fat lady and Mary drinking their tea from slender cups whose pink floral patterns matched those of the saucers.

My father, still in his tie, white shirt and dark suit from the morning's Mass, took coffee and smoked cigarette after cigarette, standing near an open window, out of earshot, as the women traced the delicate lines of acquaintances' lives, many ending, like Davy, in the grave.

The little white-haired woman was like a doll or a drawing in a book. By the time I was nine or ten, I towered above her. It fascinated me that she could speak at all, much less go on at length as if she had ever stirred from that parlor where lace doilies shrouded the arms and backs of all the chairs. Mary's small feet fluttered above the carpet. Her little doll shoes were black with low thick heels and perforated on the sides so that the holes made somber little designs; they were laced snugly and the plastic tips of her shoestrings nestled against the polished leather.

My father rarely joined the conversation, though occasionally he approached the two women where they murmured together, sighing and shaking their heads sadly from time to time. Unaccustomed to such tiny cups, my father finished his coffee quickly and required numerous refills. It tickled me as I sat, my ankles carefully crossed, sipping my warm ginger ale, to see him struggling to extricate his thick, nicotine-stained index finger from the narrow handle of the cup. I watched his lips silently shaping some obscenity as he fought the impulse to fling the damned flowery tormenting devil of a thing against the papered wall of the parlor. But it was Sunday and the doilies subdued him too.

Instead he'd light another cigarette, making ghoulish faces at me behind the old lady's rigid back. As always, he sought my support in his skirmishes with flypaper woman-hood; as usual, I couldn't hold out. Snorting bubbly ginger ale down the front of my Sunday dress and choked with fizz and laughter, I succumbed to the sacrilege in his blue eyes, just as the two women were lowering the afternoon's latest corpse into its untimely grave, observing, as they shoveled in the first spadeful of dirt, that the good do indeed die young. Irritated, and distracted from the eulogies by all the commotion and mess I was making, the fat lady would shush me and pat at my dress with a linen napkin.

Mary's cheerful morbidity persisted well beyond her golden years. The older she got, the more she relished put-ting on the finishing touches, lightly, delicately applying the rouge to those who preceded her down that dark, but by now familiar, path. She had a willing apprentice in my mother with her limitless capacity for ecstatic participation in the misfortunes of others. They ate their cookies tran-quilly from the thin plates, took their tea with sugar and cream, as youngsters were thrown from horses, heads of families were crushed beneath endless streams of John Deere tractors, and young mothers bled serenely to death after giving birth for a final time, leaving their brood in God's capable hands. Like God coolly watching the sparrow tumble out of the sky, the two of them didn't even blink. There in the quiet Sunday parlor, they just ate their cookies, grateful to be still above ground.

As her hearing ebbed away, Mary demonstrated no cor-responding loss of interest in the comings and goings of her fellow creatures. She relied more heavily upon my mother to do the hunting and gathering, but she listened eagerly. The fat lady, of course, was eventually reduced to shouting at the old woman. What was it that got him finally? Mary would inquire for perhaps the third time. GALL BLADDER, my mother would scream, GALL BLADDER, I SAID!

Tight skin and a pain in the face, my father muttered out into the open air.

⋙ FIFTEEN ⋘

O, Mary, we crown thee with blossoms today
Queen of the Angels and Queen of the May.

Scratch the dust with horny yellow claws. The head cocked sideways, fierce jet beads of eyes sort trash and shiny pebbles. Listen for the fat lady. Who's there? What if bones snatch me, drag me down into their silky metal houses filled with blackness and the hum of composting? You're all we've got to live for. Oh, please.

Tiptoe. Don't wake her. Listen. Hear the fat lady banging on the wall. Hurry up. She's lying in bed, the shade still drawn. Above her, St. Cecilia, hearing music, gazes skyward. She lies in bed beneath her heap of a belly always pregnant, never pregnant again. You tricked her womb and deafened her. Now she's stuck there, trapped beneath herself, loathing, lonesome. Get away, fat lady.

Tiptoe. A white-bread sandwich for the big, black, man's lunchbox. Mixie Hurlbut has a plaid one. Where's the

waxed paper? St. Anthony finds things; he found her wedding ring once. The fire's gone out in the coal stove standing in the middle of the kitchen floor. Mick and I used to
melt crayons down its hot sides to watch the colors run and
to make her angry. This apple's wrinkled. It's winter and
yesterday's oatmeal still sits in a saucepan in the icebox.
Eat it cold and get out. Heavy woolen leggings lined with
flannel are clammy from yesterday. Good-bye, fat lady. So
long, sucker.

Thin slippery child slams the door and runs, fat lady,
down to the stop sign on the corner to watch for the red-
and-white-and-blue bus. The mare's foggy muzzle pokes
through the wire, stretches soft whiskery lips toward the
apple. Horse and I stand like the two figures on the hooked
rug in the dining room that Aunt Gerda made for us.
Apple balances on fingertips. The horse's lip is raised, its
ragged neck extended.

The doors flap open and the driver's lip draws back from
his rotten teeth. Good morning, Mexican. This bus is cold.
The heater's broke. It's always broke. Inform the bishop.
The bus rattles across the railroad tracks, grows noisier
with the morning. Pat Spumone shares her orange with
me. Mixie Hurlbut sucks her M&M's, one by one, staring
straight ahead. Mixie Hurlbut's father runs the dry goods
store with his two brothers. He is a convert, henpecked,
and wears his trousers up under his armpits; my father
laughs at him because of the way he struts around like a
bantam rooster when he's out of his wife's sight.

An hour and a half later the bus is full. It's against the
law, but the last eight or nine stand in the aisle. Phillip
Wonder, a Protestant whose mother is divorced, jostles me.
His blond hair goes back in a lovely wave from his fore-

head. When I hit him with my lunchpail, the sandwich flops around inside. You can tell by my belt that I am a safety patrol.

Inside two cold rooms, the black-and-white nuns are waiting. Christ up near the clock is half-frozen, miserable in his slipping loincloth that he can't reach down to fix. The thermostat is turned down to save the diocese money. When it gets too bad, Sister Mary Virgin turns the thermostat up and posts one of us at the back door to watch for Father Himmel. He suspects her, and always checks the setting whenever he comes over from the rectory, but Sister Virgin is too cagey for him. I lean back against the radiator to warm myself and rub my backside twice with the palms of my hands to encourage circulation. Sister Virgin sees me, frowns, and shakes her head no. Jesus. It doesn't even feel good; I was only cold.

The oak vestibule with brass hooks for our jackets and a dark hallway separate two large classrooms that make up the main floor of the red brick building. Though their dimensions are identical, the room on the right, Sister Mary Martyr's, is called the little room because the lower four grades meet there. Sister Virgin's is the big room and houses grades five through eight. The top floor of the building is a gymnasium with a proscenium stage. Father Himmel's predecessor, Father Lily, had great plans for plays and basketball games, but Father Himmel screwed down the valves on the radiators and turned the lock in the door. In the basement are two smelly bathrooms and a dim chapel Father Himmel has never asked the bishop to consecrate. The Mexican doesn't clean the toilets regularly and extra desks are stacked in the chapel. Sometimes big boys grab a weaker littler one and shove him through the door of the girls' bathroom. Regulation and control of bathroom traffic consume a good deal of the nuns' time; they worry about it a lot.

The school's population varies some across the eight years but roughly sixty-five souls arrive each morning. We have a dozen Mexicans, the bus driver's dazed and numerous offspring, as well as the children of stranded migrant workers who sort cucumbers in the pickle factory during the summer months and shiver in their drafty shacks by the railroad tracks in the wintertime. We have D.P.'s, Lithuanians who, like the Mexicans, could speak no English when they first arrived but, unlike the Mexicans, have since caught on just fine. Now they always have their homework done. They will shorten their name to Kimber and go to college. Not the Mexicans. Lorenzo is already fifteen and he's only in the sixth grade. Gangly, he laughs a lot with his big teeth but he can't multiply. His sister Mary is smart but she'll have babies very soon. The younger brother, Lupe, bites and kicks.

A number of red-headed children, once Irish Catholics who turned hillbilly, and a few Protestant hillbillies, discipline problems thrown out by the neighboring county school, emerge each day from ratty cockeyed little houses whose sagging porches sport three-legged chairs and busted washing machines. Old rattletraps with disheartened chickens roosting in them perch on cement blocks in front of the houses. Grimy curtains, dismal flags, flutter out through broken panes of glass in upstairs windows. The fat lady has explained to me that, while these people are God's children with souls like our own, they are trash.

The rest of us are children of the Catholic farmers scattered about the countryside or town kids from four or five small villages whose parents belong to the parish and don't want their children in the local public schools.

All of us are bussed out into the country with its lightly rolling hills and black onion fields to Sts. Cyril and Sebastian's to learn to know, love, and serve God. Some of us even learn about rivers and long division. I'm one of them. The nuns are excellent teachers; they do it for God. Most days I go home with a star stuck to my forehead. The fat lady is not impressed, though she quizzes me from my spelling list each night. She likes words. She also teaches me that George Erwin's old grandmother rode a pig home yesterday is how you spell Geography. I like that because George Erwin is my grandfather's name.

An embryonic dentist, Jimmy Dutch, and I compete daily for eight years. We are well-matched; heaps of holy cards accrue to each of us. We will both go on to fame and glory; he fills teeth now in an expensive suburb of Detroit. I am jealous of him. His mother is elegant and reserved; the collar of the coat she wears to Mass on Sundays is trimmed with fur and she speaks graciously. I chew M&M's whenever I get ahold of any.

The very first day of school ever, sitting nicely in my green socks at my new desk, I watch Sister Martyr dragging a boy into the classroom by his shirt while his mother shoves him from behind. His arms straight, locked stiff against the doorjamb, he cries no no, finally buckles and comes tumbling in. That day Jimmy Dutch and I learn to spell Vatican. At the picnic on the last day of school that year Richie Poker writes t-i-t with his toe in the sand on the beach at the lake and I discover I am not wearing a shirt.

Sister Martyr's black habit makes a soothing sound as

she passes between the rows of desks and she seldom raises her voice. Her slender hands are lovely; she touches the crucifix on her breast while she describes for us the beauty of God's love and her gold wedding band gleams. Sister Martyr is a bride of Christ. At noon, Mixie Hurlbut, Pat Spumone, and I tie scarves around our heads, hang rosaries from our belts and play nun. For several months in second grade I write the letters J,E,S,U, with special care whenever they appear in other words. I hope Sister Martyr will notice and at least bring this extraordinary manifestation of piety to Father Himmel's attention, if not to the bishop's. I will be modest, dovelike even, while enquiries are made; everything will be duly noted for future hagiographies.

Forsaking heathen lusts, I sell my soul for silver stars. It's easy enough to be good at what they want from me and, each day during Lent, I put aside my candy money; I am saving up to buy a pagan baby. Sister Martyr praises all my good works and permits me to clap erasers, correct arithmetic homework, and, in the spring, I'm allowed to clean the rock garden over behind the convent. White and purple violets grow there in great profusion and each year I take a long rake and clear away the dead oak leaves that clog the bottom of the small pear-shaped pool. I love it. The water is icy. It pleases me to pluck twigs and dead leaves from the paths of the violets shoving themselves upward with such might on such slender stems.

A Belgian nun, Sister Mary Midget, takes care of us at noon. In the spring she leads us out into the woods way out behind the baseball diamond. Ordinarily we're forbidden to go into the woods, just as we're prohibited from entering the sheds where the booths and benches and long tables for the Italian picnic are stored. It's damp and shadowy in there but sometimes the older kids sneak in anyway. They get sent to Father Himmel if they're caught. The priest threatens them—there are sins black and sticky like pitch —and their parents are called.

With Sister Midget we scour the budding woods for puffballs, wading ankledeep through May apples, trilliums, and rampant violets. The puffballs are huge and Sister Midget's joy is boundless whenever we uncover one. I never see a deer but know they must be watching. Hill-billies from the county school trudge across several muddy spring fields to heave rocks at us, shouting Cat-lickers, Cat-lickers. With their own dopey drawls, they mimic Sister Midget's accent when she scolds them. Their freckled faces have a mean crazy look to them. I'm amazed God doesn't kill them, jumping up and down in the muck like monkeys and yammering that way at a nun, who's one of His wives, even if she is just the dumpy little lunch nun. She doesn't teach but cooks and cleans for the other nuns and washes and irons the altar linens. She's very kind. She referees the softball games for the big kids and somedays she plays fruitbasket-all-upset with us on the rocks that line the gravel driveway. It's fun to see the black puffball laugh and run, her rosary and Christ and everything swinging and clanking when you yell APPLES, RASPBERRIES, AND PEACHES!

There's yet another nun, Sister Mary Psychopath, who's old and very fat like a spayed cat. She's not sweet; actually she's crazy but still she's a nun. Her job is to supervise the Safety Patrol and the altar boys and also to teach music, which really only means that she comes over to the school unexpectedly and starts to play the piano. Sister Martyr tightens her mouth and hurriedly distributes the yellow songbooks. We sing along as best we can, happy enough.

During the winter, because she's old and the sidewalks are slippery, someone has to accompany Sister Psychopath back to the convent when she has worn herself out at the piano. One grey afternoon I am chosen. Though I'm holding her beneath the elbow, she loses her footing on the bottom step, pitches forward, landing on all fours up to her black elbows in the snow. Oh, God. She must weigh five hundred pounds; you'd need a crane to budge her. I tug at her hopelessly, then start to laugh. Hearing me, she glares up over her shoulder and, balancing herself, wobbly like a three-legged dog, she shakes a black fist at me. Giggling, and in terror for my immortal soul, I flee, leaving her teetering there, a holy Brontosaurus about to disappear into the slush. Sister Martyr and four eighth-grade boys rescue Sister Psychopath, finally, and restore her to the convent where Sister Midget can comfort her. I observe her resurrection from behind the door of the school; she'd shiver my soul with one look if she saw me now.

Ever after, she hates me, accuses me bitterly one afternoon all alone in the convent parlor of having taken over the Safety Patrol and of now trying to move in on her altar boy operation. Squat and lunatic, her black bulk obscuring the entire piano bench, she screams up at me. Her moustached upper lip is drawn back over her yellow teeth and her eyes are glinting nuttily behind her thick rimless glasses. Squinting in through one of her bifocals, I see her bleary pupil magnified and swimming in rage. Jesus, let me out of here. Go ahead, hit me, she shrieks, hit poor Sister Psychopath, you know you want to. Go ahead, do it! I don't want to, I try to reason with her. Why would I want anything to do with the altar boys? I don't know Latin; I couldn't serve Mass if I did. I'm a girl, Sister Psychopath, I'm just a girl. Please, stop it. Hit me, she howls. Go ahead, hit me. No, no, I save pagan babies; I don't punch nuns. Leave me alone, you crazy old witch with your damned pie-dough face. Leave me alone. Reaching out a swollen paw, she makes a grab for me and I run from the parlor with its green shades and tranquil saints, slamming the front door behind me. Sister Midget runs out onto the porch, drying her hands on her white apron, and calls after me. I pay no attention. My ears are pounding and my legs are shaky as I slide into my seat. Sister Martyr's telling the class about Father Isaac Jogues, a French missionary to the Indians whose thumbs and forefingers the savages chopped off so he wouldn't be able to say Mass but Father Jogues got his bishop's permission to use his remaining fingers to elevate the Host at the Consecration but then the Indians scalped him and tore his tongue out and I almost hit a nun, Jesus, she got me so rattled finally yelling at me.

Father Himmel, who is also bald but has all his fingers, comes over regularly from the rectory, not only to check the thermostat, but to teach us music and to quiz us from the catechism. He just walks in, never knocks even. Everything stops. Somedays he plays the piano and suddenly, just like when Sister Psychopath comes, we're singing De Camptown Races, Daisy, Daisy, and sad and mournful Old Black Joe. The only Negroes I ever see are in the butcher shop in Meckleton where the fat lady shops on Saturdays but, staring into their dark faces, I know it must be awful. Their heads do bend low.

Occasionally, instead of banging on the piano, Father Himmel carries over John Philip Sousa records from his private collection, plugs in the Victrola that stands over in the corner by the supplies cupboard and we all get up from our seats and shuffle around the classroom while Sister Martyr, who was about to tell us about Mesopotamia, tries to look gay and military.

Father Himmel holds himself accountable for the state of our souls as well as for our musical education. We are the lambs; he is our shepherd. Skippy, a little rat of a brown-and-white thing with a dented-in face where he once got hit by a pickup, is his dog. Father Himmel is gruff and all business when he examines us. You stand up by your desk, repeat the question and then answer it word for word as it appears in the dark blue Baltimore Catechism. Usually, swell little parrot, I do fine, preening and glowing beneath his praise after I sit down again.

One third-grade November morning though, truly in innocence, I raise my hand to inquire how God, omniscient, and infinite in His mercy, can manufacture certain souls, knowing beforehand that they will wind up in hell. Father Himmel finds the question irksome, blusters something about free will. Yes, but, the bad parrot pursues, He knows ahead of time they'll use their free will for sin and isn't He just making some people to suffer forever in hell? How can He do that if He loves us? Father Himmel is irate, comes closer, towers over the desk where I sit, hands folded and ankles crossed. God can do anything, he roars down at me. His nostril hairs are quivering and one eyebrow waggles up and down, a centipede caught up in his frenzy. I shudder, hearing the gates of heaven clang shut against me. His face is blotchy with anger, the way it was that Sunday after the vandalism in the church. From the altar he railed against parents who refuse to discipline their children and, pointing a shaking finger over at the scorched face and breasts of the Blessed Virgin, he screamed, The more you love them, the more you'll beat them! Beat them! Father Himmel told my father after Mass he'd found human feces on the main altar and that, while he suspected the hillbillies, he couldn't be certain it wasn't one of us. The church was never locked in those days, not even at night.

Even though it's November and there's no heat in the church during the week, Father Himmel orders me to go and to pray for faith. I don't argue. Slipping in through the heavy doors, I shiver in the dampness, then bless myself with icy holy water. Now my mitten's wet. The next to the last pew at the back of the church bears my father's name and I slide into it. The day outside being dreary, the stained-glass saints in their tall windows are gloomy too. I can see my breath and a hundred miles away, way up at the front, the sanctuary lamp glows red like the Devil's eye. Off to the left, before the repainted Virgin, fat little candles flicker in ruby glass in wrought-iron racks that have slots for your money. The small flames represent peoples' prayers, requests for a quick recovery maybe or a new washing machine.

My footsteps going up the aisle make a racket in the still shadowy valley between the glassy-eyed saints who, unblinking and morose, watch my progress. Above the main altar under a dome tinted blue like heaven, Christ hangs, looking down at His punctured feet. Nearly as large as life, He is withdrawn, endlessly absorbed in the agony of His own dying. Beneath Him, behind a white curtain, behind two little doors that swing outward when Father Himmel unlocks them on Sundays with his small gold key,

I know a fancy chalice gleams in the darkness. That's where God is, baked into thin little wafers, consecrated Hosts that taste like goldfish food, not in the plaster or the glass or the flames.

Two years ago when Mick held the paten under my chin and Father Himmel laid God on my tongue for the first time, I arose all white, even my shoes, from the railing and walked giddy back to my place beside Mixie Hurlbut. Burying my face in my hands as Sister Martyr had taught us, I started to make my Thanksgiving. God made me wobbly, however, and, overwhelmed suddenly with all that grace, my eyes filled and I nearly passed out. My nylon veil was damp and stuck to my lips whenever I tried to suck in a mouthful of the hazy air thick with incense. Damn. I clawed with my white cotton gloves at the back of the pew in front of me as the blackness in my head sent me reeling against Mixie. Without even glancing up from her own Thanksgiving, Mixie jabbed at me with her pointy little elbow, catching me just above my right ear as I slid past on my way to the hard red-oak floor.

When I came to, Sister Martyr was bending over me all black, her soft face anxious. She pulled the veil away from my mouth and nose and stopped Mixie, who had been prodding my shoulder with the toe of her shoe. Gently Sister Martyr tried to lift me up, but my right shoulder was wedged in tight under the kneeler; most of the rest of me was sprawled beneath the pew. Everyone in the second row had to get up so that the kneeler could be raised and my shoulder freed. I spent the remainder of the holy sacrifice of that Mass, my first real brush with God since my baptism, vaguely propped up against Sister Martyr.

Standing now before the varnished oak railing, I peer

past the red eye at the tabernacle, where God abides behind locked doors. When I was young, before I started school, I asked the fat lady one Sunday what was inside the little house on the altar and she whispered Baby Jesus and I saw Him lying in there, diapered, leaning on one elbow, bored with the drone of Father Himmel's voice and wishing He weren't so cramped and there was room to stand up.

Now I know better; I can even spell Transubstantiation. Still, how do you pray for faith, I wonder, and I think about fallen-away Catholics. The flesh of lepers falls away too. Noses drop off. You have to wear a bell. The snowy lamb the Shepherd carried so tenderly upon His shoulders has become a tough black sheep with a mournful bell. Mutton. My feet are cold. How long do I have to stay here? Give me faith, please, God. St. Joseph looks kind, with Christ and a lily in the crook of his arm. The stations of the cross march around the perimeter of the church and I tag after them, watch Christ, bloody, scourged, and full of sharp thorns, fall and get up and fall down again beneath the cross heavy with our sins. There's Veronica. Out of pity, she wipes the face of Jesus with her veil and, when she draws it away again, it's stained with the gruesome image of His suffering, a souvenir. I wish I had something like that. What does God think about all those pagan babies with their pot-bellies in Africa and China whose parents sell them for ten dollars to the missionaries? Would the swollen babies have gone to hell too? You can't pray for faith. I am uneasy, hearing the first crack in my plaster.

Poking around for a while, up into the choir loft with its huge organ and all those steam-whistle pipes and then back down the narrow stairs curling round like one of my

Sunday ringlets, I hold the rope as thick as my arm that
drops all the way down into the basement where it lifts the
archangel with his bad teeth up off his tiptoes when he
rings the bell high in the belfry for the Angelus or calls
us indoors for Mass.

Settled back in my father's pew, I determine to wait
until either I hear voices the way Joan of Arc did or it's
noon and time for lunch. God has twenty-five minutes to
show His hand. It's cold but I listen very hard. The hands
on the clock above the confessional move slowly, absent-
mindedly. Not a peep out of God. He wouldn't need to say
much; He doesn't even need to speak; any kind of sign
would do. St. Joseph could wink his staring brown eye just
once or waggle the lily. Nothing. St. Ippolito's lips are
sealed as usual.

St. Ippolito is the Roman officer who was in charge of
St. Lawrence when he was in prison before they broiled
him to death. St. Lawrence converted and baptized St.
Ippolito. The emperor ordered St. Ippolito scourged and
demanded that he renounce his new religion but the saint
refused, so they tied him by the feet with a long rope that
was fastened at either end to two crazy horses who dragged
him all over, across rocks and through ditches and bram-
bles. His blood covered the ground and the trees and stones,
and other early Christians soaked it up with handkerchiefs,
knowing it would be valuable someday. St. Ippolito's body
was badly mangled and worn away up to his waist, which is
why his statue only shows him from the waist up. Even on
his pedestal, you can pretty much look him right in the eye.

During the Italian picnic, they tie ribbons to St. Ippolito
and he's carried through the crowd after Mass and the
Italians pin big bills to the ribbons. My dad says there are

even a lot of hundred dollar bills by the end of the day. The money buys fireworks and beer and pop and water- melon and the prizes for next year's picnic. My dad says that the parish gets a cut too. We come every year with the Spumones even though we're not Italian. Italians drive in from Detroit and all over Michigan, lots of them pulling up in big cars, with their mothers in black headscarves and black dresses in the back seats. That Sunday, Father Himmel doesn't read the Mass; a curly-headed priest from Lansing, a cousin of the Spumones, recites the Latin and delivers the sermon about what a fine thing it is to be Italian and how you have to be especially holy if you're Italian because of the Pope living in Rome. Everybody laughs a lot and shakes hands.

St. Ippolito doesn't break his seventeen-hundred-year silence to pass on any messages from God. At noon, the Mexican, having come over to the church to ring the Angelus, asks me what I'm doing here all alone. I remem- ber St. Maria Goretti and the Italian farmer with the dagger and get nervous, but he grins at me with his broken teeth and just tells me to go back to school and eat my lunch before I catch cold. He's probably right and, besides, Father Himmel must be back over in the rectory by now sitting down to the lunch Mrs. Aprons has cooked for him. I dip the tip of my mitten again in the font and run relieved back across the gravel driveway to the school. While Mixie Hurlbut glares, Sister Midget folds me in under the black batwing of her woolen shawl and rubs my cold cheek and tells me to be a good girl and not to bother Father Himmel and that God loves me.

I open my lunchbox warily and not very wide so Mixie won't see the breadwrapper covering my peanut-butter-

and-jelly sandwich; she makes fun of things like that. For a long time, down at the stop sign, before the bus would come, I'd take off the big socks of variegated wool that the fat lady knit for me to wear over my shoes inside my boots to keep my feet warm during the long bus ride. I'd stuff the bulky red-and-yellow-and-blue-and-green-and-purple socks into my lunchbox along with my sandwich so Mixie wouldn't laugh and tell me how queer they were.

When Sister Martyr comes back after lunch, she calls me out into the hall to assure me that God knows what He's doing no matter what and she reaches in under her starched white bib and hands me out a holy card with St. Jude's picture on it and tells me to pray to him. Sure, I will. You bet. I do too, when I remember. I even say whole rosaries to him at night with the glow-in-the-dark beads I keep under my pillow.

Sister Martyr, who used to teach in Detroit, tells us that afternoon about the Jews who are so pious they won't even open a letter on Saturdays or ride in automobiles, and they even hire someone not Jewish to switch on the light in their synagogue. We should practice our religion more like Jews. I decided never to iron on Sundays and, a year later, when the bishop slaps me on the face as he confirms me, reminding me that someday I might have to die for my faith, I'm ready for him; my jaw is steady and firm, my mind empty of vagrant impure thoughts. I'm one of the three Father Himmels points out to him to catechize before we are all called up to the railing to be anointed and slapped. I decide not to inquire of the bishop what plans God has for unpurchased pagan babies; the unransomed will have to shift for themselves.

That evening Mrs. Limbercar takes Dolores and me and

Mixie to the movies to see *Alice in Wonderland* for a treat in honor of our confirmation. I'm fine until the fat red queen chases Alice around the garden waving an ax and screaming OFF WITH HER HEAD! OFF WITH HER HEAD! I start to cry, spill my popcorn, and try to crawl in under my seat until Mrs. Limbercar leads me snuffling out into the lobby. She buys me a new bag of popcorn and keeps me company until the movie's over. They conclude it's just all the excitement of confirmation; I got too worked up answering the bishop's questions. In school the next day Mixie tells the others what a crybaby I am and, howling, pretends to climb under her desk. Mixie's one day younger than I am and every day for twelve years, all the way through, even in high school, she sits beside me with her sharp ferret face and nasty puckered little mouth.

At noon one day we are playing out by the side of the school beneath the lilac bushes. We've all brought our dolls to school that morning in brown paper bags and have them dressed and sitting up on the ledge of the basement window. We are playing school and when it's Mixie's turn to be teacher, she asks Pat Spumone's doll what's eight times twelve. Since Pat doesn't know, her doll can't answer and, before Pat can stop her, Mixie grabs the doll by the head and shakes her, accidentally loses her grip on the curly hair, and flings her across the barbed wire fence behind her into the neighboring field where she lands, little gingham hat and all, in fresh cow dung. Sobbing, Pat tears her arm on the fence retrieving her blinking baby. When Sister Midget calls Mixie into the school to confront her with the damage, Mixie is teary. She doesn't know how it happened. It's awful. Oh, what can she do? Returning to our window ledge, Mixie sneers. Anybody knows eight times twelve.

The last day of school the year that Mick finished the eighth grade, he went wild on the bus on the way home. Lots of times before, the Mexican had just stopped the bus and made Mick walk home. Sometimes I'd get out and walk with him if the day was nice. I didn't like it when the bus pulled away and left him there. Mick was throwing lunchboxes and leftover food and tearing up report cards. He got Mixie's and I was glad. She shrieked at him and clawed his arm but turned white and shut up when he told her to go fuck herself. When Mick started throwing bus seats out the windows, the Mexican pulled the bus over to the side of the road, collected the cushions from the ditch, and then threw Mick out the door. I gathered up my sweater and the big black lunchbox, found Mick's tan jacket, and joined my brother. We had a long walk home but it was a nice May day and we saw red-winged black-birds and an indigo bunting.

Today, when Sister Virgin hears the tires on the gravel outside, she cautions us all to button our wraps before going out to the bus. There's more snow forecast for tonight. God bless us. Through the frosted window, I wave down at her where she stands shivering, with her nose getting red and her hands tucked up inside her wide black sleeves, and I hope she doesn't get too lonely.

We're quiet and cranky during the ride through the flat grey countryside. Cows huddle up together against the sides of barns, their backs to the wind. Crossing the railroad tracks on the way into town, we drop off Mary and Lorenzo and Lupe. Their little sister in her thin dress comes with bare legs to open the door of the shack for them. Then past the cemetery to the Tomalwinches, and the two sisters, fat and ruffled, climb down from the bus. The older one has diabetes and injects insulin every day. They both design and stitch up clothes for Martians who visit them at night. The fat lady maintains it's because their mother is divorced and works in an automobile plant in a town twenty miles away.

At my stop, I wave good-bye to Mixie and the Mexican. Pat Spumone I'll see later. Running the block from the stop sign, I hear the mare whinnying after me but I have nothing for her. Freezing, I can't get in. Every day it's the same. Tick tock, double lock. I pound on the door, kicking it with my boot finally to roust her out. Who's there? The curtain is pulled aside and she squints out at me, her hair all wrinkled. Who the hell did you think it was at three-thirty in the afternoon? Fat lady, can't you see my star?

⋘§ SIXTEEN §⋙

Like so many small towns, Pinkerink was filled with peculiar people like the Tomalwinch sisters, but mostly I never noticed. Like the elms or the noon whistle, the G.A.R. Hall, or the railroad tracks and the Chevy garage, they had always been there and they would never change. It's worked out that way too. Those people are frozen in my head, bugs stuck in chunks of amber, or like those people in Pompeii I saw once who were talking to a neighbor or giving the dog some water when it happened. They're all in there lined up on shelves, not getting any greyer or any crazier, way in the back, Christmas merchandise that didn't move, dusty and mostly benign.

Next door to the Spumones, right on Main Street in a

house that was never painted, that winter had gnawed right down to the grey wood, lived a man named Claude who kept four Weimaraners out in the barn behind his house. Claude kept his lawn cut, so no one ever bothered him, and Mrs. Spumone used to knock on his back door with plates of hot food every now and then. His dogs were sleek, nervous creatures who flung themselves at the wire of their run when Claude went out after supper to feed them. He warned our mothers to keep me and Pat away from them because he said they weren't used to people. The dogs slept at night in the barn.

Sometimes Pat and I crept up on Claude's back porch and peered through the rusty screen door into Claude's murky kitchen, where the big iron range stood. It was a wood-burner and a hole had been cut through the wall of the house for the pipe to lead the smoke outside, but Claude never cooked much. The springy metal handle for lifting off the cover to where the fire should have been stuck up in the air like a thrown knife. Forks still poked into bites of food; stacks of dirty metal plates formed wobbly towers on top of the cold stove and sat in all the available chairs, and empty tin cans hid the porcelain tabletop. Claude must have stood up to eat. Only a little light leaked in through the windows, but over in the corner, leaning against the oak cupboard, you could see the short, knotted whip that he made pistol shots with when he worked his dogs.

Pat and I watched Claude sometimes in the evening from the window of Pat's bedroom when he brought the four dogs out into the backyard. They sat all at once together, quivered, waited, a crack flight squadron in leather jackets waiting for the general to bark their orders at them. Actually, they were half-naked with ribs threatening to poke out through their thin hides and their tan eyes were lunatic like the eyes of some anchorite who didn't eat enough locusts.

Fritz and Herman and Harry and Max did everything that Claude told them to do. They were like something you'd see on Ed Sullivan. One after another, again and again, they sailed over the old oil drum that Claude rolled out of the barn every evening. Then he'd make them stand up on their skinny hind legs and turn around and around in circles all together like the German kids who come out of the cuckoo clocks when the hour strikes. Then, with Claude's whip popping in their ears, the dogs did backflips or crawled on their bellies like John Wayne's infantry clear across the backyard. When they were finished with maneuvers, Claude froze them sitting up, backs rigid, weird eyes front, with their forepaws dangling in midair. He held them there with his voice until my muscles ached. My dog had her own chair and wouldn't even come when you called her.

One December just before Christmas when I was about eight, Mrs. Spumone sent Vince over to see whether Claude was all right because she hadn't noticed him outside with the Weimaraners for a couple of days and they were howling out in the barn. Claude didn't pay any attention when Vince pounded on his back door; Claude just lay there on his face, stretched out in front of the stove with his jacket and boots on. The sheriff's men came and knocked down the door. Vince said it stank something awful in there. The undertaker came and carried Claude down the snowy steps on a stretcher. Then the sheriff's men unlatched the barn door and loaded the dogs, whining and snarling into the trunks of the patrol cars. Harry and Max and the others had to be shot; they really weren't used to people and all that talent didn't save them either.

Pinkerink had only about eighteen hundred people so, of course, you knew about anything that was going on. I was playing with Mixie Hurlbut one day after school out in her backyard, crawling around in a packing crate from the refrigerator her family had just bought. The day was cold and rainy; the leaves had already fallen and were turned black and muddy underfoot but it still hadn't snowed yet. Mixie and I had nailed an old tattered blanket over the opening of the crate to keep the wind off us. We were pretending the crate was a cave and that there were wolves outside, which was all right, but Mixie kept accidentally on purpose mashing my fingers with her boots and I was getting mad and thinking about going home early when Mixie's brother Jimmy tore away the curtain and stuck his head inside our cave to announce that Della Myers had been murdered and that he'd seen the police car and the ambulance and everything. We didn't believe him but just then Mixie's mother, Fricka Hurlbut, slammed open the back door and, shouting my last name at the top of her lungs, yelled at me to go home, that my mother had called and wanted me to come home right away before it got any darker. Fricka Hurlbut made Mixie come in out of the packing crate too.

When she was younger, Della Myers had been either an Alternate Associate Matron or a Worthy Matron in the Eastern Star—I'm not sure which—and she had traveled by Greyhound bus all over Michigan on official visits to other chapters; she'd gone to Paw Paw and Dowagiac and Vandalia and Imlay City and all over, kind of reviewing the troops and attending buffet luncheons. Della still got out on Mondays for the meetings of the local chapter, but for the last four or five years she hadn't been herself; some days she didn't even walk the block to the post office to fetch her mail. I used to see her down there when I ran in after school to get ours.

Della always wore white gloves and a hat with a long, pearly-headed pin stuck through it, but some days she wouldn't remember her combination or even her box number and tears would come into her eyes. Her father had been a justice of the peace in Pinkerink and it embarrassed her to forget things. Della still corresponded with a bunch of the Grand Matrons even though she no longer could go see them, so after a few days when her mail piled up and nobody came to collect it, Mr. Trapp, the postmaster, phoned Della's house but got no answer.

When Mr. Trapp and the local deputy broke into Della's little yellow house that afternoon, they found her lying, like Claude, alongside her oil burner in the kitchen, but she wasn't all dressed up like Claude had been. A ratty old mauve wrapper was all Della was wearing; she wasn't wearing anything on her feet even though the day was so damp and chilly. Della's hair was all frizzled and going every which way and there were bruises and burns on her body that whispered foul play to our policeman, Wilbur Pilk; Wilbur even sent out for a piece of chalk and marked the linoleum before he permitted the undertaker, who was also the coroner, to cart out Miss Myers's remains.

As I ran home from the Hurlbuts', the November evening was hurrying in and the streets were mostly empty; the people I did see looked strange to me. A murderer in Pinkerink. It could be anybody. Who would murder Della Myers, for God's sake? Those jewels they gave out in East-

ern Star were just colored glass; even I knew that. Pat
Spumone and I had watched an initiation once through a
crack in a basement window of the G.A.R. Hall. Imitating
the mumbo-jumbo for weeks afterwards, we laughed ourselves stupid, calling one another Sister Cora and Sister
Nettie. My mother said that Catholics couldn't join because those people hated the Pope and, besides, they were
all nuts anyway.

I flew across the railroad tracks. Boxcars with shadowy
open doors stood on the sidings. Maybe it was hoboes. The
fat lady always warned me to run if I ever saw one and
lots of times down in the woods I'd come upon the ashes
and tin cans from their suppers. God. A hobo and Della
Myers. The streetlight had just blinked on when my mother
unlocked the front door, yanked me inside, and hooked it
again. Later on, after he'd come home from football practice, we told Mick that Della Myers had been murdered
and he laughed at us. Who the hell would kill that daffy
old bat?

Mick was right. The coroner's report indicated a lot of
alcohol in Della's bloodstream and he speculated that she
had just fallen against the hot stove and had smacked herself real hard on the way down and then on the floor when
she hit. She had just lain there unconscious until she died;
nobody helped her at all. The newspaper naturally didn't
say a word about Della being all liquored up when it happened, and several Worthy Matrons contributed a nice
piece of poetry to the next issue of *The Pinkerink Republican* in honor of Della's demise. I cut it out:

> *Not dead! What a beautiful thought*
> *To cheer us through life's dreary way.*

Not dead! But bloomed into life
Where time is eternally day.

Not dead! 'Tis a glorious hope.
How it lessens the burdens we bear,
As we lay our beloved away,
To know we shall meet over there.

Pat Spumone and I memorized it and we sang it together, leaping high in the air and shouting NOT DEAD! at the top of our lungs at people we passed down on Main Street.

Actually I kind of missed Della; I liked all her dopey hats and that pearly pin. She was always dressed up like something important might happen any minute and she wanted to be ready. She must have been mortified to find herself in a bathrobe at God's radiant feet.

Sadie Fraley always wore a hat too, but that was because she was going bald. Sadie's hat, a small round one of knitted red wool, rested on the back of her head like a doily or a big maraschino cherry. Mick and I called Sadie "Your Eminence" and asked if we could kiss her ring when she came to our house for supper; she was so hard of hearing, it didn't matter much what you said to her so long as you smiled a lot. A huge old lady, Sadie ate a lot of cookies and never even turned down the awful oatmeal rocks my mother made with drippings from the bacon. Always puffed up, flushed, and all squishy, Sadie moved slowly and carefully, like a strawberry Jell-O with the fruit cocktail left out.

Sadie lived down the street from us right next to the railroad tracks. Only a row of bridal wreath sheltered the house from the racket the trains made; the china in the dining room cabinet did a little tap dance three or four times a day but Sadie didn't mind. Sadie lived alone except for her brother Jimmy who didn't make much difference anyway.

When she was younger and perhaps less plump, Sadie had been a schoolteacher and for many years had taught out in the country in a one-room schoolhouse. Lots of her former pupils had gone on to become farmers in the surrounding area. Sadie had turned down many offers of marriage, my mother often said, shaking her head sadly, and she a well-educated woman, too. Mick observed that most of the farmers who had proposed to Sadie wouldn't have been able to handle her feed bill anyway and would have had to auction off their other livestock.

Sadie moved into town along with Jimmy when her sister Alice died. Alice, the only one of the three Fraleys who took the plunge, had married Pat Clampitt. Pat and Alice were nearly a hundred each when I was old enough to begin to notice them. My dad didn't come home from the prison until ten-thirty at night, so my mother and I visited around a lot in the evenings.

Pat and Alice were tiny and feeble. Pat walked with a stick and one of his high-topped black shoes had a lift under it. Alice was so frail it took her forever to make the tea in the evening. The kettle had to be filled from the pail in the kitchen and then settled properly on the flat top of the coal-burning stove that stood in the middle of the living room. Alice wouldn't let my mother help her and made separate trips back to the kitchen for the tea, the pot, the cups and saucers. She wiped out the cups with her apron.

Pat kept his shoes on the fender, drawing in what warmth he needed through the soles of his feet. Heavy,

dark curtains hung at the window that faced the street.
During the day, Alice tied them back, but at night she let
them fall closed again. A cloudy kerosene lamp stood on
the wobbly table where Alice poured out the tea finally,
but it was midnight way off in the corner where I sat
fiddling with a silky tassel from the cover of the daybed.

Everything in the room was black, the stove with its
blushing cheeks, the scuttle, Pat's shoes and his saggy suit,
Alice's long dress and even her apron. My mother's had
flowers anyway. The chairs creaked when Pat and Alice
leaned forward to add milk and sugar just as if their bones
had weight like anybody else's. I had to call them Grandpa
and Grandma because they were so old and their mothers
and fathers came from Ireland. My mother taught me to
respect my elders even if they didn't mean anything at all
to me, but especially if they were Catholic.

Pat and Alice liked my mother a lot because she came to
see them and liked to talk with them about dead people
and sigh and twiddle her thumbs. I watched her from my
corner on the daybed where I sat with my legs sticking
straight out in front of me and I tried to twiddle too but
wasn't really very good at it.

From where I sat, I could see through the archway into
the dining room. In the dim light, I could make out the
big table pushed up against the wall and piled high with
newspapers, Sears catalogues, bits of old mail, a stray sugar
bowl whose contents had turned to rock years before.
There were calendars, long deceased, on the walls and that
Indian, his feathers drooping, slumping over the neck of
his spavined war-horse.

Opposite the worn-out Indian, nailed to the china cabinet were toilers who, hearing the ding dong of the Angelus

wafting across the noonday fields, leaned on their hoes and bowed their heads. Everyone's head was bowed, even mine. The kerosene, the heat from the stove, the thin, gibbering voices of the old people bickering over whether someone now moldy had been a second or a third cousin once removed made me drowsy. My eyes itched and my thumbs stumbled.

After nearly seventy years of an utterly fruitless marriage, the two old people upon whose heads the years had dropped a lot of snow nodded off finally within a week of one another. Pat with his broad translucent forehead was lifted from the big old bed and carried out through the curtained doorway, past the stove, past the Indian, and buried. Alice took it poorly and died before the following Sunday. My mother had scarcely had time to put her black hat with the shiny feathers back in the box under her dresser when she had to get it out again.

Sadie had come in to town to stay a while with Alice after Pat died. When Alice, like some library card that had fallen down behind a bureau, expired, Sadie just emptied one of the drawers and moved in. She sent my father out to fetch Jimmy and installed the lunatic in the upstairs bedroom. Sadie had had it with country living and here in town there was more for Jimmy to watch; the Wingers across the road had a pair of English Setters, Nip and Tuck, in their backyard that Jimmy could see from his window. Jimmy kept Sadie company downstairs during the daytime, but whenever my mother and I arrived for a visit, Jimmy lit out up the stairs, a furtive little rat of a man with his nose twitching as he scurried up into the gloom above. None of the three of them—Alice, Sadie, or Jimmy—ever produced a child. They were dead ends.

Most Sundays we picked Sadie up and took her to Mass with us. Jimmy never came. My dad wouldn't toot the horn at Sadie and she couldn't have heard it anyway, so I had to run up onto the porch and hammer on the door until she'd notice the curtain move and then she'd open it. Sadie would just put her Sunday hat, which had shiny black eyes like a fox's all around the crown, right on over her everyday red one; then she'd walk out with me to meet her maker. Jimmy watched us from the upstairs window as, grabbing on to my shoulder, Sadie steadied herself coming down that little hill in front of their house. The only time I ever worried was in the winter when it was slippery underfoot; Sadie would have crushed me if she'd ever landed on me.

Mick opened the back door for Sadie and smiled at the beaming mashed potato as she settled herself in with a fur-topped boot on either side of the hump. Wedged in between Sadie and the door, my shoulders almost met in front and I tried hard not to breathe in the odors of dried walrus and rancid whale blubber that came off the stale old schoolmarm. Exhaling as long and as often as I could, I blew holes in the frost on the window to pass the time.

My mother, shouting back over her shoulder at Sadie, tried to carry on a conversation over the noise of the heater and the Chevy's engine. My dad just watched the road while my mother screamed at Sadie about the Heeney's new baby girl, the price of a loaf of bread, or how hard it was to make hens meet. Sadie nodded and clucked, no matter what my mother yelled at her; nothing wiped that grin off her face—earthquakes in Turkey, millions drowning in pools in Afganistan, the Pope's new frigate—they were all one to Sadie.

One Sunday, I felt my brother's hand tugging at my coat collar. He'd slipped his arm around Sadie and was resting it along the back of the seat. While Sadie leaned forward to watch my mother's lips, Mick leaned back, leering and winking at the beady eyes on the back of Sadie's hat. My father watched in the mirror as Mick let spittle run down his chin and urged Sadie, baby, to give him a kiss. My father swung his big fist around and, dusting Sadie's startled chin, smacked Mick's head up against the side window. Dad probably figured things wouldn't work out between Sadie and Mick.

After Mass, Sadie usually came home for breakfast with us. I stood over in the corner of the kitchen on a stool, watching the toast, opening the two doors before it started to smoke, flipped it, and shut it back up again. Feeding toast to Sadie was like shoveling virgins to a dragon; when I got worn out, Mick took a turn. When I was older, I read about amoebas oozing along nice and easy on their little pseudopods until they bump into somebody, then, no trouble at all, just flowing all around whoever it is, surrounding the little tyke and digesting him, and I thought about Sadie, sitting blissful in the pink of my mother's kitchen with Buddha-butter glistening on her lower lip.

Jimmy died suddenly one afternoon watching Nip and Tuck. Keeled right over. The wooden milk crate by the windowsill where he rested his stubbly chin went right out from under him. Whee. Bam. His eyes slammed shut, toaster doors, on the black and white spots and that was that. The Mexican dug a hole and buried Jimmy's old bones and beady eyes.

A couple of years later, a distant cousin, some slick from out of state, showed up in a silk tie, sold the rattly old house by the railroad tracks and packed Sadie in her hat that never missed a trick off to a nursing home twenty-five miles away. My mother shook her head but said Sadie had been getting forgetful and might have burned the house down all around her some night. My dad drove my mother and the cookies to visit Sadie every couple of Saturdays for a while until Sadie didn't remember my mother anymore either so she stopped going altogether. The cousin got everything, even the catalogues.

Before, back in my corner on the daybed, I used to squint through the murk, night after night, at the shiny ladies in red dresses with their vacuum cleaners and sets of flowered dishes. I wanted them, their spark plugs, their plaid husbands cheerful with gun racks and toilet articles, their fluffy boys and girls with durable sleepers and plastic phones and little cash registers. Life was all gingham and electric there and teeth were real and ravishing and stayed in at night in the mouths of mothers who cooed at their children. It was great and you could send away for it, using the form in back that folded up into an envelope, no postage necessary.

The last time I saw Sadie, she was waving good-bye to us through the steamed-up picture window of Sleepy Cedars; as we pulled away, her mouth made an O suddenly like the hole of a doughnut, like the rim of Etna.

SEVENTEEN

Pinkerink was full of patriotism—my dad said the town positively shook with it—and nearly everybody got all worked up on Memorial Day, but I almost passed out in the early heat. Because I was tallest, I had to carry the American flag in the parade and Mixie marched beside me with the green-and-white Girl Scout flag protruding on its wooden pole from somewhere near her belly button. Both of us wore broad leather belts fitted out with a special slot for the end of the pole so you wouldn't drop the flag when the breeze grabbed hold of it; it was a sin to let the flag touch the ground and you had to burn it if you did.

Our entire troop, all twenty-six of us, had assembled outside the G.A.R. Hall at nine-thirty that morning. Our leaders had lined us up and checked our uniforms, straightening yellow scarves and adjusting our sashes with their bright machine-embroidered achievement badges. I had a bunch of them and so did Mixie.

The badge with stacked wooden blocks that read A,B,C indicated that we had watched a real mother bathe a real baby, then had taken turns on a rubber doll using the same tepid water, which we checked first with our elbows. It was a girl baby and looked just like the doll. Afterwards the mother showed us all the big vat on top of the gas stove where she boiled the baby's bottles with their rubber nipples.

Next to the child-care badge was the pet-care badge I had earned by feeding Boots and changing her water for a solid week. I also taught her how to sit when you pushed down on her hips. She didn't like it, though, and growled at me when I did it. The fat lady told me to leave her alone, that she probably had arthritis or fleas.

I had lots more; they were easy to get. You did about ten things for each one, like showing you could thread a needle without poking out your eyes for the sewing badge or learning to distinguish oaks and elms for the tree badge.

For grooming, you learned about deoderant and how to clean your comb with ammonia. We met in the basement of the G.A.R. Hall after school on Tuesdays and, once we'd pledged allegiance, we sat with our ankles crossed and discussed our progress.

Once a year, usually in autumn, we sold cartons of cookies that were shipped out to us from National Headquarters. First, Mrs. Elmo Byrum, one of our leaders, would read us the story about Lord and Lady Baden-Powell to get us fired up, and then we'd get together in groups and plan our strategies, dividing up the town and assigning sections to pairs of girls so that we wouldn't pester the same people twice. For a couple of wet, grey weeks Mixie and I worked opposite sides of the street every afternoon until it got dark and, at the end of the sale, we were each presented a dark green comb with a green plastic sheath that had the gold Girl Scout emblem stamped into it. That meant you'd sold at least thirty boxes.

The combs came with the cookies from National Headquarters and, like the cookies, were not available in stores. Mine was usually lost by Thanksgiving, but Mixie kept all hers from previous years together in one place in the top left-hand drawer of her dresser, and each year she'd just add the new comb to her pile. By the time we quit Girl Scouts, Mixie had a whole mess of them. I don't know what she did with them; you couldn't sell them; it was against the law, just like you had to cut all the buttons off your uniform when you outgrew it so the person who was going to get it next couldn't use it for deception.

Besides selling cookies for National Headquarters and learning to keep our nails and hair clean, we also Christmas-caroled in the snow outside the doors of old people who lived alone and to whom hardly anyone paid any attention the rest of the year. I never minded singing for Sadie even though I knew she'd never be able to make out the words because she always bought lots of mint and peanut butter cookies from me and Mixie.

Our last stop was outside the waterworks by the tracks to sing "Silent Night" to George Kitley, who hadn't been able to hear a pin drop for nearly forty years. George was my mother's friend; sometimes in the evenings when it was warm outside, they sat together on the rickety bench that leaned up against the orange wall of the waterworks and played checkers until it got too dark to see. George couldn't hear any better than one of his kings; I doubt he even knew we were out there shivering in our boots unless he happened to glance out his window. Through the closed door and brick wall, though, we could hear all that racket inside. If it weren't for the box of chocolate-covered cherries my mother wrapped up with silver paper and sent down every year to surprise him, George probably wouldn't have known it was Christmas.

When it was all over, we trudged back to the G.A.R. Hall and drank hot chocolate made with water and gave Mrs. Byrum and the other two leaders the brooches we had bought for them at the dimestore. We always bought them identical presents so that none of them would feel slighted; we didn't want to cause hard feelings. We also cut up folded construction paper into snowflakes that we inscribed with personal messages. I think they were all moved a lot. They said they were.

Mrs. Byrum told us how wonderful it was to work with young ladies and how we could do it too when we got older. Mrs. Byrum was the chief leader and the other two ladies were her assistants. In their pocketbooks they all carried little white cotton hankies ironed into small stiff squares and edged with white lace or some crochet work. Mrs. Byrum's husband, Mr. Elmo Byrum, taught band up at the high school. He and Mrs. Byrum had no children but Mrs. Byrum liked to lead the troop anyway.

The greatest thing about Mrs. Byrum was her neatness. She was always tidy; the green Girl Scout anklets that she wore with her uniform never slid down inside her shoes. Once when I gashed my leg sledding on Meeker Hill and had to go inside her house to ask for a bandage, the first thing she did was put down newspapers on the linoleum in her kitchen so my blood wouldn't get all over her wax. The whole house just gleamed.

I had set my alarm early for that Memorial Day morning so that I'd have lots of time to get ready. Out in the pink kitchen I sat alone and ate cornflakes and read the box over twice even though I no longer believed in their offers.

Pulling the bobby pins out of my hair, I brushed it a hundred times and then my teeth. Next I applied a Five-Day Deoderant pad to my underarms; the first time I bought a jar of them from the drugstore, I read the instructions and figured out you were supposed to stick one of the saturated cottony discs under each armpit and leave it there for a week, but they kept coming unstuck and falling down my sleeve and onto the floor. Today I was especially careful because I knew I would soon be carrying the American flag right up the middle of Main Street in front of hundreds of men, women, and children.

When I was all set, I buttoned on my light green uniform, slid the yellow scarf around my neck, smoothed the collar down over it, carefully tying the ends of the scarf into a square knot the way they showed you in the book, and pinned my pin right in the middle of the knot so that my nose, chin, pin, and belt buckle made a straight line down the front of me. When I reached in under my bed for my brown tie shoes, Boots snapped at my hand; she was still half asleep and had no way to know who was reaching under there.

I grabbed my dark green tam off its hook in my closet and was standing in front of my dad's shaving mirror that hung over the kitchen sink, trying to line up the insignia with my nose, when my brother sauntered out into the kitchen in his underwear. Leaning up against the sink, Mick watched me fiddle with the hat, then suddenly he snatched it off my head and flung it across the kitchen. It landed next to the stove, nearly in the dog's water. When I swore at him, Mick laughed and told me I looked like a fucking elf. He retrieved the tam, brushed it off, and jammed it down over my ears with the yellow trefoil glancing back over my left shoulder. The fat lady's bed creaked as she rolled over; I was anxious to leave the house before she got up, crabby and eager to complain about the cost of my uniform the way she did every time she saw it on me.

The porch door slammed behind me. Running across the lawn, I cut through the opening in the hedge, past the knotty old purple lilac and the giant spruce that marked the edge of our property. I didn't slow down until I had crossed the tracks and had nearly reached the lumberyard. Overhead the sky was cloudless and already the day was warming up.

Behind the barbed wire fence, I could smell the sliced

trees, all laid out and stacked up so neatly, layer after layer. Both the lumberyard and the grain elevator stood alongside the railroad tracks and ordinarily you could see farmers and other men in overalls inside, jostling one another and drinking coffee from heavy mugs, while Ike, good-natured and bald, beamed down at them from the calendar on the wall behind the counter. Ike was surrounded by the other presidents, lots of them with mutton-chops and high collars, but today, since the offices were closed in honor of Memorial Day, he grinned out at nobody in particular. Two elevator cats, one a big orange tom whose right eye was gummed shut, watched me from the steps outside the grain office. My brother said lots of rats came out at night but I never saw them, though I did hear things scrabbling around under the wooden ramps sometimes.

Most of the others were at the G.A.R. Hall already, either sitting on the concrete steps, the skirts of their uniforms smoothed under them so they wouldn't wrinkle, or balancing doubled over on the metal handrail. Mixie stood off by herself at the foot of the steps; she was mad because she'd had to hold both flags until I got there. When it was almost ten, I asked Trudy Hendershot, whose buckteeth made her so shy, to hold Old Glory while I strapped on the special leather flag belt and pulled up my socks. Mrs. Byrum lined us up the way we'd practiced last Tuesday at our regular meeting with me and Mixie out in front and then four rows of six behind us. The leaders walked beside us so they could count cadence. Mrs. Byrum looked especially snappy in her green overseas cap and spotless white gloves as we marched off to join the other groups.

The V.F.W. and the American Legion came first with their rifles, then the Masons, the Eastern Star, and the Boy Scouts. We were next, followed by the Cubs and Brownies and then the Pinkerink High School Band. We made a pretty impressive sight, sorting ourselves out there beneath the stoplight. Don Braynes, the deputy, scattered a few of the Eastern Star ladies when he roared up in the patrol car, but he shut off the siren finally when V.F.W. Commander Yerby yelled at him. Deputy Braynes opened the door for Mayor Jake Fetcher to get in, then inched the dark blue Chevy, red light flashing, to the head of the parade.

Pinkerink was a Class C school, which meant it had at least three hundred kids in the high school, so the band was good-sized and had lots of braid and nice black-plastic rims on their hats. I glanced back over my shoulder at the tubas and all that brass glinting in the sunshine, saw the drummer give the bass drum a good thwack when Mr. Byrum gave the signal. Movin' out, snarled Mixie.

It was really something. People were lined up along the sidewalk on both sides of Main Street. Farmers and their wives in town for the day set their kids up on top of the cabs of their muddy pickups. The kids cheered and banged the metal roofs with the heels of their shoes when they caught sight of all the guns and flags. Paul Spumone stood outside under the green-and-yellow striped canvas awning of his store, leaning against the big plate-glass window, his hands buried deep in his pockets under the white apron he always wore. Frank, drying a coke glass with a towel, strolled outside to join his father.

Frank could have marched with the V.F.W. if he'd wanted; with his skull plate and glass eye, he was entitled, but he never did. Pat Spumone had quit Scouts three weeks after we joined because it was dumb, so she wasn't marching in the parade either. When our troop passed the store and Paul and Frank spotted me, they grinned and waved and yelled, Hey Irish! They made me laugh and, when I dipped the flag a bit and waved it at them, Mixie hissed.

We passed the Dairy Queen, the red-and-white-and-blue pole outside Doug Cutler's barber shop, the dimestore with pink, plush Easter rabbits still peering out through the green cellophane grass in the front window, the Motorola TV repair shop, Edie Gignac's bakery, and then the post office with its own giant flag flying. When our tubas and drums penetrated the early-morning gloom of the Electric Bar next door to the post office, five or six men tumbled out into the sunlight, raising foamy glasses aloft and cheering wildly; their red faces and beery guts were all excited. Out of the corner of my eye, I could see the three or four others who had stayed inside the long, dim, narrow room; perched on high stools, they stared straight ahead into the big mirror that covered the wall behind the bar.

Don Braynes swung around the corner by the Shell station and the V.F.W. and the rest of us stepped briskly along behind. We passed the dry cleaners and the pool hall, where the sharp crack of the balls sounded very military coming out through the screen door. Mick hung around the pool hall after practice even though my father threatened to kill him if he ever saw him in there. Mick and his friends played pool with the old pensioners; they smoked cigarettes and drank beer with the old men and won quarters away from them at the beginning of the month when their Social Security checks came in.

The day was growing hotter and, when we made our first stop, before the honor roll near the edge of the park where we played baseball, my scalp started to overheat as the sun soaked into the dark green wool of my tam. Without breaking ranks, we gathered in front of the yellow brick wall that had set into it the names of all the young men from Pinkerink who had ever been shot down or blown up or drowned or just dismembered for us. Lots of the Spanish-American War boys would have gotten old and died by now anyway, I calculated.

The Baptist minister stepped out from behind the brick wall where I guessed he'd been waiting since early in the morning and asked us to bow our heads for a moment of silent prayer so that our Heavenly Father might bless us. I didn't bow mine because he was Protestant, just like when we sang "Away in a Manger" outside in the snow, I just clamped my mouth shut. Reverend Pixley's thin blond hair was slicked down; dandruff had drifted like grace over the shoulders of his dark blue jacket and he was balding fast.

In a nervous, nasal voice he read the names, one by one, of all the dead men. The list was long and lots of the last names were familiar. The V.F.W. men, already wearing their uniform jackets open to accommodate fat they'd put on since their service days, began to fidget, shifting their rifles from shoulders to sidewalk and back to their shoulders again. The Eastern Star ladies mopped their brows with white hankies; new home permanents frizzled in the heat. When I muttered, God, it's hot, to Mixie, Mrs.

Byrum frowned and shushed me. The stars and all the stripes hung limp and heavy on their poles.

When Reverend Pixley finished finally, the band struck up "America the Beautiful" and we all sang it together before setting out for the cemetery that lay in a hilly part of town north of where we were. Just before the end of the song, the Reverend bowed his head and stepped quietly behind the yellow wall, disappearing again into the honeysuckle bushes where the pop flies always landed. Lovely, murmured the Eastern Star ladies in their white blouses, and I began to worry that my deoderant might give out.

O.K. So we went up one side of the town and down the other, waving our flags to cheer up the dead. The sun climbed as we marched past the bowling alley and the boarded-up Sunoco station. In front of us, I heard heavy breathing as the Eastern Stars and Legionnaires labored together up Fowler's Hill toward the cemetery. Beside me, Mixie counted cadence between gritted teeth. Behind us the Brownies began to whine. On either side of the gravel road that turned into the cemetery stood Mr. Yupp's two assistants handing out miniature American flags to the townspeople following the parade as they walked through the iron gates; Mr. Yupp was Pinkerink's undertaker and he told my dad once that giving away flags was good for business. Ranks grew ragged as we trudged up the hill.

It was nearly noon by the time Mayor Fetcher climbed out of the patrol car and stood waiting while Deputy Braynes unlocked the trunk so he could get at the wreath they'd brought along to hook onto the foot of the metal W.W. I soldier who stood atop a chunk of granite on a little rise looking out over a bunch of tipsy, pitted old tombstones and some more modern shiny ones. The butt of his rifle was down by his boot and his metal fingers curled around its muzzle. He was young, not fat like the other veterans. From beneath the round brim of his hat, his flat eyes stared morosely out at a huge old crab apple tree whose unruly pink blossoms, humming with bees, blocked his line of vision.

Mayor Fetcher hooked the wreath of red carnations over a piece of metal that stuck out from the soldier's boot, then turned and looked significantly at all of us for a few moments before introducing Reverend Circumspect, the Congregational minister, who had suddenly turned up. I tried to figure out where he'd been when we first got there; none of the headstones was big enough to conceal his bulk unless he'd gotten down on his hands and knees and I couldn't see any sign of grass or dirt on his creased white trousers; maybe he'd been hiding up in a crotch of the crab apple amid all that pink where you wouldn't think to look.

Drops of sweat rolled out from the silver waves of Reverend Circumspect's hair and ran down his smooth, chubby cheeks as he told us how terrific the dead were and that because of them we could go to church any time we wanted and be Girl Scouts, proud of our badges, instead of slaves. I thought it over and wished I had some gum; my mouth was getting really dry. My stomach growled and I felt queasy and light-headed from the heat and prayed that the shiny-faced preacher would stop, but he didn't, and just kept on about Freedom and how wonderful it was to be dead and with God.

All around us, the air was sweet from lilacs and, high up in an elm, a male cardinal sang out, sudden and scarlet, like a pulse in the clear sky. A small breeze came up the hill, shaking bees and petals out of the crab apple tree. It snapped my flag to attention and I clutched at the wooden pole to keep from whacking the Grand Matron across the back of her blue head. Mixie, who'd grown sullen and sleepy like a lizard in the sun, told me I was going to get it.

At last Reverend Circumspect quit, a warble in his voice bringing tears to the eyes of the ladies as he vowed for all of us there that we'd always remember and never forget. When I tried, I couldn't even see in my mind the faces of my two cousins whose planes had been shot down.

The Legionnaires roused themselves and pointed their rifles at the sky and when, at a signal from Mr. Byrum, the bugler, Calvin Pratt, a senior with pimples who hadn't made the basketball team all four years, stepped forward from the ranks and raised the brass mouthpiece to his lips, the fat men with their musty unbuttoned uniforms fired their guns and fired them and fired them and fired them while Calvin played taps on his bugle and the air cracked and stank from their guns, and first I was worried they'd hit the cardinal but he flew away, and then we all sweated back down the hill and left the metal man with his round hat there glaring out at the bees.

Mick was sitting on the porch steps in his blue jeans eating green rhubarb from the garden when I got home. He crossed his eyes and gave me a dopey salute as I walked across the front yard. Forest green sweat rings stained my uniform and my arms ached from lugging the flag all over everywhere and my sash was a wrinkled mess from the leather belt. Mick followed me into the house, hooting and saluting and waving his rhubarb.

It made my head hurt.

ᘍᕽ EIGHTEEN ᕽᕽ

I walked into the Corianders' house one early summer morning not long afterwards looking for Pat Spumone. The Corianders lived almost directly across Main Street from the Spumones in a big white house with a bay window and nice bushes. I'd never been in their house before. The Corianders were Protestant and Mrs. Coriander taught third grade in Pinkerink's elementary school. My mother said Mrs. Coriander taught because Mr. Coriander, who had thick wavy black hair and sold insurance, couldn't earn a living; I think she said he drank too.

Clara, Rena, and Lila were their daughters; all three were kind of oversized and wore horn-rimmed glasses and had shiny straight dark hair. Lila, the youngest, was a couple of years older than Pat, but sometimes Pat played with her because they lived across the street from one another. I think that they played dolls or something; the Corianders were very refined so Lila never ran around much; mostly she just read a lot and was very tidy.

My mother really had it in for Mrs. Coriander, though sometimes she did allow as how Mrs. Coriander worked hard and had to raise those three daughters by herself. The older two attended some Methodist college in Indiana and were studying to become teachers like their mother. The fat lady liked to think almost everyone in Pinkerink was trash, but the Corianders stumped her, even if Mr. Coriander did drink.

That morning I ran up the wide wooden steps of the Corianders' front porch and banged on the screen door.

The inside door stood open and I saw more polished wood than I'd ever seen anywhere besides church on Sundays. A crystal bowl of red and white peonies glowed in the sunshine on a small table by the bay window that looked out on the side lawn. At my knock, Lila's cat, a fluffy grey Persian with eyes huge and orange as harvest moons, bounded down from the chair where she'd been sleeping and rubbed up against the screen to say hello.

I heard Lila's voice from upstairs. Who's there? When I told her, she called down that the door was open and I should come up. Never having been in their house, I was unsure where I was going once I'd walked inside. It really was like church. Oak and mahogany gleamed. Curtains, white and immaculate as nuns' bibs, hung motionless at the open windows. The two green chairs in the living room matched the sofa, and the rug that lay before the fireplace was a deep ruby red like the glass around the sanctuary lamp. On the mantle, along with two pale blue porcelain ballerinas and a small vase with four or five white narcissus, was a gold clock with four little gold balls. Everything was so still, I tiptoed.

Having located the staircase, I climbed slowly, trailing the tips of my fingers along the cool smoothness of the banister. Where are you? In here. I followed Lila's voice down a hallway whose walls were covered with framed pictures of Clara, Rena, and Lila in organdy dresses at birthday parties, piano recitals down at the Grange Hall, out on the front porch with Lila's cat, or all dressed up with white hats and gloves and white purses by the forsythia bushes outside at Easter. The shiny glass reflected the light from the globe in the hallway, so I had trouble seeing their faces right.

The white enameled door of the bathroom stood open. Lila lay back in the tub. Bubbles rose up under her chin and her hands, reaching up out of the bubbles, held a book about collies. Near her on a shelf at the edge of the tub rested a tumbler of iced tea with a piece of lemon stuck on the lip of the glass. I'd never seen anything so sophisticated in my life. A yellow ribbon caught up Lila's dark hair and held it out of the foam. A fuzzy white rug lay alongside the tub and all the towels were thick and the same shade of blue. It looked like Hollywood.

Lila peered nearsightedly out over the bubbles at me; her glasses were over on the sink. Except for the squint, she looked like a princess or something out of *Streets and Roads*. Hi. Hi. Is Pat Spumone here? No. Do you like dogs? Some, but I'm allergic. I nodded, but I had no notion what allergic meant; I figured it probably had something to do with being Protestant. Cats don't bother me, she explained. They don't bother me either, I volunteered chummily. I liked cats. We'd never had one because the fat lady said they were sneaky old things and that we couldn't afford to feed one, though we were able to feed our dog and she gave scraps to the neighbor's calico with the seven toes and I'd even seen her pet it sometimes by the back door.

Lila climbed out of the tub and, after drying herself with one of the powder-blue towels, doused herself with Lavender Splash and pulled a red flowered mu-mu over her head. Her breasts were starting to grow and her nipples looked dark and serious, not at all like mine. I decided to save up and buy some of that Lavender Splash; I'd seen it in the dimestore next to the barrettes.

Lila asked whether I wanted to see her dolls, so I said

sure, and she led me down the hallway and around a corner to her room. Her damp feet left faint prints on the waxed floor. My red sandals with the holes in a flower pattern across the toes were dusty and I hoped I wasn't marking up the finish on the floor. I noticed that my bare ankles were dirty too where they came up out of my sandals.

Lila's room was all pink—the rug, curtains, bedspread, everything—a pink stuffed cat even sat on her pillow. The bed had a pink roof and a pink ruffle ran all around the border of it. I'd never seen anything like it; it looked like something out of the palace where Cinderella went to live after the shoe fit. Across from the bed against one wall was a little table with a mirror and a pink skirt. A matching pink wicker seat stood in front of it. Next to the musical jewelry box with a picture of Snow White on top lay Lila's brush and comb set and a box of scented powder with a big pink puff.

On the wall near the door hung a picture of a sort of honey-colored Jesus with a stick in his hand, knocking on somebody's door. His head was cocked like a dog's when he hears your stomach growl or you talk funny. Taped to the wall over next to the mirror were pictures of Esther Williams and Doris Day that Lila must have cut out of movie magazines. They both looked really perky.

Lila pointed to the far wall. On each side of the window, I saw three rows of white enameled shelves that Lila told me her father had built to hold her doll collection. Lila had more dolls than the toystore in Meckleton where I bought my Nancy Drew books. There must have been a hundred of them, all about seven inches high.

There were fairies with wands and ballerinas with

sequins and princesses with diamond tiaras, a Scottish doll with a kilt and her leg in the air, a Swiss doll with a flowered pinafore, French and German dolls wearing kerchiefs and aprons, and even a freckled Irish doll dressed in green. Bride dolls wore long veils and white dresses and even clutched little bouquets in their stiff little fingers. Some of the dolls had their feet glued to shiny wooden platforms and were covered by snug little glass domes that kept the dust off. Other dolls smiled out from behind clear plastic covers like the one that protected the white satin robes of the Infant of Prague Father Himmel had brought my parents once when he'd come back from a trip. His arms couldn't move either and he didn't have anything on underneath his outfit. The Infant's curly wooden hair was painted brown and two fingers of his right hand stuck up in the air like a railroad crossing sign. Father Himmel had blessed him for us when he brought him over and my mother kept him on top of the TV.

I crossed the pink rug to stand over next to the window so I could get a better look at them. Outside, a breeze passed like a shiver through the leaves of the elm that stood in the Corianders' backyard, and I saw an oriole, her breast a ripe peach in the sun, take flight from the long branch where she'd suspended her pouch of a nest. It was still early in the summer and the elm's leaves were pale, not yet the dark crayon green they'd become later in the heat.

I squinted in through glass and plastic at the rows of tiny faces with their red wooden lips, mouths that wouldn't open, and little dots of eyes, dull and staring like squirrels run over in the road. With those small round patches of red on their white painted cheeks, they all looked like

Snow White and Sleeping Beauty after they'd eaten the apple or been pricked. When I reached for the Scottish doll dancing the hornpipe, Lila cautioned me not to touch her. She told me she didn't handle them either, just once a month when her mother helped her lift them down and they dusted the covers together.

My dog had fleas. I put powder on her sometimes, but she still had a bunch of them. I let her climb up onto my bed at night anyway. I'd rather have had her in my room at night, in my bed even, than to have had all those shelves of brides with their feet glued and no grooms or the dancers with their net skirts and their legs fixed like warnings in the air.

You've got a lot of dolls. Do you like horses? No, replied Lila, I don't. I decided not to tell her about my Aunt Gerda's horse Queenie or the two china horses my father had bought for me when we went on vacation last summer. One is brown and long-legged, a foal who stands on a little hill that says St. Thomas, Ontario, and the other is black and shining and her mane and her tail stream in the wind as she gallops and her forelock is beautiful and tangled on her broad forehead. In the dark before I fall asleep, I watch her galloping, galloping in the night across hills, down moonlit courses of rivers, her long legs lifting, falling, force gathering, flowing, exploding almost into flight. Her fine hooves glitter so brief on the earth. There are no fences, no roads, just the swelling of hills and the winding of water. She startles the owl and the black-faced fox, scatters deer come down for a drink.

Lila raised the pink bedspread and dragged a big carton wrapped in silver foil from under the bed. Do you want to see my paper dolls? She held up two stiff-legged, smiling girls in striped bathing suits. No, I've got to find Pat Spumone. I've got to tell her something. It's important.

The screen door slammed after me and I laughed at the clatter of my red sandals on the painted steps. Across the street, I still didn't see Pat, but I spotted Bunkie, Pat's dog, a red Spitz with a black tongue, trotting along the sidewalk on his way downtown to the store to see Paul, so I yelled to him to wait up, then grabbed his head in my hands and, my lips tickling his soft furry ear, I told him, Bunkie, listen—I run, Bunkie—I run everyplace I go.

⊷§ NINETEEN §⊶

Over the way, across the street from our house, big Harleys smoked and roared and summers were yodeled away beneath bright clouds that the afternoons shaped into mountains and cows, then blew away with a poof. Babies crawled about in the dust outside the door where grass couldn't grow; their mothers, grandmother, and aunts swatted them when they bit.

At fifteen, resting on the sagging wooden step, Salome lets the sun warm her pumpkin of a lap; she's flunking all her business courses anyway. Some days I play with her sisters, Blanche and Phyliss. Even though Blanche is older, she is pale and her voice quakes when Phyliss attacks her. Phyliss is short and mean and round like her mother and she's got bangs too. Her blue plaid dress, tied in a bow behind, is a disguise. She's a thug.

One morning Phyliss caught a striped snake in the garden out behind the house; she twined it around her bare arm and, squeezing the small head with its terrified

tongue between her thumb and forefinger, she chased
Blanche who screamed, turned whiter still, then stumbled.
Phyliss fell on her and her eyes glittered while Blanche
shrieked and sobbed. Phyliss rubbed the snake's head like
snow in the winter all over Blanche's face. I made Phyliss
quit when I caught up with them and had to pretend it
didn't bother me at all when she waved the snake in my
face. Every spring when school got out, Phyliss asked me if
I'd come to Vacation Bible School with her and every
spring I told her we were Catholics and didn't do that.

Blanche and Phyliss lived across the street from us all
my life and every Sunday ate Jell-O and mashed potatoes
for dinner when their father stepped out on the back
porch and blew the whistle for them to come inside. Their
oldest brother wasn't their father's and neither were they
nor their little brother. The two older girls and Eck Jr.
were his. Then something had happened to their father
but their mother kept having babies anyway.

There was a hole in the floor of Blanche and Phyliss's
upstairs bedroom where a stovepipe used to go, and we'd
pile pillows on the couch below and drop down through
the hole like Alice. One afternoon I landed next to their
mother, who was feeding the new baby. Belle's breast was
round and swollen and flattened out the baby's nose; his
head was round and red and bare like his mother's breast.
They looked like blind things that live underground and
only come up at night for fear of dogs.

Their mother had a leather outfit with studs that she
wore when she and Eck went to rallies on weekends.
Sometimes Belle rode with Eck, climbing up behind him
on the broad leather seat. The visor on her cap snapped
down and off they went. Black and glistening, they looked

like two frogs mating. Roar. Roar. Dust rose and dogs barked. Other times Eck hitched on the sidecar for Belle and she climbed over the side and settled in, as snug as an egg in its crate. Vroom. Vroom. My father, watching out our kitchen window, loved it and promised my mother he'd get one for our car so she could ride to Mass on Sundays in it. She told him to come away from the window and never mind gawking at people.

The day after my brother came home from the army, Eck Jr. knocked on the front door and asked to see Mick. He sat down heavily in one of the kitchen chairs and spread his corduroy legs very wide. He asked Mick how he'd liked the army. Mick said it was all right and then Eck Jr. asked Mick did he want to drag. Jesus, Mary, and St. Joseph, marveled my mother under her breath.

Eck Jr. had the thick bearlike gait of his father, the same broad grin and dim, flickering light in his eye. He never amounted to anything. He impregnated some hapless high school girl, got a job in Pinkerink's screw factory, and settled down to plough several acres of land across the creek next door to his older sister Marlene and her husband Rodney and their kids.

During that summer Salome brought her record player out on the porch and played her little pile of 45's over and over while she watched her baby brother Olie and Marlene's kids scrambling about in the dirt and made sure they didn't go in the road or pull the Harley over on themselves. Roy Rogers's wife sang all summer long at the top of her lungs and Gene Autrey and Hank Williams and there was lots of twanging and yodeling and Salome skedaddled and kept up with the babies as best she could in her condition.

Salome had to watch Olie on those afternoons when her mother was out at a demonstration party. Belle sold Tupperware products and went to people's houses to show them how to put their leftovers in and snap the cover down tight. They came in all shapes and sizes and had a million uses, Belle said, when she asked my mother if she wanted to order a set. My mother said no, she saved cottage cheese cartons and they worked fine. My mother thanked her though. She was always polite to Belle, even with those bangs, because, she said, regardless, they were neighbors. But my mother never walked across the street to visit her or set foot in their house or anything like that, and once when I asked whether I could spend the night with Blanche and Phyliss, my mother just said, you bet, and laughed at me for asking.

For a long time Eck worked at the prison with my dad, but, even when they were on the same shift, they didn't drive to work together. Dad tried it once for a week but it didn't work out; Eck was never ready to leave for work as early as Dad was and, at night after work, Eck liked to stop at a bar for a while and my dad always came right home and had a beer in the kitchen with my mother and then watched the eleven o'clock news while he ate a ham sandwich or a piece of cold chicken. My dad always said Eck was good-hearted, though, and a decent man the way he took care of those children he knew full well didn't belong to him. Lots of men wouldn't, he pointed out.

Belle's oldest son A.C. wasn't Eck's either. Belle had him before she and Eck got married. A.C. was a sweet sunny young man whose right arm had been withered by infantile paralysis. It just dangled shrunken and lifeless from his shoulder. When he played baseball with us after

supper, he'd bat with his left hand and send the ball
zinging high up into the air over our heads anyway. He
married early too and moved out of the house. A.C.
brought his bride over to meet my mother and my mother
told my father that night when he came home from work
that A.C.'s wife was quiet and refined; that meant she
wasn't a hillbilly. My mother had said lots of encouraging
things to them about settling down and making a little
home and a family someday for themselves. She always
talked like that to people, like it was the best thing
ever.

In the shed at the back of the house where Eck kept
the black Harley in the winter months, Phyliss let some of
the neighborhood boys touch her for a nickel. Blanche
tried to make her quit it and threatened to tell on her but
Phyliss said she'd beat her up, so Blanche didn't and
Phyliss bought a lot of *True Romance* comics and Juicy
Fruit gum.

Blanche and I played in our backyard. We were still
making dolls out of hollyhocks and toothpicks and serving
pretend tea at the low red-painted table in metal cups and
saucers, while Phyliss was already out making something
of herself.

Blanche was frail and afraid of everything. My mother
said she was probably anemic, but I liked to play with her
anyway because she was quiet and happy to imagine dolls
talking to each other about their cats and whether the tea
was still too hot. She wasn't bossy like Phyliss and you
didn't have to look out all the time around her. Years
later, in high school, on the day we were supposed to give
career reports, Blanche made her way to the front of the
class, blushing and squeaking like a little bat, and told us

with a kind of sob and a glance down at her damp 3x5 cards that she wanted to be a beauty operator. Mrs. Curtis said, that's wonderful, dear, and called on Larry Limetruck.

❦ TWENTY ❦

There were lots of others in Pinkerink, people whose lives left traces on mine the way you find somebody else's paint on your fender after a scrape in the supermarket parking lot. Vinnie Trickett, who was probably in her late fifties by then, lived at the lower end of our street by the railroad tracks in a small dark-green house. Patches of moss grew on those parts of her roof that the big maple in her side yard kept shaded most of the time. Pigeons nested in the cornets of Vinnie's gables and every spring the maple sent millions of little helicopters twirling down into Vinne's gutters where they rooted and sprouted into millions of small maple trees that nodded and jostled one another up there whenever a wind came up. Along the edge of the front porch ran a ramshackle wooden railing with most of the uprights missing. The whole house had that look of disheartened bravado that caved-in jack-o-lanterns develop a couple of weeks after Halloween.

Except for her dog Jake, Vinnie lived all alone; her parents were dead and she'd had no brothers or sisters. Vinnie had been raised in Pinkerink a long time ago, but she'd gone off to Kansas City as soon as she grew up. She'd gone there, she told my mother once down at the post office, to make a life for herself; Vinnie claimed she'd met a young man, that they'd planned to be married, but then he died of meningitis, so Vinnie became a schoolteacher instead. But now, she told my mother, she was going to live out the rest of her days in Pinkerink. She'd taught geography, Vinnie added and inquired whether my mother knew that four-fifths of the earth's surface is covered with water.

Doesn't any fool know that? my mother snarled after Vinnie had left and we'd picked up our mail. That old devil couldn't make O in the gutter with a stick, she fumed. Aren't there as many oceans as there are continents and haven't I seen more of the Atlantic Ocean after crossing it three times over in a ship than that old tinker could dream of? My mother thought Vinnie was lying about what she had done in Kansas City; Vinnie, she maintained, was too ignorant to teach school and, besides, no woman with any self-respect at all would deck herself out the way Vinnie did just to walk downtown to do her shopping.

When I asked her what she thought Vinnie had done in Kansas City if she hadn't been a schoolteacher, my mother got all riled up and told me not to poke my nose into things that didn't concern me. I knew that Kansas City had been a wild place during Prohibition because I'd heard my father talking about the Prendergast mob; I remembered about Kansas City because my father's mother's name had been Prendergast, so I wondered whether my mother figured Vinnie had been a bootlegger or had maybe taught school for hoodlums.

Besides the way she dressed, Vinnie's hair got to my mother. Vinnie's hair was a flaming red—like some old rag doll's, my mother said—and, when I reminded her that Aunt Tess's hair was red too, my mother closed her eyes and sniffed and told me not to be comparing my Aunt Tess with that old trash, that God had given my aunt her red hair, but that Vinnie had bought hers down at Robinson's Drug Store. Huh, I thought.

Vinnie did always use a lot of rouge and lipstick and powder and you could see that she penciled in her eyebrows. In warm weather Vinnie wore silky flowery sundresses that came down quite a ways in front so you could see the beginnings of her dusty breasts and, right after Memorial Day, she pulled out those white high-heeled shoes that she polished up and wore all summer long. Even so, I never understood why my mother had it in for Vinnie so bad until my dad told me, laughing, that one fine summer morning before I was born, while my mother was back in Ireland with my brother to visit her parents, Vinnie had rapped on our front screen door in one of her flowery dresses and asked my dad whether he didn't need a woman to come in and do his cooking and washing for him. My dad told my mother he'd thanked Vinnie for the offer and said he guessed he'd carry on by himself.

My mother was gone for almost two years. She had promised her father when she came out here that she would come home again to see him and she did. Soon after she and my brother landed back in Ireland, Mick became terribly sick and nearly died; he broke out in boils that the doctor had to lance and he ran a high fever for such a long time that my mother prayed and prayed Mick wouldn't die because she couldn't imagine facing my father again if he did. All the doctor could tell her was that the climate didn't agree with Mick and to let him drink lots of good strong tea.

Eventually Mick recovered from whatever it was and, the day before they left to come back home on the boat, my grandfather stood Mick up on a chair with a towel pinned around his shoulders and, while my mother and grandmother watched, my grandfather cut Mick's hair for the first time ever and my mother cried, she said, and gathered up some of the corn yellow curls that fell to the floor that morning into an envelope that she saved always afterwards in the top drawer of her dresser right inside her jewelry box. She took out the envelope lots of times when I was little to show me and each time she'd start to cry because of her father and because Mick was so nearly lost. The coils of blond hair were hard for me to connect with Mick because by the time I'd been born and had grown up some, his hair was the same light brown color as mine, though mine had started from jet black, my mother said. But those yellow curls made me feel awful too when I saw them and thought about ever trying to be alive with Mick dead. Anyway, my brother didn't die and my mother came home and I was born and Vinnie never got a chance to cook for my father, though she'd wanted to.

The woods below our house reached almost up to Vinnie's back steps and, from my perch on a branch of the box elder, where I used to sit sometimes with a book in the heat of the summer day with my bare knees drawn up to my chin and my back propped against the rough trunk, I could see out through the dense leaves to Vinnie's back porch with its torn screens and the rows of empty bottles and piles of stacked-up newspapers.

Lots of afternoons Vinnie would come out and sit in the shade on her back steps with Jake and smoke a cigarette and talk to Jake about his water dish always being tipped over or how bad his fleas were biting him. Even though Jake was just a mutt, he had a lot of terrier in him and the patch of black over his right eye made him look like he'd been socked in a fight in a bar. Jake watched Vinnie closely. Vinnie looked kind of saggy sitting down there talking with Jake, not peppy and high-heeled the way she did whenever I saw her downtown. I always figured when she got so quiet sitting there with her arm draped over Jake's back that she was thinking about that blond young man a long time ago who had caught meningitis, but one muggy evening after dinner when I'd climbed back up into the tree and settled down to wait for the rain that had been threatening all afternoon, Vinnie walked out her back door and, nearly tripping on the bottom step, gave Jake's water bowl a vicious kick that sent it flying off into the weeds. She lurched back to the porch steps then and sat down heavily against the rickety handrail. Her eyes half-closed, she wiped her mouth with the back of one hand and with the other steadied a tall half-empty wine bottle that she'd carried outside with her.

Thunder rumbled in the distance and heat lightning started up again. The sky was growing darker, but even in that fading light I could see the bright smear of lipstick on the lower part of Vinnie's cheek and again on the back of her hand. All that powder on her face was smudged with tears. I started to think I ought to slide down out of the tree and light out for home, but I didn't know how to get out of there without Vinnie catching me spying on her.

Vinnie reached into a pocket of the tatty red bathrobe she was wearing and pulled out a pack of Luckies and a man's Zippo lighter; the lighter gave her trouble, sputtering a lot, and the hand that held the cigarette shook badly, but she finally managed to get the Lucky lit. Taking several deep swallows from the wine bottle, she slumped back against the railing and, in a voice as soft and low as that far-off thunder, Vinnie began to curse.

You can rot in hell. I hope you die of cancer covered with scabs and stinking in the gutter. I hope your flesh rots and falls off in huge stinking chunks, hunks of it that you choke on, you rotten dirty son of a bitch. I hope you fall down into the sewer and lice and rats eat out your eyes, you bastard and all you bastards, the whole lot of you, you devils, you dirty rotten liars.

Vinnie's eyes almost closed and she lifted them up toward heaven, the way Father Himmel rolled his eyes back in his head during his sermon on Sundays and then sort of tipped his head back so that it seemed as if he were mainly trying to get to the people up in the choirloft with what he was saying. He'd pause sometimes between ideas that came to him just like Vinnie was doing, as if he were waiting to find out what God wanted him to say next.

At first I thought Vinnie was just mad at that guy for dying of meningitis, but as I listened, that didn't make much sense. I didn't understand what she felt so bad about or who had made her so mad and I wished I wasn't stuck up in that old tree with the thunder coming closer and the rain starting to fall but, when her voice just died away after praying that rats would eat his liver and her head with all that orangey hair fell forward into the palm of her hand and she started to sob, something in me wanted to cry too, watching the faded rosy-red of her robe turning dark and splotchy like the powder on her cheeks from the rain.

His legs and belly covered with muck from the banks of the creek where he'd been hunting frogs, Jake trotted up out of the woods and stopped in front of Vinnie, his tail wagging just a little. Leave me alone, God damn you, you stinking liar, Vinnie cried and shoved him away, so Jake lay down in the tall grass by the edge of the steps as the warm late-summer rain fell lightly on Vinnie and me and my library book and the trees and that mossy old roof and, after a while, Vinnie stopped weeping and, all worn out from the wine and the grief, slumped over against the grey rotted-out wood of the handrail, she slept, holding with both hands her head that glowed down there in the near dark like an overblown poppy.

While Jake with his patched eye kept watch, I slid down and ran for home through the rain and I lay awake in my bed that night afraid like in a dream where you open a door to step out and suddenly there are no stairs, just a vast dark space where you can't make out any of the edges.

When I asked Mick the next morning about Vinnie and told him I'd seen her crying outside her back door, he laughed at me and told me not to worry about the old tart, that she'd get along all right. She always has, he assured me.

⋞ TWENTY-ONE ⋟

Sister Poinsettia arrived late in the spring the following year, just before school ended, to replace Sister Psychopath, who had to be put away finally after one day over in the sheds where the picnic tables were stored, she strangled a stripey orange cat right in front of a bunch of third graders who were out for recess. Some of their parents complained to Father Himmel that evening and said that was the last straw, that Sister Psychopath was bats even if she was a nun, so Father Himmel called the mother-house and had them come pick her up. When my nun caught us watching out the window as they loaded Sister Psychopath and her two black valises into the back of the station wagon that had been sent from Kalamazoo, Sister Mary Virgin scolded us and told us it would be more in our line to be saying a prayer that Sister Psychopath and the others have a safe trip back to Kalamazoo. Yeah, I thought, she might just throttle that poor skinny, sheepish-looking driver with her rosary.

Sister Poinsettia wasn't a whole lot better, though she never killed any cats. She did feel very keenly about hygiene, however, and taught us during the noon hours when she came over to supervise us that God loves clean fingernails better than almost anything. On those days when she substituted for Sister Midget, before she'd even let us open our lunchboxes, Sister Poinsettia would line us all up, girls on one side of the room and boys on the other, way over by the radiators, and she'd inspect our hands to make sure they were all right to touch food. Kids whose weren't got sent to the lavatory in the basement to wash up and were reminded before they left the room that their bodies were temples of the Holy Ghost. After lunch Sister Poinsettia would check the desktops for crumbs from our sandwiches because they encouraged vermin, she told us. I wasn't sure what she meant; I thought vermin was what the Pope and rich ladies wore.

Sister Psychopath was fat and waddled; from behind, that vast expanse of black backside looked like a semi moving down a rutted country road at midnight. Sister

Poinsettia, though, had no fat at all on her and looked like one of those people in the church history books who'd been left too long hanging on a cross by the side of a Roman road.

Sister Poinsettia always wore black cotton gloves, even in May when lilacs were out all around the sides of the school. One blustery afternoon when I had to run over to the convent to fetch Sister Virgin her umbrella, Sister Poinsettia was outside in the wind bringing in flapping sheets off the clothesline before the rain came, and I noticed she was wearing the gloves then too. Some of the kids bet she had the stigmata and just didn't want to brag about it, but the fat lady said she probably had a good case of eczema.

Sister Poinsettia was filling in for Sister Midget that Monday at noon when Mixie Hurlbut's period arrived for the first time. Mixie, like me, was only in the sixth grade, so none of us really knew much about what was going on. Sister Poinsettia chased the rest of us away and hustled Mixie off the baseball diamond and into the convent to lie down. I'd seen a little blood on the inside of Mixie's right knee, but I just figured she'd probably scratched a mosquito bite while she was out in left field. After she'd stowed Mixie away in the convent and called home to have Mixie's father come and get her, Sister Poinsettia came back out to the ball field. Her sharp nose was twitching like a rabbit's when it smells either a carrot or the fox and, when we crowded all around her to inquire about Mixie, Sister Poinsettia just rattled her rosary and waggled her eyebrows significantly toward the boys and urged us to say an extra little prayer for Mixie. One of the fourth-grade girls had died during the winter from pneumonia, but Mixie hadn't even sneezed that morning on the bus as far as I could remember. I figured I'd say a Hail Mary anyway; it couldn't do any harm.

Mixie returned to school the following Thursday, bragging to us about her belt and her cramps and the rest of her apparatus. She and Pat Spumone and I had carried our peanut butter sandwiches over to the big flat rock near the driveway and we'd just spread them out on a piece of waxed paper when Sister Poinsettia, spotting Mixie from the convent window, made a beeline for us.

With Pat and me standing there dumb and with peanut butter stuck to the roofs of our mouths, Sister Poinsettia railed at Mixie about the Blessed Virgin and impure thoughts and those sins as black as pitch and just as sticky. Mixie just kept looking down at the ground and scuffing around in the gravel with the toe of her shoe. Mixie's face was red by the time Sister Poinsettia finished with her, but so were mine and Pat's, and we hadn't even done anything yet. Pray to God and to Our Blessed Mother, Sister Poinsettia hissed at Mixie, shaking her black index finger in Mixie's face. Pray to the Little Flower whenever Satan sends you vile thoughts and foul notions. Flush Satan out of your soul and out of your heart; you are the bride of Jesus and of the Holy Ghost.

Sister Poinsettia was garbling her canon law, of course. She was the Bride of Christ. She was the one with the glittering, feverish eyes. She was the one who wore those wacky black gloves to make sure nobody could ever see any of her except that starved-looking bit of face that poked out through the white starch beneath her black bridal veil. Mixie and Pat and I were just dopey and flat-footed, puzzled, flecked with peanut butter and strawberry jam, not pitch, and during the next few years, with the help of God, we might learn to pray and to entertain impure thoughts at the same time, if all went well.

On the last day of May that year, a beautiful day, Sister Poinsettia rode with the other nuns in Mr. Fleming's car out to Guffy's Resort at Bluegill Lake for the big end-of-the-year picnic. The Guffys had been parishioners forever and one of their grandsons was even studying for the priesthood. The hotel they ran was kind of ramshackle and needed paint but every spring they turned the dining room and grounds over to us and we loved it. There were big yellow bags of potato chips on the tables, enormous watermelons, a huge red cooler filled with floating blocks of ice with lots of cherry and orange and grape pop, and toward afternoon hundreds of steamed hot dogs appeared, along with vats of mustard and catsup and platters heaped high with potato salad and relish and chopped onion.

Sister Poinsettia wouldn't touch any of it. She spent the entire day sipping lemonade, sitting on a folding-chair in a corner of the wide screened-in porch that ran across the front of the hotel. With the tips of her gloved fingers, she traced circles in the mist on the side of her glass and visited with Ella and Jane Guffy, the two unmarried aunts of the couple who ran the place.

Jane Guffy sang in the choir and every Sunday morning drove her sister and herself to early Mass in an old black Ford as rheumatic as they were. Jane and Ella had lived together all their lives and, when they'd retired from schoolteaching fifteen or twenty years earlier, the two of them had moved back for good into this hotel where they'd grown up. Ella was sweet and a bit vague, but Jane, with her stiff narrow back and thin pinched face, looked a lot like the old maid in the deck that you didn't want to draw when it was your turn, the one so grim in her black hat with the pin stuck through it because, unlike all the others, she had no mate.

Jane and Sister Poinsettia scarcely budged off that porch the whole day, although the other nuns played volleyball with us and badminton on the broad ragged lawn that stretched down to the edge of the water. Sister Midget even pulled off her shoes and socks and hiked up the dark heavy skirts of her habit to wade out a bit into the lake while we swam in the still chilly water. As I watched her standing there sturdy near the shore with her wonderful broad feet planted in the sand of the beach and with the small waves we made with our splashing washing up all around her ankles, I loved her a lot. The sun at noon that day caught the soft gold of her glasses and again warmed with its rays the weary body of Christ who hung from the cross on her breast. Sister Midget ducked and laughed there in the shallows when we rose up dripping and surrounded her and threatened to douse her. The hem of her habit was soaked, but she didn't mind and, when Mary Flannery's skinny little brother came up out of the water all covered with goosebumps and with his teeth chattering, Sister Midget hugged him and rubbed him to warm him with a big orange towel. As we all trooped toward the dining room for our hot dogs, Sister Poinsettia scowled down at the sand on Sister Midget's bare feet, shook her head slowly, and sighed a great sigh to Jane Guffy.

After lunch Jane and one of the young men who

worked around the hotel walked through the shade of the tall elms that stood on the lawn and crossed over the narrow wooden footbridge spanning the little creek that flowed into the lake through a culvert beneath the road from the golf course across the way. Jane took a key out of the pocket of her brown sweater and removed the padlock from the rickety double doors of the roller-skating rink that the Guffys operated in the evenings during the warm months.

We all swarmed after Jane and the man who rented the skates and changed the records and sold the pop, but we didn't bother with the bridge at all; we just jumped one after another like startled frogs from one weedy, mucky bank of the creek to the other and crowded around Jane while she fished the right key out of her saggy pocket. The skinny young man in tight Levi's with his pack of Lucky Strikes tucked underneath the sleeve of his black T-shirt swung open the two broad doors with their flaking green paint and hooked them to the outside wall of the building so they wouldn't slam shut again in the breeze.

Inside, the rink was dim and vast and solemn like a church when nobody's there; we could barely make out in the dusky light the rows and rows of shelves behind the high wooden counter with all their tall leather skates, toes in, their sizes printed on the backs with black or white paint way down by the heels. We lined up on benches to pull off our shoes while the man, his dark hair long and slicked down, slammed open, one after another, the heavy wooden shutters that came down like eyelids over the wide screened windows. Sunlight, bouncing brilliant off the surface of the water, skittered along the ceiling, lighting up the bare rafters. The red-and-white Coca-Cola sign on the back wall flashed on, the young man lowered the arm of the record player, and a sudden blast of organ music sent us reeling.

Milling about the counter in stocking feet, yammering at the tops of our lungs, one by one we traded the man our sneakers or sandals for skates and a tag. When the lean young man with his long sideburns handed the tall white skates across the counter to me, their wooden wheels were already spinning. I stuck the metal tag with the number on it into the pocket of my shorts and sat down next to Mixie Hurlbut's older sister Mary Kate to put on my skates. What happened next astonished me.

While I'd been waiting my turn at the counter, through the open door I'd noticed some kids I didn't know standing on the steps outside in the sunlight. Now one of them was standing in front of the bench where I was sitting, his black skates flung across his shoulder, one in front against his chest and the other dangling down his back. Out of the bunch of kids outside the door, he was the one I'd particularly noticed; I liked how he looked out there, long-legged and easy, not twitchy and pushing and shoving like the others. His thick hair was the color of an Irish Setter's and the sunlight had kindled it.

Want some help? I heard his voice but didn't look up, assuming he was talking to Mary Kate, who was dark-haired and pretty and in the eighth grade. Mary Kate wasn't at all like Mixie; she wasn't catty or mean and she even told you if she liked your blouse or pin or something else you were wearing; at Confirmation, she'd chosen the name Bernadette because she liked the idea of the Blessed

Mother appearing to the young French shepherdess with asthma out in the middle of nowhere. The nuns usually picked Mary Kate to be the Blessed Virgin in the May procession and in most of the plays, so it wasn't odd of me to be so sure that the tall boy was offering to help her with her skates. But he wasn't. I heard him ask again and felt the slight nudge Mary Kate gave me with her elbow, so I looked up. There he was, smiling down at me with quiet hazel eyes. I got all rattled and frowned and blushed and just muttered, All right.

Kneeling there in his blue jeans with that flaming cloud of hair drifting down across his forehead, this boy reminded me of that picture in our reader of young Roland alone at midnight in the chapel, calm and at peace before the tumult that was to come. I scarcely had the wits to pull up my socks before he had the long laces crisscrossed and tied securely and was inquiring whether they were tight enough. I nodded, thanked him, then stood up to go out onto the floor. Hey, wait and I'll go with you, he said, his fingers holding my wrist for an instant. Out of the corner of my eye, I saw Mixie glowering at what was happening; she narrowed her eyes and set her mouth in that nasty, tight-lipped way she had.

His own skates on, this lovely boy took my hand and drew me along the long row of kids, some of them scuffling with one another and others bent over tying on their skates. He just reached over and caught hold of my hand as if it were the most ordinary thing in the world— nothing to it—just as if anybody else had ever done it before. His name was Andy Sullivan, he told me, and he lived a couple of doors away from the hotel. When they'd heard the loud organ music starting up so early in the day, he and his friends had come over to see what was going on; the rink usually didn't open until after dinner.

Andy asked my name and, as we rolled slowly out onto the floor, he showed me how two people are supposed to skate together, arms crossed over, his right hand holding mine and his left my left. I felt lightheaded and was a little afraid that I might pass out just like on that bright Sunday morning years ago when I'd received my First Holy Communion, but Andy was nice and easy with all of it and I forgot soon how strange it was to be skating with a boy I didn't even know and who was probably a Protestant too, even with that name, since he went to the public school. But he was a wonderful skater, and after the first couple of circuits I felt myself remembering what to do; in the wintertime, I skated a lot on the pond behind Dr. Parker's house and this wasn't really very different.

Andy steered us along the outside edge of the rink so we wouldn't bump into slower skaters or any of the little kids who were falling down and getting up and falling down in the middle and, as we headed into the patch of bright sunshine coming in off the lake, that crazy organ music rose up and crashed in our ears like a tide and our strides lengthened and I leaned into the shimmering sunlight, into the music, first toward him, then away from him, and then back again. Taking the corners with easy rapid cross-overs, we gathered speed and flew so fast down the long sides of the oval rink that I started to laugh and he glanced over at me with those lovely eyes and we went faster still. I was glad my legs were so long beside him and I felt strong and fast and the millions of wooden wheels around me made songs inside my head.

We never stopped except once for two cold bottles of Coke that Andy bought from the man with the Lucky Strikes. As we leaned on his counter to rest while we drank, the man asked Andy when his old man figured they'd be heading for Columbus and Andy replied mid-July. His family was moving because of his father's job; none of them wanted to go at all, Andy told me, but they had to. His little sister had cried, he said, when she found out. Rolling the cool green glass of the Coke bottle across his forehead and holding it an instant against his flushed cheek, he looked serious and full-grown and worried suddenly and he told me then, half-shouting above the clamor of the organ music, that his parents fought a lot and he didn't know what would happen once they moved and that he'd never even been to Columbus. I wanted to say something to take the pain away from his eyes, but all I could think of to say was that I wished he didn't have to go, that it sounded awful, but maybe something would happen so he wouldn't have to leave.

But nothing did happen. For the next hour and a half we skated around and around as fast as we could go, past Pat Spumone with her pigtails flying, past sullen, crabby Mixie, past Sister Midget, who, leaning toward us across the railing, rose up on her bare toes in her black habit and swayed to the music and blessed us like the breeze that blew in through those fine wide windows. We skated through shadows of willows that the sun flung and the wind tangled and swirled in our paths. No ordinary devil could ever have caught us, we fled so fast along the edge of that afternoon, holding on a moment longer before the wave gathering behind us would break over our heads and send us sprawling.

At four o'clock sharp Sister Poinsettia left the veranda and her bitter lemonade to instruct the man behind the counter to shut down the music and to announce over the public address system that the bus had arrived to carry us home. Andy kept me company while I located my towel and wet bathing suit and asked me just before I climbed into the bus whether I'd come skating again sometime before he left. I looked down at his hand on my wrist and said I would if I could and I'd try.

The bus was already moving up the dusty track up to the main road when I found the seat near the window that Pat Spumone had saved for me. The muscles in my legs were trembling and my feet felt odd and numb in my sandals down there on the floor with all the orange peels and crumpled waxed paper and bits of old sandwiches. Through the lowered window, I waved to Andy who stood near the wreck of a young elm that an early storm had blown over. Calling out to us to have a good summer, the nuns and the Guffys were waving good-bye. The last things I saw that day as the bus made its turn were Andy's blazing hair and that woman's black glove.

By the next Sunday, all the nuns had left for the motherhouse in Kalamazoo for the summer. On the first Sunday in September before school began again, they were back, but Sister Poinsettia wasn't among them up there in the fourth pew from the front. I was glad; over the summer, I'd begun to know how deadly she was, even if she was a nun.

❧ TWENTY-TWO ❧

When he got older, Elvis Presley grew fat and took drugs and one night, like some ninety-year-old man, while taking a crap, the aging punk dropped dead of a heart attack— keeled right over with his silver jumpsuit coiled around his ankles. Like a cat, his girlfriend tried to cover it up. She claimed Elvis had a big overstuffed chair in the bathroom where he used to read at night for hours on end. The world wasn't convinced. Elvis's mansion, like God's, had many rooms and probably lots of lamps.

When Elvis first appeared on the Ed Sullivan Show, I was twelve or thirteen. Pat Spumone and I eyed the singer closely. Though the camera remained above Elvis's waist during the entire performance, Pat and I shrieked in chorus with the rest of adolescent America that night. Everyone knew what was happening down there where we couldn't see.

Pat and I used to embrace the wooden uprights in her basement that supported the kitchen floor above our heads. We took turns caressing the columns, and made up steamy scenes with Tab Hunter and Farley Granger and occasionally a favorite from the Pinkerink High School basketball team. Except for an old cash register from the store, some garden tools, and the snow tires from the Olds, the musty basement was empty and no one ever disturbed us.

We derived our notions about love and sex in part from the tepid romances we checked out of the tiny public library housed down in the G.A.R. Hall. We also drew extensively upon Doris Day movies, which revealed to us only that sexually active adult women changed their pastel outfits a lot and always looked fresh. They also kept their powder dry.

Pat and I had access as well, however, to a stack of detective magazines my father used to bring home from the prison in the pocket of his raincoat. He hid the magazines in a back corner of our garage under some gunny sacks.

Once a small foil-covered package dropped onto the dining room rug from my brother's wallet. When my father saw it, he slammed Mick up against the wall with one hand and slapped him repeatedly across the mouth with his free hand. My father cursed Mick for bringing rotten degenerate filth under this roof where his own mother and little sister lived. Likewise, I suppose my father didn't believe that detective magazines belonged on the coffee table alongside the current *Messenger of the Sacred Heart*.

When my dad wasn't saying his rosary up there in the glassed-in tower where he passed most of the afternoons and evenings of forty years of his life, he probably whiled away the lonely daylit hours gazing at the sprawled, mostly naked bodies of women who were garroted, punctured, pummeled, or dismembered and the pieces stuffed into burlap bags for having indulged unwisely in eroticism. Jealous husbands and lovers or random lunatics regularly avenged themselves on these women. Thousands of them had been strangled with their own black-mesh stockings but, somehow, their stiletto heels always remained in place. The magazines claimed that the photographs were either obtained from police files or were authentic representations in which professional models had been substituted for the original victims. Sprinkled throughout the magazines were shots of blood-spattered trysting places with lamps tipped over and underclothing and sodden bedding strewn about. Shallow graves abounded.

Summer afternoons, Pat and I pulled the garage doors shut behind us and there, amid the cobwebs and the turpentine, we peered into the dingy yellowed pages spilling over with their antic dead. Was this the inevitable result of entertaining impure thoughts? No wonder our mothers had never breathed a word. Jesus. But nobody had gotten Doris Day yet. Did my own silent father, eyeing my lumpy blathering mother across his breakfast oatmeal, imagine her chair upended and her tongue stilled finally by the pressure around her fat neck of the purple belt from her chenille bathrobe? Was that what gave him strength to go on? Was that what he was praying for up there day after day all alone in that tower with his only company the skunks who prowled about the base, waiting each night for him to throw his dinner down to them?

Pat and I peered at the pictures and at Elvis and at the geography lessons to be had from the sheets of instructions that came in her sister's Tampax boxes. We stared at the sweaty basketball team on Friday nights and thought about it all. One Sunday before Mass, when I whispered guiltily through the grill to the priest in confession that I had on several occasions during the week not only entertained impure thoughts, but had even touched myself immodestly, Father Himmel inquired whether I had caused the seed to flow. It took Pat and me most of the following week to figure out that the priest had assumed I was a boy; apparently penance was doled out according to the degree of illicit pleasure achieved.

Pat and I were enormously interested in any and all manifestations of that energy that was making Elvis a millionaire even as it threatened the two of us with the eternal fires of hell or at least temporal disembowelment by suitors and strangers off the street. Along with this passionate interest came the endless cycles of guilt, confession, and resolve toward more Marylike behavior that inevitably gave way before the force of thoughts so impure that no half-hearted Hail Mary could dispel them. The concept of eternal recurrence took on meaning for us at an early age.

It's difficult to know to what degree our preoccupation was hormonally induced and how much was simply a delighted response to the uproar a singer's pelvis was able to provoke in an otherwise obdurate world. Even our mothers broke their old-country silence on the subject of sex to tell us that night that we should switch off the television, that Elvis was like an animal strutting around Ed Sullivan's Catholic stage.

Actually, my mother was never any use to me at all. When I was still quite young I awoke from a nap one summer afternoon in the half-light of my room where my mother was also resting. Staring up at the designs in the border of the wallpaper where it touched the edge of the ceiling, I let my eyes slip out of focus. The patterns began to sway with a motion lovely and soothing as the waters of a womb or the green glowing after-image of bright light drifting in the blackness behind your eyelids. I wondered from what wave I'd been born, how I'd come out of the darkness to be lying there watching those graceful blurry shapes swaying above me like seaweed. Turning my head, my eyes found the dim bulk of my

mother across the room where she lay asleep on the
narrow cot. Her face looked betrayed and angry even
in sleep, and I knew I would never ask her such things,
that something in her nature, a substance now deep in
the cells of her body, was inimical to anything fragile.
Nothing ever shook that conviction.

Something had made her the natural enemy of whatever was delicate; it had to be hidden away and sheltered
from her. Except for her flowers, which she did love, all
her life my mother was suspicious and intolerant of anything much more subtle than one of the spuds from her
garden. For the most part, life bewildered her and in
her bewilderment she was often mean. Thinking always
in block letters, she knew only a few things; whatever
hinted at a larger world was hateful to her. She had
cleared a small anxious patch of this foreign wilderness
and now she patrolled its boundaries with a dogged
ferocity. Something had made her sad and savage and
had defeated her so that she wanted sometimes, like
Sampson, to bring all the world down around her.

I learned to be wary of her, to hide away from her
whatever I cherished lest she ferret it out and rend it.
Little between us flourished; parts of me survived, stunted
and grotesque, like plants grown in some moldy corner
of a basement. I knew enough to ward off those definitions
that emanated from the dilapidated hulk my mother had
wrapped about her soul, but I lost nearly half my life to
resisting her, to defying her insistence that the world is
flat and small and mean, to shoving against the walls
that her sullen bulk pressed in upon me. I didn't know
what any of it was, but surely there was more than that.

Ignorant and aflame, Presley was right, pacing arro-

gantly about like a young cougar, and she was wrong
when she came out of her silence a second time one day
years after I was married to tell me that your husband
had to have it and you gave it to him because he was
a man and couldn't help the way he was but no, you
didn't enjoy it.

I'm still not sure what it is, but it isn't that. We
shouldn't feel shame for wanting to know and, surely
to God, it's not something to be murdered or mutilated
about. It lives in our fists of hearts that grab and let go
and grab again, in our lungs as they suck the world
inside. And once, in the middle of the ocean, I saw it
gleaming on the back of a whale as she rose up, shattering
that wall of water between her and the air remembered
from long ago. Whales know; their joyous lovemaking
goes on for days and can be heard for miles inland.

⤙ TWENTY-THREE ⤚

Duck your head. This vale of tears is a tight, cramped
place—and stay inside the lines when you color.

Father Himmel and the nuns made it clear that you
don't have much leeway; a random impure thought, far
more deadly than any typhoid virus, could hurl you down
into the flames of hell to sizzle and splutter like a strip
of bacon frying for all eternity. So could a bite of baloney
sandwich swallowed some bright Friday morning just as
you stepped vaguely off a curb into the path of a cement-
mixer making a U-turn.

Don't expect much—there's not a whole lot to go
around.

My mother, weary of washing fingerprints off enameled woodwork, often lay in bed for entire afternoons, listless, puzzled, dreary, and cross, locked up tight as a drum in her pumpkin-shell house. Other days she pounced like some fat idle cat with trouble on her mind, dropped on me suddenly like a hungry spider from its hiding place in the rafters when it feels its web quiver. She cornered me somedays, tormenting me for no good reason or not much of any reason that I could make out. My throat tightened. It was hard to breathe. But there wasn't much to say or do anyway until she was finished and you could duck out. She was just crazy.

When I grew older, I read about menopause and I learned the word "irrational," so I called it that but it didn't make much difference to either of us. Back then, I just wanted to scream, to stop her mouth somehow, to bash her face in, to run, but I could only stand there trapped, my shoulders stiff, my soul squirming with rage and pain and loathing, impaled on her craziness like some damned hapless beetle.

During those same afternoons, while I shifted from one foot to another, banging my lunchbox against my knee to keep from flinging it at her, my father was out earning my bread by watching with his sharp blue eyes from his own glass cage high on the tower near the stone wall that enclosed all the murderers, thieves, and rapists, that collection of aberrant impulses whom he had sworn to blast to smithereens with his rifle if ever he spotted one creeping out over the wall. One night, toward the end of his shift, his owl eyes caught something moving there in the dark. He switched on the floodlights, slid open the glass, and there the guy was, some murderer or pimp or car thief, scrambling down by a rope from the wall.

Raising his rifle to the night sky and firing three times, my father shouted, Stop, or I'll shoot! Stop, goddamn you! Stop! You son of a bitch! Three times he roared out through the murk at the man who ran, then laid his cheek against the stock of the rifle and found the man's back with its number so clear in the circle with its crossed hairs, the middle of his back in the middle of the sight, just like any pheasant frozen in flight above a winter cornfield or a rabbit in terror flushed out suddenly from a pile of brush, and my father swore again and swore some more and shifted the muzzle down and slightly to the right and shattered the man's femur and dropped him, not dead, in his tracks.

But one morning during the summer that I turned fourteen I was out swimming in the middle of a green and shimmering lake, swimming slowly and silently underwater, watching for bluegills or turtles, when a boy, my friend, dove deep off the pontoon raft and in a swarm of bubbles swam right up before my startled eyes, and with his cheeks puffed out slightly, his hair drifting soft like seaweed around his head, he touched my face with his hand to draw me closer to him and kissed me there beneath the water in the midst of all those deep and quiet slanting shafts of warm sunlight.

Don't ever kiss anyone on the mouth, my mother cautioned me. So many germs in peoples' mouths—your father and I don't even kiss one another on the mouth.

Are you going steady with him? she inquired one evening before he drove up in the old blue Pontiac that had once caught fire in an accident and always afterwards smelled of smoke. Don't worry about it and leave me alone, I explained. Don't ever forget who you are, she urged me lovingly, shaking her fist in my face. You're a clean, decent Catholic girl with pure Irish blood in your veins—not like the trash that's all round us.

She really didn't need to worry. At the end of his junior year, Skeet moved away and Jesse, with the soft gleaming black hair that fell down across his forehead, who one day in biology class wrote me a note that said, Roses are red, as red as the sea. I love you. Do you love me? died the following summer of hepatitis, which he'd contracted somehow picking peaches day after day in the heat. None of us understood how that worked, but when we stood in front of the coffin to pray, we could see even under all that powder they'd patted on him that his skin was jaundiced. They said that if the hospital there in the town next to ours had had an iron lung, Jesse probably would have lived, so our tenth-grade class took up a collection and made a donation to help buy one.

Jesse's grandfather, a friend of my father's, worked at the prison and his mother ran the general store in a nearby town that was even smaller than ours. His father was rarely home because he was crazy—too nervous, my father said—and had to be shut up most of the year in a sanitorium. He'd come home every now and then and try to help out in the store, but he always wound up having to go back. Two attendants brought him to the funeral, and he sat stiff and upright in one of the wooden folding-chairs and shook hands with people when he had to. His hair was thick and black like Jesse's, but his face was drawn and white and his eyes had a shut-down look to them.

Do you ever wonder whether there's really a God? I asked one of my best friends, who was sleeping over with me after the Friday night basketball game and record hop. We'd talked until nearly two about Pendleton skirts and boys and my mother had hammered on the door of my room several times to tell us to turn out the light and go to sleep. Raising herself up on her elbow, Petra readjusted one of the pink plastic picks that held her brush-rollers in place, then looked over at me with her Noxema nose all wrinkled up. God, no! she confided and switched off the light.

Are you a beatnik? my mother finally demanded one Saturday afternoon after circling cagily around me all morning. I'd come home one weekend toward the end of my first year in college. My hair was long—no longer the pageboy I'd left home with—and I no longer wore make-up. Like most of my new friends, I usually dressed in Levis and black or navy turtlenecks. Before I'd ever left home, Father Himmel had warned me solemnly that the big state university where I was headed abounded with atheists—professors and students alike—and that I was to shun like the very Devil himself those rabid proponents of sin and disease. Others before me had lost their faith in that desolate and godforsaken place. Remember Maria Goretti and pray to the Little Flower daily, he urged. Right, Father, I sure will, I replied, nodding and carefully checking out the toe of my loafer.

The night before my parents drove me and my new pale blue luggage to college, I lay awake all night, too excited to sleep. This was it—the real thing—the big

world—what high school never had been—what Pinkerink certainly wasn't! Jesus. I couldn't wait for the elevator doors to shut behind my parents.

I did find friends—good friends—and the whole lot
of us laughed and argued and drank and smoked and
listened late into the night to Miriam Makeba and Bob
Dylan and Joan Baez, to the Beatles and to Ray Charles.
Sometimes we cried. We read everything—Cummings
and Whitman and Dylan Thomas and Yeats—and began
to write passionate intense poems cluttered with seagulls
and the sorrow of fluttering grey doves. I read *The Sound
and the Fury* three times that first September and my soul,
parched for so long, spun and whirled with all that
lightning and all those words roaring in my ears like a
sudden violent thunderstorm after that long, long dry
spell. I scrapped my major in Political Science.

After several long shuddering months of reading the
theologians and John Donne in the vast fluorescent under-
graduate library or closeting myself with Father Hugo,
the student chaplain, who responded to most of my questions by admonishing me to pray for faith and by warning
me about the dangers inherent in necking in front of the
dorms on Saturday nights and not contributing ade-
quately to the collection basket on Sunday mornings, I
concluded that, since human misery flourished so in this
world where millions of innocent people sickened and
starved and died, either there was no God or I hated his
guts.

Now, glancing over at my mother standing before the
curtained windows in her pink kitchen, I assured her,
No, Ma, I'm not a beatnik. Beatniks, I told her, usually
have grey hair like yours and they get permanents and

wear black tie shoes with stumpy heels like those you've got on. You sure you're not a beatnik, Ma?

I'm an orphan, I explained to my friends' mothers during Mothers' Weekend at the dorm.

I'll write to you, Sal promised, kissing me and Ricki good-bye just before he swung down from the train with two suitcases under one arm and the guitar he'd just been playing under the other. It was three o'clock in the morning. Ricki and I were off to New York for the summer and Sal had ridden as far as Rochester with us. A sleepy-looking man in a beige cardigan patted Sal on the back and took one of the suitcases; his father worked for Kodak and looked just like Perry Como. Sal, all rumpled and curly, turned and waved before he climbed into the station-wagon beside his father. Stretching my legs out across Ricki's stereo, I rested my bare feet on the empty seat opposite, watched the taillights disappear, and sighed, Do you think he really will?

He did. His job as a nightwatchman in one of the warehouses left Sal lots of time to write his dark, brooding poems and to send off several long rambling, lonesome letters that I read over and over in the fourth floor MacDougal Street sublet that Ricki and I shared that summer with several thousand cockroaches and a scruffy ill-tempered black-and-white spinster cat that belonged to the regular tenants who were off to paint in Mexico. The roaches swarmed over the butter whenever we forgot and left it out and the cat snapped peevishly anytime either of us absent-mindedly reached down to stroke her scraggly fur, but Ricki and I didn't mind.

Ricki worked in a Wall Street office as a receptionist and read novels most of the day. Every morning I pinned

my hair up into a French twist, sprayed it, caught the Fifth
Avenue bus beneath the monument in Washington Square
up to 42nd Street and ran into the Savarin Restaurant in
Grand Central Terminal in time to serve the early com-
muters their coffee and Danish. After lunch, my tips
jingling in my pockets, I browsed through the Doubleday
bookstore across the corridor from our restaurant, invested
in stacks of paperbacks and, climbing up into the heat and
racket overhead, caught the bus back down to the Village
where, unpinning my hair, I washed the spray out and,
with it hanging cool and loose down my back, crossed
the street to pick up a piece of meat and a box of frozen
vegetables for dinner from the small cluttered grocery
store run by a querulous old Italian couple.

Ricki's rich lovely voice rang in the grimy stairwell
as she sang coming home late in the afternoon. Peter,
Paul, and Mary sang with her continually that summer
in the white-painted front room near the window where
we'd set up Ricki's stereo. They sang over and over about
a man of constant sorrow and about missing the train I'm
on and I thought about Sal and about pain and about his
beautiful dark eyes that were so troubled so often and I
loved him more and more and read his letters so often
I could have recited them.

Trying to make sense of it makes little sense. I loved
him because he was beautiful and restless and sad and
because something in me answered him; the mass of soft
black curls, dark uneasy eyes—his soul swaying to the
music of the poets with whom we'd bombarded one
another during that first green year when, former altar
boy and never-nun, the two of us had turned our backs on

the Church, on salvation, saying No, we won't buy your death, and set out, scraped and raw and afraid into the world.

All that summer I loved him quietly and waited and Ricki and I talked long nights in that candlelit, streetlit room with the dingy white walls where the roaches darted and skittered like sudden impulses. Saying yes to the sounds drifting up through the open windows from the noisy streets below and to the music from the stereo, our souls stirred and ached and stretched and we talked all night Ricki and I and, often, another friend from school, the tousled young man with grey eyes she loved who some evenings rode the train in from his parents' house on Long Island to spend the night with Ricki in the small room off the kitchen where the painters' children used to sleep.

The three of us talked, argued, and exchanged revelations all that muggy summer long. Earlier, during that first year, nine or ten of us, a couple of tense Jewish kids from New York, several Catholics trying desperately to fall away from our faith, and two or three kids from the suburbs of Detroit, all of us birds of those same odd, anxious feathers, had drawn together for solace, for aiding and abetting, out of the intensity of our discomposure as our beliefs and our lives disintegrated and reassembled themselves, each of us seeking an authenticity and engagement we'd found lacking in the lives that previously had been laid over us like so many coats of paint of someone else's choosing. We floundered, barked our shins, nursed one another with a solicitude I've seldom seen since, a rawness and receptivity, an attunement I'd never known before and have often longed for since.

That first year we spent most of our days and many of
our nights crammed into a long red-plastic booth in
the student union, some of us venturing out occasionally
to work or to attend a class—letting their hair and beards
grow, Sal and Murray and John and Carl cut the com-
pulsory ROTC meetings and played pool instead—but
mostly we exhorted and comforted one another over and
again in our struggles to shake off coils of tattered belief.
Like snakes shedding old skins, we suffered blind and
frightening moments. Sliding across the red plastic seats
toward one another, grieving some days or bumptious
others, maddening often, we mostly constituted for one
another a litter from which we might one day emerge.
Day after day that first year, Sal had tumbled in beside
me, his shoulders bumping mine, grubby in his Levis and
sweatshirt and with black stubble on his cheeks. Silent
some mornings, he was playful and silly others, but often,
digging deep into his canvas bookbag to read us what
he'd been writing, he stoked my ears with poetry.

It's all right if you really love someone, Ricki and I
agreed that summer on MacDougal Street. I did and I
waited, tired of my chastity, not believing in it anyway,
despising, along with Auden, "the perversions of ingrown
virginity." I longed to be relieved of the burden; positing
one's identity on the maintenance of a layer of tissue was
absurd and I wanted to be over it, to be past the careful-
ness of it. I wanted to redeem my life from the mindless
marketplace insistence that had declared virginity our
major counter in the endlessly manipulative power strug-
gle between men and women. No man will ever respect
a woman he's had his way with, my mother had explained

to me. No decent man would ever marry a woman who'd given in to him. What kind of a man wants a slut for a wife and the mother of his children?

But the sun's gonna shine in my back door some day, Nina Simone sang to us from Carl's battered stereo set up on cinder blocks over in a corner. One night early the next September, when school had started again, we all gathered in Carl's dim basement apartment near the Law School to drink cheap Chianti from bottles that came wrapped in straw. Candles stuck in empty bottles flickered in the main room off the kitchen where we sat or lay about on the floor, leaning against one another, glad to be home. The black woman and Ray Charles and the others restored us to a rich and swirling world, deep, mysterious, and abundant, which held out again to our disinherited souls all the hymns and incense, all the Latin, the litanies and the absolution without the spirit-crippling falsehood.

Toward the end of the evening, I walked out into the kitchen to pour myself more of the red wine and found Sal standing alone by the sink. All evening long, stretched out alongside him on Carl's rug, I had stirred to his every movement. With my mind, I understood the desolation he felt, turning away, maybe toward perdition, from the known world; unsure whether we even had souls, we nevertheless feared terribly for them. But besides our mutual terror at the murky uncertainty, we shared something else, some wrenching inward grief that always lurked about the shadows of our hearts, some kind of gloom, too dark and too early, like a December night, that often threatened to swallow us up.

I walked blinking out of the candlelight into the kitchen and he turned and reached for me suddenly with a cry and, suddenly, I held him weeping, his tears wetting the collar of my shirt. It was the first time ever and I held him and, startled, caught the fingers of my hand in his thick curls and, for the first time ever in my life, for that moment anyway, what someone else felt mattered more to me than I did, and my soul leapt out toward him, flew toward him, a speckled bird kept too long in its cage.

That was the first time ever.

The very next morning I caught a seven o'clock bus back to Pinkerink to be a bridesmaid in Pat Spumone's wedding. Whistling softly under his breath, Sal walked me and my suitcase to the Greyhound station. Around us the morning was spectacular, the early September sky clear and blue and a million miles way high up over our heads. Just before I climbed into the bus, Sal raised his hand to the side of my face and kissed me. All during that long ride through the bright autumn countryside, smiling at my own reflection in the window, I kept telling myself my news over and over, trying to get used to myself again before the bus pulled up in front of the Rexall Drugstore.

What's his name? Mrs. Spumone demanded, inquiring whether I'd found a boyfriend. Benequisto, I whispered in her ear. That was all she needed to know; her face lit up and she kissed me noisily on both cheeks.

My pale peach dress with the dyed-to-match shoes hung in Pat's closet next to the long lacy gown she was to wear the following morning. Earlier that evening, during the rehearsal over at Sts. Cyril and Sebastian's,

Father Himmel had lined us all up and had asked Pat and her earnest crewcut Greg those questions they would be answering for real during the next morning's Nuptial Mass. The church was dim and the air, heavy with beeswax and stale incense, hung damp and chill around us. Pat's voice trembled slightly when she responded and later she didn't seem to be paying attention when Father Himmel and her older sister Josie asked her where to place the huge arrangements of white blossoms the florist had delivered that afternoon.

How's Miss College Student? Father Himmel pried, eyeing me closely from behind his rimless glasses as we all turned to walk back down the aisle. Terrific, Father, I replied, bouncing the palm of my hand along the backs of the pews as we passed them. He was suspicious. You watch your step at that place and stay close to your faith—no education in the world is worth an eternity in hell. You remember that. I surely will, Father, I nodded, looking him right in his rheumy eye. Overhearing our interchange, the tall apostles in the dark windows and the plaster saints in their pastels on the altar groaned and shook their heads mournfully. For shame, they muttered. A good Catholic girl.

In the car on the way home, Pat asked me to spend the night with her and, later in her room, while Josie rolled up Pat's hair and her mother sat on the bed, fussing with the fringe of the spread, Pat began to weep. I'm afraid. I don't want to go away with him. It'll be awful. I know it will. The two women sighed and then chided her for being silly. Laughing, they assured her they had both felt the same way before their own wedding nights. It'll be over before you know it, Pat's mother promised her. Her

sister filed and painted Pat's nails for her and then her
mother kissed the two of us good night.

With our pillows propped up against the pink padded
headboard of the Hollywood bed where, growing up,
we'd spent so many nights, Pat told me again how frightened she was, and I wanted to much to assure her that
it wasn't awful, that it didn't really even hurt, but I
couldn't. Instead I just patted her arm and told her not
to worry, that it would be all right and that I bet they'd
be happy. She and Greg had gone together all through
high school and then for two years afterwards while
they'd worked and put money aside, but it made no difference tonight. After we turned out the light, trying to
fall asleep, Pat lay on her back, rolling her head from
side to side, rhythmically, over and over, the way she had
sometimes when we were kids. No. No. No.

The next morning she was pale and a little quiet, but
the ceremony went off fine. Pat and Greg listened intently as Father Himmel droned on forever about children
and founding a home and the sanctity of marriage and,
standing there beside my friend before the tabernacle, I
stared down into the small buds of white roses I held,
following the inward turning edges, thin precipices curling ever in upon themselves and disappearing finally into
possibility.

Stubbornly I resisted his voice rasping at my ears,
but then everything I'd ever heard about the snares of
the flesh, the defilement of the temple of the Holy Ghost,
the sins as black as pitch—all that terror stored away
in my cells, setting one cell against the other—welled
up and, suddenly catching sight of Christ up there behind
the altar wretched with thorns digging into his skull and

blood dripping down from his wounds, my eyes blurred. I shook my head from side to side to clear it. No sulphurous hellfire, the flames blazing on the altar were only the six tall white candles that had been lit for the High Mass. And Father Himmel was no furious burning prophet thundering out of the wilderness to rain down damnation upon the heads of luckless sinners; he was a crotchety old man with the sensibilities of a Prussian barber and an ugly black mole on the side of his bulbous nose. Something in him made even my dog growl.

Still, after the wedding breakfast and before the reception that afternoon, while Pat's mother and my own were still drying their eyes and the Mexican janitor was sweeping the rice from the floor of the church, I fled. Flinging the pale peach dress and shoes in a heap on the chair in my old room, I pulled on a pair of Levis and a wrinkled cotton workshirt and slammed out the front door, ran, nearly suffocating, up the long hill to the bridge by the creek, scrambled down the slippery bank, ducked down under the strands of hot barbed wire that kept the cows from the road, then ran back through the tall grass where the cows grazed, moony and knee-deep. Back there at the edge of the field where the woods began, I spotted the big granite boulder and I raced for it and reached it just in time. God, what if they ever knew?

Leaning against the roughness, I slid my back down the side of the rock all warm from the sun, closed my eyes, settled back, and let the sun in that rock warm my shoulders, hush my jagged breathing, calm the uproar in my soul. They don't know. They never will.

Bees buzzed in the Queen Anne's Lace.

❧ TWENTY-FOUR ❧

Sometimes I try to skip this batch but they're stuck, like slides jammed in a projector. Everything goes black and quiet and you wait, hoping the next one will show her, the sturdy peasant, laughing with the sun, out in her vegetable garden maybe or standing before the flowerbed that ran along the side of the house. She'd hold up the heads of her favorites for the camera, cupping them steady in her hand the way you do a baby's wobbly head. Dozens of others could turn up, images, floodlit, of a random kind of happiness—a contentment, anyway—that visited her sporadically, but these always intrude, superimposing themselves on the others, crowding in, out of order, insisting, making chaos of my efforts. It's all wrong, boiling it down that way to the last days I saw her, while she was still maybe as much alive as dead, and then later, when she wasn't.

In one, she sits on the disposable paper sheet of an examining table. Her feet in their black leather shoes dangle above the low step she has just used to raise herself onto the table. We had waited a long time out in the holding area before the nurse called her name and she is tired. The nurse hands her a folded white cloth and tells her to strip to the waist. The doctor will be along soon. Clipping her folder to the inside of the door, the nurse leaves us alone in the little windowless rectangle of a room. Bright fluorescent light is cold on my mother's fingers as she undoes the buttons of her dress. Her left hand trembles. Carefully she slides the straps of her slip and brassiere first over her left shoulder, then the right. She places the sandbag that they gave her a month earlier beside her on the table and prepares to wait.

I try to talk with her to ease the waiting. Drawn and frightened, she sits there, her feet dangling that way like a child's, her thin shoulders rounded in upon themselves, sheltering the catastrophe. I try not to look at it, get up from the chair where the nurse has put me. I stand alongside my mother, leaning back against the edge of the stainless steel table. My hand brushes the fake breast and I nearly cry out. Though we both face the pale green wall opposite, out of the corner of my eye, I can still see the wall of her chest, bare now like a man's on the side nearer me. I'm startled to see the pulsations of her heart so visible beneath the dangerously thin layer of skin and rib. My eye traces the narrow line where the surgeon had stitched her together again. She is proud of how well the wound is healing. The doctor had removed the breast that harbored the crazed growth, but outriders, terrorists, cells as elusive and equally lunatic, right now are scaling her spinal column, assembling for the assault on her brain that will kill her ten days from now.

Outside, the January day is bitter. Pipes freeze and burst and cars skid out of control. She shivers a little. I drape the white cloth over her shoulders and bring it together in the front to warm her but also to shut away her lopsidedness. Her breasts had been big and heavy and soft like the pillows she made for our beds from chicken feathers and goose feathers.

Nearly a month before, just after Christmas, my brother and I had driven through the cold morning darkness to be with her before they carted her off to surgery.

Tears had started quietly down her cheeks, even as my brother was saying stupid things that made her laugh. Looking up at us, in that white gown, she was terrified. Someone she knew once had died under the knife, as she put it, and she feared she would never wake up again. The doctor planned to do a biopsy and then decide while she was on the operating table whether to remove her breast.

When they let us see her again, she was still groggy from the anesthetic. She asked me whether her breast was still there. I told her it was gone. She shut her eyes and drifted back into the drug again. The next time she surfaced, she asked us whether they had gotten it all. I told her the doctor was hopeful though he couldn't know yet for sure, but that she had come through the surgery itself in fine shape. She was comforted by having done her part well and laughed softly when Mick told her he had asked the doctor to do a hemorrhoid transplant on her as long as she was going to be out anyway. The transplant, he assured her, had been a great success.

Her initial recovery really was rapid; she worked hard at it. Soon, when I arrived in the morning, her bed would be empty and I'd find her padding about the ward, admiring snapshots of other women's grandchildren, displaying her own, fetching juice or a nurse for someone, and generally finding out everything about everybody. Watching her, gregarious and open there in the crowded ward, I felt how dreadful her isolation had been—those years of long days, alone in that silent house, cut off from her own, from all she had known, and stranded in that town that made no sense to her and offered her little solace. The ward, it turned out, was filled with two kinds of women—the God-love-'em's and the God-help-'em's. The former were merely wounded and had hope; the latter were dying.

Before releasing her, they taught my mother exercises to help her reclaim her left arm. They had sliced through muscle tissue in order to fish out the lymph nodes. The doctor told me and my brother that it appeared the disease had already spread but that, being post-menopausal, she might last comfortably another five years. He had removed the breast partly for cosmetic reasons, he said. The old clothes-pole wound had been draining; now she was tidy anyway. By the way, he added, he was prescribing a hormone for her that, in most cases, slowed the progress of the disease. Occasionally, the opposite effect was achieved. Oh, I thought.

This particular morning I've brought her back in for her check-up. The intern, palpating the tissue of her right breast, grimaces slightly. He hasn't learned yet to freeze his features like a proper doctor. She chats with him, inquires whether he's married and does he have children. Maybe he'll spare this breast if she can distract him. He obliges her, asks about her brogue, teasing, is she from Scotland? She is indignant. He laughs and asks her what she weighs now. She is evasive. I'm pleasingly plump. She isn't really, not anymore. The disease is eating her. She's almost thin for the first time since I've known her. He praises the marvelous scar tissue she has formed and she beams, proud, the bright pupil with the gold star. She's doing it right. She shows him how high she is able to raise up her left arm now. Wonderful. He touches her grey hair with his hand and tells her to cover up now so she won't catch cold. He'll see her next month.

When he's gone, I see again how exhausted she is. Slowly she arranges the eerie rubber breast and smoothes the soft wool of her dress over her real one. I hold her arm. As she eases herself down from the table, she tells me her ribs hurt her. Why didn't she tell him? What does it matter, she says.

My husband Ernie and I are buying a house. Much of the down-payment has come from my mother because paying rent, she says, is throwing money out. Our belongings are mostly in boxes so my mother is staying with my brother whose wife is kinder to her than I've ever been able to be. She grows drowsy and vague in the car as we drive through the frozen countryside. I wonder whether it's the warmth from the heater or the drug that makes her sleepy. I ask her a question or two but she just sighs heavily and leans her head against the cold window; her performance for the intern has depleted her. I wonder was he taken in but then, recalling his expression when he encountered the lumps, I'm sure he wasn't.

That evening after dinner, I lean down to kiss her good-bye. She sits, half-propped up in the chair by the pillows she has wedged in against her side. Her eyes are closed but she rouses herself to thank me for picking her up and bringing her back. She squeezes my hand and I tell her to rest. Be sure to take the vitamins I bought for you, I urge her foolishly. She nods, but her blue eyes are shut again.

Driving home in the dark, I wonder about the medicine. Maybe it is doing it all wrong the way the doctor said it might. Mick and I had spoken with him earlier about how tired it seemed to make her, but he said it probably hadn't begun to take effect yet. When I pull in for gasoline, the attendant,, apparently referring to the swirling snow, shouts into my face, She's a real bitch, ain't she? No.

Two days later, an ambulance rushed her to a hospital near my brother's house. When the attendants tried to lift her from the bed onto the stretcher, my mother screamed with pain, Mick told me, and pleaded with my terrified little nephew to help Grandma. By the time I arrived, she was unconscious. They had given her shot after shot of morphine to knock her out. They kept her under for a couple of days, then stopped, realizing there was no need for it anymore. Circuit breakers in her brain had tripped. Her soul, refusing to identify any longer with the frenzy in her cells, had withdrawn, drifting farther and farther from the chaos.

For the most part she was gone. Though she held tight to Mick's hand or mine, her eyes never opened again. At first she would murmur the names of people I'd never known, or my father or grandfather, and others whose names I hadn't heard since I was little. Holding our hands seemed to comfort her, but she had no notion whose hands they were.

She would still swallow sups of water and once took several spoonsful of custard the nurse brought for me to give her. They had her raised up, half-sitting, in the bed, strapped in, with the rails up. Several times, afraid she might choke, they tried to take out her false teeth, but she grimaced and clamped her jaws shut until they left her alone. Neither would she let them take my father's ring from her swelling finger.

The doctor told us she might last for six months that way. People did, he said. Besides, her heart was very strong. When he left the room, my brother sat next to the bed, holding her hand through the railing and drinking bourbon from a thermos. I looked out the window. The sky was rotten. I looked over at her. The nurses kept her clean and each morning I brushed her grey hair back from her forehead. Her fair Irish skin, always soft, was rosy and flushed as if she'd just come in from the garden. I knew, however, that she was pink because her blood pressure was climbing steadily as her various systems faltered and began to give way. Looking over at her, I tried to remember whether I had ever hated her so much that something this vicious could happen to her. A semi was running down a small child.

We kissed her good night that night but I knew, though her flesh was warm, that, in spite of us holding her hand, she had died already sometime three days or so before. I had turned my head for an instant and she had slipped off the black wet rocks and been washed away, refuse from the breakwater, washed out upon a sea where she would float forever, and neither I crying MOTHER MOTHER nor any trumpet blast would ever recall her.

Her body stopped altogether that night and the next day my brother and I drove home to talk to the man who had buried my father for us. On his little finger, the undertaker wore a large ring with an ugly blue piece of glass for a stone. Leaning forward across the financial records of my father's burial, he inquired in a hushed voice whether he might recommend a particular model for

Mother, just like Dad's, he assured us, only more feminine, he said. Puke, I thought, and my brother nodded agreement.

The rubber breast was in place. Mr. Unctuous cleared the room just before they screwed the lid down for the ride to the bleak church through the blasted month of February. So you can say Good-bye to Mother, he oozed and backed out of the room. She was my mother, you son of a bitch. Mick leaned over and kissed the cold powdered stone forehead. I couldn't. I looked at her thick fingers with the Irish rosary looped through them and I looked at the lovely white-gold ring my dead father had given my dead mother and then Mick and I climbed into the limousine.

That's the last I ever saw of her if you don't count when I dream about her or see her in my mind suddenly when I'm just walking along and thinking about something else altogether.

◄ξ TWENTY-FIVE ξ►

My father was worn out and a little distracted when I poked my head in the side window of Mick's car to kiss him good-bye. He was anxious to get home to mow his lawn and trim the hedge. The day before, he and my mother had come back from Ireland with my brother and his wife and son; they'd all spent the night at my house and we'd had sort of a party.

Mick and I had stayed up long after the others had gone upstairs to sleep, my mother first, shaking her fist, threatening us to never mind the booze and come away to bed. Bag it, you old bat, said Mick. When we laughed at her, standing there at the foot of the stairs, she offered us each a peg of a fist, which she promised would stiffen us. Her stockings with their elastic garters were rolled down around her ankles and one of her clip-on earrings was missing; she'd had a long day and a few beers herself. You're a sexy broad, Ma, Mick goaded her. Ye old devils . . . when I'm dead and buried . . . God help us.

We kissed her good night and kept drinking. Mick told me about their trip. When I'd taken my parents over to Ireland before, it had been my dad's first time back in over forty years; time and again he had marveled at how old-looking one or another of his friends had grown. Besides the electricity and a few new houses though, the mountain and the bay below hadn't really changed much; he wondered aloud what had ever provoked him to leave. Aunt Nell, Mick said, still had no running water; she carried it in buckets from the stream behind her house where the water flowed down the mountain on its way back to the ocean.

Aunt Nell was my mother's sister, older than my mother by only eleven months. Their faces were alike and, together in the same room with them, my back turned, I couldn't distinguish their voices. Early mornings I kept Aunt Nell company out in the small stone barn. Johnny was already out in the fields.. My soft-spoken cousin was over forty and had never married; Aunt Nell worried what would become of this big awkward son of hers should something happen to her. When my mother pestered him about marriage, Johnny inspected the toes of his boots and mumbled that he was waiting for Mrs. Right. Steaming milk soon filled the metal tanks that Johnny and the horse drove down later in the morning to the main road where my cousin hoisted them onto the creameryman's cart. He carried empty ones up home along with news of the parish.

Milking and kneading and hauling had made my aunt's hands larger and far stronger than my own. Watching her, I leaned my back against the cool dim wall and listened as great flat yellow cow teeth all around us rhythmically crushed the grain doled out earlier by my cousin. Aunt Nell warned me against one of the cows, an orange-and-white one, who stamped and lowed out her irritation at waiting her turn. Bridie's a bad-tempered old thing, kicks, you know, but who wouldn't to be a cow. She doesn't kick me, of course, but she will a stranger. She means no harm; it's just her nature.

The dark skirts of her dress and apron covering the tops of her tall Wellingtons and her grey head protected against the dampness by an old flowered scarf, Aunt Nell moved from cow to cow. Overhead in the shadows, dusky amber bellies of swallows flashed as they looped in and out through the barn door. Clutches of their young filled nests tucked in among the rafters. Aunt Nell called out to the birds and, laughing, told me that many mornings, their own children fed, the swallows would stop to admire her milking. Mrs. O'Malley, they'd say, surely you're the finest milker in the parish of Keel; there's none can compete.

Neighbors down the way, she said, had a black cow and, when the old woman of the house died one fine day, the cow wouldn't let anyone next or near to take the milk from her poor udders and the farmer was driven desperate with the loss of his wife and the miserable bellowing of the cow until finally the woman across the road thought to throw the dead woman's old shawl across her shoulders and head before going in to the cow to milk her. They get attached, Aunt Nell said.

Several years earlier, wasps had built a nest in the chimney of the parlor, a room seldom used, whose walls were lined with saints and dead relatives. Finding Johnny on his knees before the hearth, laying on tinder for a fire to smoke out the wasps, Aunt Nell stopped him and told him instead to board up the chimney down below. Wasps need somewhere too.

Afternoons my aunt cleared the long green table and, bringing out the round metal flour box and wooden dough board, she pounded and kneaded and patted into being heavy loaves of warm bread. After dinner by the fire, Aunt Nell tilted back in her chair and sighed and laughed with us. She demanded everything at all we might know about her other Yankee nieces and nephews, what work they did, their children's names, and who did they take after. She told us about her own two daughters and her younger son, away in England, their babies and their visits once in spring and then all together at Christmas. There was no work for them here at home, but at least they hadn't gone off to America. Aunt Nell herself had tried America for two years when she was young. That's enough now, she said, and came away again. Buffalo was too much dirt and excitement. When she grew tired, I mixed a teaspoon of sugar into the glass of brown stout that she carried upstairs to help her sleep.

Right from the first, when Aunt Nell had pulled me dripping into her firelight out of the rainy, blowing night, I gloried in her, heedlessly, like a cat warming its calico soul. Leaving her for what turned out to be the final time, I could scarcely steer the rented van down the long rutted track to the main road and I wondered why was I going at all. When the door of the van slammed shut, Aunt Nell had covered her face with her dark apron and wept, and in the jiggling mirror she's still standing desolate there above with Johnny at the narrow bridge.

During this last trip, Johnny told Mick my aunt had called out for me the following winter when she lay so ill that her daughters had to come from Manchester. But I never saw her again after that time in the mirror and she's dead now, but when I first got home I bought a young Newfoundland for my son and named it for her. I wrote to tell her how beautiful and how gentle the dog was and that my son loved her. My mother and Aunt Nell took my son between them one summer for a walk with a bucket to pick black raspberries from bushes that border the stream. He's forgotten both their faces but remembers the pail full of dark berries.

Mick and I drank too much that night and shouted and swore at one another. Mick flung his glass across the room finally and slammed out the back door, wandered off and fell asleep in somebody's bushes somewhere. I followed after him but, even with the moon, I couldn't find him. During the night the police picked him up and held him until morning, then gave him coffee and a ride home.

In a foul temper and hungover, when Mick arrived, he cuffed his six-year-old son and sent him sprawling on the side lawn. Timmy howled and ran to me. I cursed Mick who seemed startled by what he'd done but turned his back on the two of us and strode off again, muttering that Timmy was a goddamned crybaby anyway. The child's face was hot and wet as he burrowed in against my neck. Bastard. I hated that bullying, befuddled piece of my brother. Timmy's mother, blond and herself nearly as small as a child, tried to shield her son but she was half-afraid of Mick too.

Indoors, leaning against the kitchen counter, we rocked back and forth. Around the corner of the kitchen my own son tootled, sweet and rumply from sleep and gripping his empty juice bottle. Eyeing Timmy, he insisted on being taken up too. When my father came down a few minutes later looking for his morning coffee, he asked where was Mick and laughed when I told him the police had brought him home just a while ago. My father worried that Mick drank too hard, but sometimes he seemed proud of what a jackass my brother could be. Dad inquired why had Timmy been crying and rubbed the child's narrow shoulders and told him to forget all about it, that his father must not be feeling good and surely didn't mean any harm and that he was a good boy. Then, scowling across at my son, he ordered him to go along and change his wet old diaper for himself, a notion the child found hilarious.

I carried coffee and toast and a plate of eggs and bacon out to my father on the front porch. The morning was still cool and bright and the edges of the roofs and trees were keen again. Gaunt with his seventy years and tired from the journey, my father was still a splendid man with his long, angular frame and beautiful head. He had his mother's strong cheekbones and broad forehead and eyes so blue and deepset you thought they'd never quit. I bummed a cigarette from him and drank my coffee while he ate. When I mentioned Mick, that he should talk to him about Timmy, my father concentrated on his eggs. No, it wasn't good, but it wouldn't hurt the boy. Hadn't Mick felt lots of the strap himself? I started in, but my brother walked up the sidewalk.

Mick needed a shave, his shirt and trousers were wrinkled, and now, for Christ's sake, his eyes were red too. Spare us, O Lord, but the litany began: he was no good; he was a bastard; he'd hit his beautiful Timmy, his own son; he didn't deserve even to have a son. I'd seen this before. Last night he'd known better than anybody; now there was no one worse than he was. Whatever's going, he's got to be the biggest. My father tried to stop Mick's tears and his lament, reminding us, laughing, that once, before either of us was born, after a long night drinking with his own brother, he'd found himself one morning in the middle of the main intersection in Meckleton directing rush-hour traffic. Go easy, he urged my brother, just go easy.

It's as hard not to forgive Mick as it is to trust him sometimes and, once he had everybody packed into the big Buick for the drive to Pinkerink, the two of us hugged each other. Earlier Mick had delivered a long, maudlin apology to Timmy. The Prodigal was now in his usual bumptious state. When Mick kissed me good-bye, he grinned and recommended that I not buy such flimsy Scotch glasses in the future. Right, I said, renewing the contract.

When I picked up the phone two afternoons later, Mick choked out my name. Now what the hell does he want? It was ninety in the kitchen and my son and I had been uneasily discussing diapers when the phone rang.

Mick repeated my name, crying now. Shit, he's drunk. What—what do you want from me now, damn you, Mick? Tell me—it's all right. The old man's dead.

I hung up the phone and picked up my son who'd been tickling his bare feet with the dog's thick black fur and I cried and I cried. Warm and sweaty, his skin smelled faintly of vinegar from all the apple juice he drank these hot days. He patted me and kissed my eye when I tried to tell him my father was dead so he wouldn't worry that it was about diapers, but I couldn't say it right. A friend came later and took him and Nelly and some toys away to stay with her.

I couldn't find the right clothes; it was nightfall by the time Ernie and I left town. Before long, the full moon rose, lighting up the empty backroads. Vaughn Monroe sang a song called "Racing with the Moon" that I had heard on the car radio when I was a little girl eating an ice-cream cone standing up in my nightgown behind my father as he drove through an August countryside lit by the same moon into whose face I now peered. He'd come home from work at the prison that night through the heat and had taken me and Mick and my mother to Spumone's and then for a drive in the country to cool off in the night air. Tree frogs and crickets screamed at the moonlight. I'd been asleep and now I was eating ice cream and driving through a night in which the clumps of bushes along the ditch of the road and the tall maples standing alone in the fields were distinct both in outline and detail. Though it was the same road we drove to Mass on Sundays, it was all changed now and I was eating my tin roof ice cream so fast it didn't drip down the side of the cone and my dad, whose face I couldn't see—only the back of his head was visible to me, so close I might have kissed it between bites of my ice cream—my dad was telling me about Vaughn Monroe or the person in the song who, having loved someone, raced along in his car with the moon and was looking so hard at the moon that the car somehow went out of control and the person was killed when the car hit a tree. I think, standing there in my nightgown, I had understood that Vaughn Monroe had first made the record and then had done the same thing himself and was dead by the time I heard the story. It seemed likely to me then and seemed likely to me now too when I knew suddenly that his face would be hidden for good from me, and then the face on that early September moon blurred too until I wasn't able to see it anymore.

His death was a block of ice like those they sold in summer from the windowless thick-walled house behind the Shell station. Pressing against my forehead to get in, it was urgent, sure of itself. I had no room; it was too immense; it would break my skull.

During the next few days, my mother told me over and again. He mowed the lawn. He trimmed the hedge. He walked downtown to the barber and had his hair cut and he came in from the hot sun and lay down on his bed stretched out on his back and he asked me to bring him a glass of cool milk and he drank some and he told me he was dying and oh sweetheart, I said, don't say such a thing and he died without closing his eyes and I couldn't even tell for sure he was dead. Oh, I'll never get over it, she said. She didn't either and she cried something awful. The doctor drugged her finally so she would sleep at night.

My aunts came, stout widows from Buffalo, all in black shoes; cousins prosperous and decent brought their mothers on planes. Aunt Gerda arrived by train and slept at night in the bed with my mother. The Spumones sighed and wept and cooked. Mick and I bought a blanket of dozens of red roses to cover the coffin and laughed, leaving the florist, at how furious the old man would be to know what we'd spent.

Down at the funeral home, during the rosary that Father Himmel led, I knelt beside my mother and brother and remembered the responses from years ago. As I stared at the frozen, smirking face of the corpse, it was clear my father was gone, though death seemed too inadequate, too paltry a resolution to the quantity of life he'd contained even a few days ago. But death was true; his spirit wasn't anywhere anymore; he was all gone like milk from the bottom of a cup.

My mother kissed his forehead and his hands that held the rosary and then Mick and I had to hold her up and get her out to the undertaker's limousine. The casket, draped in black and surrounded by six tall, white candles, stood at the front of the church and I listened to the Mass and I heard Father Himmel tell what a good man and good husband and good father and good friend my father had been and I kept thinking about the cold body in its dark suit with no shoes on lying deaf inside its thick bronze box under the black tent shut away in there all alone in the dark with no light at all and nothing to see and not even able to hear our tears or the roses or the dirt the Mexican shoveled over him, six deep feet of it, later.

Back at the house afterwards people ate a lot and drank beer and whiskey. Ironworkers, Mick's friends, arrived with their wives, who wore short skirts and piled their sprayed hair up high. In a corner of the kitchen,

Ernie, my phony-musician husband, zeroed in on one of the women.. A favorite cousin of mine, a pallbearer, who like me had been named for my father, watching Ernie, asked why I let him get away with it and I told him I didn't care, which I didn't much anymore, and he said his wife would kill him if he ever did that and I said that's nice. Pat was tall with curly black hair and blue eyes. He was brave too. A fireman in Meckleton, he'd been cited twice for heroism; once he'd crawled in through some kind of a shaft and saved people and all of them might have been killed anytime. At a different fire, he'd pulled out a lot of children. He told me all he'd thought both times was shit, oh shit. My mother had mailed me the clipping from the newspaper with the photograph of Pat in his uniform being handed a plaque by the mayor.

My brother's burly friends were noisy and hard drinkers, so Mick led them out into the backyard down near the foot of the garden to keep peace in the house; my mother didn't like them carrying on. After a while, even that didn't work. Mick came in and told me he was taking them up to the Hilltop, out of the way. The Hilltop was a runky little bar on the outskirts of Pinkerink. I'd only been there once before when I was a kid; I'd drunk pop and watched the colored lights flashing on the pinball machines. It was late afternoon by now and Mick had been drinking along with his ironworkers. He wasn't drunk though and neither was I, but my mother sent me to keep an eye on Mick. I think maybe she sent Pat and his sister Maggie to keep an eye on me because they came along too.

At the bar we sat around dark little tables next to the dance floor. Except for a few skinny old men perched and brooding like cormorants on the barstools, we were the only people in the place. It was good to be out of the house, away from my mother and the black widows, away from Ernie and the hair spray. It was dark and smoky and there was no sunlight in here. The ironworkers played loud pounding music on the jukebox and I ordered quite a bit of Johnny Walker and crushed the ice cubes with my teeth each time the bartender brought a new glass over for me.

The music was really loud and, before long, freckled Maggie, who'd been three sheets to the wind before we left the house, got up and did a lewd dance with two of the beefy ironworkers. She was married and had small children now, but in high school she'd been wild, my mother told me once, and had almost gone wrong.

I didn't dance with anybody—I never dance anyway—but I was glad Maggie danced and danced and suddenly with all that Scotch I loved her a lot because she was crude and raunchy and half-crocked. Fuck three score years and ten.

I drank more Scotch and soon, with an arm around Mick and one across Maggie's shoulders all sweaty from dancing, I explained over and over that I didn't understand, how could a stupid medical event put an end to him, how could he be dead and not come back again anymore. I couldn't see right and my teeth were chilled and brittle and my head ached so badly it might shatter and all the pieces fly every which way and the cormorants' smoky backs swayed black to the music. My teeth crumbled when I bit down and I spat them out on the table but there were more in my mouth and I broke those too.

⊷§ TWENTY-SIX §⊷

I married Ernest Quagmire because I was young and dumb and didn't know much and that marriage lasted years longer than it ever should have. I married Ernie partly because he wasn't loud or boorish and occasionally dangerous the way Mick sometimes got when he'd been drinking; Ernie had graduated from Princeton, after all, never even raised his voice, and whenever we played chess he puffed on a meerschaum. That slippery moonless December night when a friend who knew him from music school had first introduced me to him, Ernie, standing there in his green loden coat and striped woolen sctarf, eyeing the two of us carefully and shifting from cold foot to cold foot, reminded me of something I'd seen somewhere sometime. Years later, I realized that what he had reminded me of was probably a reticulated python—they never shout either. I also think that I married Ernie because he couldn't just walk into my heart without warning anytime he wanted and settle there like someone I'd loved earlier.

I'd loved Dance so much that there had seemed no end to the shapes I'd have been willing to assume to try to please him and, like any eager shape-changer, I sometimes lost track of my self. His impress upon my soul was so powerful and so thorough that it terrified me. You're both the campfire and the wolves, I explained at 4:00 A.M. one spring morning, perched barefooted and half-drunk at the foot of his bed where he'd been sleeping.

Five years older than I was, Dance had dropped out of school for awhile to work on the freighters that carry iron and copper ore around the Great Lakes. Now he was back, boarding at my co-op while he finished a degree in English. Brilliant, quiet-spoken, and with blond hair as fine as an infant's, Dance read me the poets in his lovely low voice, then insisted that I parse and paraphrase stanza after stanza while he stood at my elbow, musing, whistling Mozart softly through the open windows into the dazzling April sunlight. Dance particularly loved Auden and torn scraps of those poems still drift in hidden inlets of my mind:

> *Lay your sleeping head, my love,*
> *Human on my faithless arm;*
> *Time and fevers burn away*
> *Individual beauty from*
> *Thoughtful children, and the grave*
> *Proves the child ephemeral*

* * *

> *But the really reckless were fetched*
> *By an older colder voice, the oceanic whisper:*
> *"I am the solitude that asks and promises nothing;*
> *That is how I shall set you free. There is no love;*
> *There are only the various envies, all of them sad."*

* * *

> *"O stand, stand at the window*
> *As the tears scald and start;*
> *You shall love your crooked neighbor*
> *With your crooked heart."*

Nightly that spring we prowled the sleeping, lilac-laden town, paddled our feet in fountains still for the night. We haunted abandoned bandshells, listened to the click of traffic signals switching from red to green as they gazed down vacant streets. Hidden away beneath a blossoming magnolia on someone's cool expensive lawn, we smoked cigarettes till dawn while Dance, himself an ex-Catholic, explained to me there in the perfumed dark where I was still able to make out the intense blue of his eyes, that we're the disinherited; that's why people like us always feel uneasy and never at home.

We made love even though I knew he was already engaged to be married to a woman who taught school in Detroit. I suppose I thought he'd never really go away, but, of course, he did. The woman became pregnant and soon Dance had a son whom he named Jacob after the supplanter who wrestled with God, who came to him in the guise of an angel.

Dance and I corresponded frequently for several years while he did graduate work at Stanford and some nights we spoke on the phone. Once, shortly before his divorce, he wrote that, while people like us usually have trouble loving one another, we are somehow able wholeheartedly to love our children. Jacob, he told me, had asked him that morning to hand him the binoculars because he wanted to smile at the woman waiting down on the corner for the bus.

By this time I had married Ernest and had given birth to a son of my own. Dance's leaving had seared my soul badly and, for a while, I was shy of the fire. I paid for my cowardice.

Ernie was Jewish and had been married once before. When Ernie invited his parents down from Springfield to his apartment in Philadelphia, where he'd found a job teaching, to inform them that he was planning to marry a shiksa this time, Mrs. Quagmire graciously excused herself, walked stiffly out into the kitchen, and threw up in Ernie's sink. His mother didn't give up easily, but neither did I.

Poor Ernie. What a tug of war. You're twenty-eight years old. Let go of your mother, for Christ's sake. You're a musician. Don't let her desiccated soul define the world for you. You killed your grandfather, his mother assured Ernie, who for years had loved the robust old man more than anyone else in his life. He had a heart attack upstairs, she told Ernie, when he overheard me telling your Aunt Gardenia that you were really going to go through with it.

One afternoon Mrs. Quagmire even called from Massachusetts to enlist my mother's aid in heading off the impending marriage, but my mother refused to interfere. So you can give them your blessing, Mrs. Quagmire asked, even though they've been living together? Whatever my daughter does has my blessing, responded my reeling mother to whom this was news, steadying herself on the handle of her floormop. My mother never mentioned the phone call to me, but she told Mick later that she'd nearly slipped on the soapy floor, she was so rattled. She smokes, Mrs. Quagmire cried finally in desperation. And don't I smoke three packs of Lucky Strikes myself every day of the week? replied my mother, who hadn't touched a cigarette since two years before Mick was born.

Won't there be trouble over religion, my mother inquired cautiously. Not unless you make some, I smiled amiably. Well—hands across the sea, my mother shrugged and, opening her arms to Ernie, she hugged him. When I asked him out on the side lawn down by the garden

whether he liked Ernie, my father was cagier. You'll be
the only one standing there when the shit hits the fan, he
observed drily, carefully checking out the leaves on his
five long rows of potato plants. He was right, of course.

A very kind Reform rabbi married us that July. None of
our parents attended the wedding; my own stayed home
partly because the ceremony took place on the East Coast
and, as they said, that was a long way for them to drive—
neither of them had flown before—and partly, I suspect,
because they couldn't bear to stand there and watch me
get married out of the Church. As it was, on the way up
the aisle Mick's left arm in his dark jacket shook so badly
it made my bouquet of white daisies tremble. Mick's eyes
filled with tears when he kissed my forehead and then
handed me over to Ernie. The two of them never did hit
it off; even so, until that night there at the end of it all
when Mick knocked Ernie across our living room and
flung a chair after him, Mick was always polite to Ernie.

Since then, I've wondered lots of times why I married
Ernie, who's often shifty and weak. Certainly, I know I
don't like to be beaten and I suppose I won and his mother
lost, but, of course, she has him all to herself again now.
Then, too, I thought he would grow up and make the
break from her, but really he never did, though it didn't
seem too much to expect from a twenty-eight-year-old
man. Also, he really was a musician then who played his
viola nearly everyday and played beautifully, and, after
all, I thought, I'm a poet and won't we have a wonderful
life together just like in Paris in the twenties? Besides,
Ernie's peculiar; he always stands too close and looks deep
into your eyes as if something really significant must be

going on; he's thrown a lot of people off that way, but it took me a long time to figure that out and a lot of water went over the dam meanwhile.

After the wedding, Ernie and I traveled for a year in Israel and Europe. Early on, though, one night on one of the Greek islands, Ernie came back late and drunk to the hotel where we were staying for free for whitewashing a room a day—it was off-season, so the hotel was empty otherwise. Besides being drunk, Ernie smelled extravagantly of Lola Trollop, a buxom young woman into whose cleavage he had been gazing intently all afternoon. With all the wisdom of my twenty-three years, I decided that night that we should have a baby or we'd probably come unglued. So we did. I was pregnant by the spring when we reached Ireland.

In Manchester on the way over, we bought an Old English Sheepdog—against Ernie's will. What the hell is this? I inquired delicately when Ernie objected to buying the puppy. Did I get married so that some dumb son of a bitch could tell me whether I could have a dog?

But I loved being pregnant; every day when I woke up, I knew what I was for. The entire process astounded me and one morning, back home, stepping carefully out of my bath, I glimpsed in the mirror the growing roundness of my belly and, circling it with my arms, I hugged the young life inside and, dripping there on the bath mat, I solemnly promised always to cherish that small mountain of a baby —whoever he was—and to keep him from harm.

My son was born during a warm break toward the end of an icy January. The doctor caught him and, with one hand behind the baby's head and the other around his ankles, he unfolded him to see what he was, then laid him, still blood-streaked like a rose and all curled up again, on my belly. Holy smoke! I whispered and, drawing him close, crooning to him, I caressed his warm slippery sturdy little shoulders and long back. I was stunned. The storm of his coming over, his cries ceased when he remembered my voice, and his dark blue eyes began to gaze out upon this world. The air was so mild that day and the next that the windows of my room were opened wide while he nursed and drowsed all day in my arms and, down at the nurses' station, the canaries and finches sang and began to molt.

Ernie and I had never been too adept at loving one another, but now our incapacities mattered more and, none too gradually, the marriage disintegrated. Ernie's primary attachment continued to be to his mother; even the birth of his son failed to disturb that arrangement. Choices and decisions he made were arrived at with an eye to securing her approval, and neither our son's reality nor my own ever truly penetrated the inmost recesses of Ernie's soul where his mother was ensconced.

Because Mrs. Quagmire wanted a bris complete with cakes and wine, on the eighth day of my son's young life, Ernie's father and mother and eight men, all but one of them strangers to me, arrived at our house. A ninth, a paunchy man in a black hat and shabby dark suit who drove in from Detroit for the occasion, strapped my son's wrists and spread-eagled legs to a plastic cruciform and then sliced away the foreskin from his penis. While my son screamed at the restraint and the pain, the others cheered joyously. Crying upstairs in my son's room, I glared out the blurred window at the slushy grey parking lot below, hating all of them and despising myself as well for not having the courage to drive them all, with their wine and cakes and lunatic laughter, out of my house.

Ernie and I had argued for days about the circumcision. Neither my father nor my brother had been circumcised. Doctors maintained that it made utterly no difference in terms of health unless the child were to spend months in a jungle unable to bathe. Circumcision had now become the medical fashion, however, I was informed, and it was routinely performed by the obstetrician unless he was instructed otherwise.

I suggested to Ernie that the procedure constituted a mindless assault on the integrity of our son's body and marked the beginning of the more sustained assault that the world would wage against him as a sexual being. They aren't just making a notch in his elbow, I pointed out. The impulse to slash at the sexual organ of a beautiful and perfect infant struck me then, and still does strike me, as diseased, born of a death-loving, witch-doctorish urge to cripple and to maim the creative powers of a dangerously intact new human.

But Mother Quagmire won. Ernie insisted that I was being neurotic and overly sensitive and, besides, our son would feel peculiar forever in locker rooms since most of the baby boys nowadays were being circumcised. The doctors laughed too and assured me that they certainly couldn't remember their own circumcisions. Massive repression, I muttered.

But I lost finally. At least do it in the hospital where he can have a local anesthetic, I pleaded. That's just silly, Ernie replied and rolled in Mother Quagmire and, with her, all the paraphernalia of a National Geographic ceremonial.

Hearing my son scream, I ran downstairs; brushing aside the glass of sickeningly sweet red wine that was held out to me, I unfastened the straps from his wrists and ankles and carried him upstairs to soothe him. His bright red blood speckling the square of gauze between his legs started my own tears again and I wept in rage and shame. We rocked and rocked, the two of us.

So that's how it's going to be, I thought.

My son soon healed, of course. Nursing eagerly and sleeping soundly, he grew and grew. Laughing aloud, he learned to roll over, to sit up, to crawl, to grab onto things and sometimes to fling them. Mornings I awoke to his chortling and to the rollicking, roller-coastering experiments that he conducted with the upper and lower registers of his voice. Daily we listened to the Beatles and to "Music for Zen Meditation" while he yammered at the sheepdog, whom I later had to sell when she snapped once at his arm as he reached across her muzzle for a green rubber frog.

Things with Ernie continued to deteriorate. Insistently pleasant and habitually manipulative, he was seldom genuinely forthcoming. Taking out the garbage and grumbling if his clean socks hadn't been mated, Ernie treated me like the idea of a husband dealing with the idea of a wife. We seldom fought. Instead, that tedious voice of his wore me down—abraded the edges of my being, shut me down and caged me in. Inside, I grew small and lonely and quiet and found it increasingly difficult to breathe.

The smattering of infidelity in the marriage never amounted to much, although Ernie's timing was superb; the first incident, when I was eight months pregnant, involved a student of his in our living room on the beige couch that his mother had given us—the noise woke me at two in the morning—and the final episode occurred again with a student, this time Ophelia Flax, a dopey eighteen year old from one of his first-year classes. I'd spent a few days back in Pinkerink closing up the house a week or two after my mother's death. Since the house hadn't been sold yet and would be standing empty for a while, I had driven a thick nail into the wooden frame of the storm door and then twisted the head of the nail so that nobody could open the door. But that same afternoon, as soon as I walked in my own door, before I'd even hung up my coat, Ernie told me about it with a foolish guilty smirk playing across his bland Boy Scout features. Upstairs in our bed? He nodded. Jesus, I thought.

In an effort to keep things even between us and to keep from hating him during those years, I made love twice with a friend and picked up a cheerful stranger during a trip to the Rockies one March for my college roommate's wedding. Mostly though, Ernie and I just sidestepped one another day after day.

Although it stretched across years, that whole period collapses in my memory into a tangle of grey stupefied afternoons spent sorting laundry and folding diapers while my son napped. Gazing out the dining room window into an endless drizzle, I smoked cigarette after cigarette and wondered dully for the thousandth time, there in the spooky stillness of my mind, whether to get a divorce.

Though I often felt numb, the thoroughgoing intensity of my son's emotions frequently stirred my own banked passions; his bright laughter pealed from every cell of his body and, angry, his small toes even curled with red rage.

He was all of a piece and the clarity of his responses dazzled and delighted me, while it simultaneously threw all the murky evasions and failures to meet that marked my relationship with his father into harsh relief. I grew ashamed of the dismal half-light through which the two of us were drifting and I dreaded contaminating the child's soul with our own miasmic exhalations.

Here's all of me, smiled my son at two, letting his Batman towel fall and turning toward me, sweet from his evening bath, as I walked into his room after letting the water go. Sudden tears flooded my eyes and, catching him up in my arms, I nuzzled the warm marvelous dampness of his neck and whispered into his velvety elfin ear that he was a beautiful, beautiful boy and that his mother loved him, though she mourned much of her self.

We've got to do something, I warned Ernie, who persisted in being happily married over my increasingly dead body. Nothing's happening between us, I observed. You're dwindling more and more for me as we get farther away from one another—it's like looking down the wrong end of a telescope. We've got to do something or I want a divorce. So we each started therapy.

My therapist, a stumpy young Freudian with lots of neckties and with a son my own son's age and a wife who, like me, stayed home all day to care for him, informed me one afternoon that, to the degree that I wasn't contented with my life and wanted more, I was rejecting my role as a woman and that, furthermore, I should learn to derive my pleasure and satisfaction from watching others grow. Huh, I thought. That one had me flummoxed for months.

Another issue, of course, was money. Ernie worked and

I didn't—I just shopped and cooked and cleaned and ran the house and looked after our son. Several friends of mine were separated from their husbands and the strings of tinkers, tailors, bankers and Indian chiefs passing through their lives often unnerved me, but worse, they were always broke and one was occasionally on welfare. I had heard her one evening, after he'd spent nine hours that day at a chaotic day-care center while she worked as a waitress, tell her three year old whom she loved as passionately as I loved my own son that he couldn't have a second glass of milk with his dinner. The child's father, a good-looking Philadelphia Mainliner, had been educated as a chemist but preferred to smoke a lot of dope and fiddle with old VW's. I'd given up a not very lucrative job in a bookshop when my son was born and, suspecting that my B.A. in English wouldn't go far in a grocery store, I decided then and there that I'd put up with a lot from Ernie before I'd ever have to refuse my son a glass of milk.

So I did. But one night, lying like a spitted sheep beneath Ernie, who had, as usual, finished hastily and then immediately fallen asleep, I noticed my teeth grinding ever so softly from side to side, back and forth, and I was startled to overhear myself wishing that I had a knife to plunge deep into his back. This really can't be right, I reflected; I rolled Ernie off me and stared for a long time at the shadows that the streetlight tossed across the ceiling of our bedroom. The next morning I told Ernie over coffee that I'd never sleep with him again—no matter what—unless I really wanted to. I carefully explained to him, there across the clutter of the breakfast table, that it was bad for my head. Ernie didn't look all that surprised; he just sort of smiled and buttered his English muffin.

Soon after, I did leave. The day following a Saint Patrick's Day party in Detroit where I'd run into Mick so soon after our mother's death, Ernie finally and fatally overplayed his hand. He had been quiet and grim in the car on the way home that night. I hadn't said much either; leaning my forehead to cool against the dark glass of my window, I'd just kept singing under my breath the part about loving the dear silver that shines in her hair and the brow that's all wrinkled and furrowed with care from "Mother Machree" and then over and over the part about sweet Molly Malone wheeling her wheelbarrow through the streets and narrow, crying cockles and mussels—Alive—alive—oooo. I suppose it got on Ernie's nerves.

He didn't say anything when we got home and I ran a long bath and hummed some more and cried some into the bubbles that blinked out when my tears hit them until I figured that Ernie would have fallen asleep.

But early the next morning, right after he'd showered and trimmed his beard, Ernie walked back into our bedroom and, in that eminently reasonable and quietly corrosive tone of his, he expressed his concern over the way Mick and I had carried on. Regardless of how patiently Ernie was now prepared to address the issue of my impropriety, for once I knew for certain that I was right and Ernie was wrong. Mick and I had done no harm—it was Ernie's mingy, tepid soul that had been out of place that night in that old run-down house in the midst of all that uproar, that exuberance, that lush sentimentality.

Ernie feared both our laughter and the weeping and he loathed the delight and consolation that Mick and I took in one another. We'd been too noisy, he complained, too raucous with our bawdy jokes there with the old men around the keg in the kitchen where the smell of corned beef and onions and boiled cabbage had run riot.

As I watched Ernie desperately trying to shove me back between the two lines he had long ago drawn for me, I saw finally that he'd bamboozled me, shaming me always for needing more than the thin meager gruel he'd kept me on for years. All that time, he'd struggled hard to keep me away, to keep me off-balance, confused and uncertain, lest his own impoverished soul be exposed to clear light. The Bible speaks of revelation, of the scales falling from one's eyes, but glaring at Ernie standing there full of self-righteousness and with a dark towel caught at his waist, I didn't give a damn anymore; regardless of whether his soul was timid and shrunken, I was just mad and wanted my own back.

No more, I told Ernie, drawing my own line. It may already be too late, but if ever I hear a whisper, a peep out of myself again, I warned him, surely I'll listen.

Well, of course, I did hear a whisper—a shout even— and I left him for another, as one does. The other, by no accident, was no drummer with a rock-and-roll band, but rather had tenure and three young children whose sad, frail mother had taken flight and left them behind clutching two empty aspirin bottles the day after my son's birth, while through it all—his coming and her dying—the birds sang, so actually the issue of a second glass of milk has never arisen again.

⋖⋖ TWENTY-SEVEN ⋗⋗

Jesus, Mick, now you too have turned to stone.

Our backs against the blistered, prickly paint of the garage, we counted one-two-three Jump, then flung ourselves, toes grabbing the concrete retaining wall as we went over, out into the sky, down, stretched way out, feet reaching, limbs tangled, slid, stretched, lied and argued, drew lines in the brown sugar sand where we landed and then climbed up the grassy hill again. Mick usually won, being older and longer-legged. I got gritty sand in my mouth, in my hair and under my nails, but everytime he yelled Jump, I did and with all my heart. Afterwards we lay in the sand and covered ourselves up to our chins carefully, patting the warm brown sand into mountain ridges that ran up and down the length of us. We breathed lightly, lay perfectly still ankles together side by side and didn't speak so we wouldn't crack the plains on our chests. Without turning my head I could see our hearts beat. Who would last? A nose twitched where a fly landed and we erupted laughing, violent, flinging off the stupid joke.

Though he was beaten for it over and again while I watched and couldn't help him, day after day, Mick rode that horse out in the field by the corner where we waited for the bus. He rode bareback and with no bridle and he taught me how to do it too, even though I was afraid and only six. My mittens stuffed in my pockets, he hoisted me up and I grabbed hold of her mane all matted and tangled with burrs. Mick swatted the fat,

shaggy backside of the spotted mare and yelled to me
to hang on, use my knees, and I did.

Often when the fat lady reached for the switch that
she kept on top of the icebox, she found it laid out carefully in a dozen pieces. Mick always fought the two of
them off, didn't give in, insisted there was more, and,
saving his own soul, he held the roof and the walls of
that house out away from mine, didn't let them bury me
either in their damned rubble.

On winter nights I went out in heavy woolen leggings
and boots with him, up the long road in the dark, past
Cleaver's shack to the hill that looks out over the town.
Mick dragged the one sled we had behind him and his
laughter made moist blossoms for me in the frozen air. I
would have followed him off the edge of the world. Back
off the road through trees bare and black, dead for the
winter, I waded through the snow to keep up with him
until he stopped at the top of a hill so steep I couldn't
see the bottom in the dark. Pointing with his mitten, Mick
showed me our house with one light burning in the room
where that crazy woman sat who was our mother.

Don't be chicken. I'll steer. Mick stretched flat out on
his belly on the sled, the icy rope tucked under him and
his feet in their unbuckled black galoshes stuck out behind. Jump on. No. Come on. I slammed down on top of
him, digging my mittens into his shoulders and burying
my face in the damp wool collar of his pea jacket as the
sled flew over the edge. Look up. Look. Trees, stumps,
clumps of bushes shrieked past in the dark. We sailed
whooshing over through soft snow. We were the wind.

The ground was uneven underneath. The right runner
dipped, rose suddenly in the air and then truly we flew,

landed thump. I saw the sled go past and then Mick rolling over and over, his arms raised, mittens covering his ears and elbows out to protect his face. I heard him loud roaring in the stillness, laughing and hooting until he came to a halt finally at the foot, where he stood up all white, his ear-muffs even and his galoshes. He raised one powdered white arm and beckoned to me where I lay stretched out on my back still halfway up the hill with snow melting down inside my scarf. Come on. Just let go. The stars above me were like lights in the town below. I didn't stir, pretending to myself my neck was broken, that if I moved the slightest fraction of an inch, I'd die.

When I shoved off with my foot, I saw Mick and the stars and the lights and the stars and Mick and the lights all over and over again until I landed near the tree where the sled had stopped. Mick's white mitten rubbed the snow away from my face. It was all over him, caught in his hair, and his eyebrows thick with it struck out from his forehead. I got cold and wanted to go home.

When I was eight I had a boyfriend for a while, a fourth grader with curly black hair and lovely eyes who got off the bus at my stop instead of his own so we could play together until he had to go home for supper. That fall we played in the woods and down by the creek, floated twigs in the current, made rafts for tiny pebbles out of fallen red and orange leaves. Day after day, though we never spoke at school, David followed me out the door of the bus, his lunch pail clattering against the handrail. David was thin and my mother said he probably wasn't very healthy. Sometimes in school he would begin to wheeze and would have to go over to the convent to lie down. His father ran the bank downtown and his older sisters took piano lessons. A stray snowflake caught one November day in David's dark eyelashes. It lay there a moment, perfect and astonishing, then melted before I could even tell him.

Mick, when he noticed David coming around, began to tease me. What's he playing with girls for? Leave me alone. He's none of your business. One afternoon down in the woods, David and I were kneeling side by side in the freezing mud by the edge of the creek; we had our mittens off and were laying twigs and small stones on the thin layer of ice that had begun to form around the edges of the creek. Byrd and Amundsen were testing the strength of the ice before sending our teams of dogs across.

Hearing Mick's laughter behind us, harsh and nasty, I looked up just as he swooped down suddenly on David, grabbed him by one arm and the back of the neck and threw him out into the middle of the icy stream. David landed face first, then staggered dripping to his feet. The water rose up over the tops of his boots and he cried from the cold as much as from the hurt. Mick laughed, watching David climb up the slippery bank and run away crying, clumsy in all his wet clothing. I called after him but he didn't turn around and Mick held me by the sleeve of my jacket. I yelled at Mick. You're a god-damned bully. You want to go in too? Leave me alone; I'll tell. You will not.

I didn't either and David never came back. When his mother called that night to complain to my mother, I ran to answer the phone and lied, telling her my mother, who was out in the living room watching Milton Berle, had gone out for the evening with Mrs. Spumone but that I'd be sure to give her the message. Sitting at the kitchen table doing his algebra, Mick looked up at me and grinned.

Years later, I called Mick one afternoon to tell him I was divorcing Ernie. Though he was all right on the phone, Mick turned up late that night drunk and furious, knocked my startled husband across our living room and threw a dining room chair after him. He'd be goddamned if there were going to be any divorces in his family. When I stepped between him and Ernie, Mick shoved me aside. Furious myself, I called the police but swore at them and sent them away again when they asked me to sign a complaint against Mick. I got him out finally and picked up the broken chair.

When I was ten, Mick joined the army. He became a paratrooper and jumped out of airplanes over Georgia. He loved it. Before they sent him to Germany, he came home for a week, wearing shiny boots with great heavy soles, and taught me how to jump out of the box elder in the side yard without hurting my feet. Mick showed me the thick muscles of his own feet, knotted up with all the training he'd had down south.

One summer when Mick was young, he was mowing the neighbor's lawn with a power mower and a stone, catching on the blade, gashed the top of his bare foot. I heard him scream and ran out. Beautiful red blood was shooting a foot into the air each time Mick's heart beat. I ran and got our neighbor and a towel and we wrapped Mick's foot in the white towel, growing red with Mick's blood, and I pressed down on it hard to make it stop while the neighbor drove. I was crying, afraid Mick would die, but away off like in a dream, over in the far corner of the back seat, Mick laughed at me though his face was white and, of course, he didn't die at all.

But of course this time he did. Suddenly, the paper said. In my own dream that night, my son's hockey coach, an Irish Catholic airline pilot who showed up at the rink at six o'clock on Saturday mornings shaved and in a jacket and tie, who taught my son to begin to know how strong he is and not to give in, was lying on an operating table. His heart needed surgery and he was crying because he was so afraid he would die and I was holding him in my arms and his head was against my breast and he was crying and I held him and rocked him and told him he would be all right. He was weeping so, and so was I because I was afraid too. I woke up suddenly then, as if there had been some great noise, but there hadn't been. It was still dark outside. I switched on the light and the clock said four. After half an hour, I slept again until five-thirty when the phone rang and the woman's voice told me Mick was dead, that there had been a wreck at two-thirty and that my brother had died in surgery an hour and a half later.

He'd been on his way home from a meeting of other union officials and probably had been drinking with them. It was late and he was sleepy and hadn't bothered with his seat belt. His eyes closed and the heavy car glided stealthily across the middle line and Mick woke up suddenly when the front tire touched the gravel and he swung the wheel fiercely and the big Buick spun around and around three times, four times before the other car struck it from behind and slammed Mick headfirst into the windshield. His heart stopped once, the surgeon told

Mick's wife, then started again before it quit altogether.

The undertaker, instead of closing the coffin, put some kind of a face and head together. The only way I knew it was Mick lying there was because his thick hair is the same color as mine and grey in the same places. Also nothing had happened to his hands. The funeral home was full of strangers and flowers and cousins again. My nephew's young back was rigid when I held him; his face looked as if he too had been awakened suddenly.

The church my brother belonged to was filled the next day for the Mass, and a priest who wore white vestments and spoke no Latin told us my brother had just gone ahead to Christ's banquet table and that we'd meet him there later. Then he talked about how funny Mick was and how great it was to play golf with him.

While Mick was loaded into the hearse for the hundred mile drive up to Sts. Cyril and Sebastian's to be buried, people ate chicken and scalloped potatoes and chocolate dessert. People I hadn't seen in a long time and people I'd never seen before talked and laughed and ate the meal Mick's parish had cooked. I sat in my black suit and drank black coffee and watched them. My pockets were full of soggy kleenex; Gabe, my new husband, had fresh ones for me in his jacket. People patted me a lot and the old woman sitting across from me shook my hand and marveled at how like Mick's it is, told me I'm his spitting image, and that he had brought her a huge ham the Christmas before and had found work for her son even though he is afraid of heights.

The September day was blue and sunny, splendid and indifferent. We took the back roads through the country to Sts. Cyril and Sebastian's. Leaves had begun to change but only a few had fallen. The Spumones and others were all waiting in the driveway near the rectory when we pulled in. My mother's friend was there, small and leaning on Vince's arm. We walked together across the road, through the iron gate and down among the listing tombstones to where Mick's bronze coffin shone in the sun. The heap of dirt next to the new grave had been covered over with a blanket of phony grass and a jeep with a blade on the front of it stood waiting a few hundred feet away. A skinny man in overalls sat on the fender, swinging his legs and smoking a cigarette.

I stepped across my parents' graves and sat underneath the canopy in the folding-chair that the undertaker motioned me toward. Mick's wife and son sat beside me and Gabe handed me more kleenex. Father Himmel, an old man now, did wear black and spoke Latin. He sprinkled Mick with holy water and the undertaker handed us each long red roses to lay on the casket as we walked away. The metal box was warm from the sun.

We drank more black coffee from styrofoam cups in the basement of the church while the thin man in overalls did his work. I walked back over across the road alone half an hour later and the canopy and hearse were gone and the bare earth covered over with flowers. The soil was sandy and warm when I knelt down beside him; I wanted to talk to Mick, to say something to make him stop it, but there wasn't anything.

Driving home later that afternoon I saw sandhill cranes out in a field. Gabe stopped the car and we got out to look at them. Six of them, huge, amazing unlikely creatures, long-legged and gawky, moved about dreamily out in the middle of the sunny field. Then suddenly I spotted half a dozen more standing motionless on a mound of dirt in the midst of the broken line of trees that marked the distant edge of the field. I pointed them out to my son. He'd seen cranes only once before and never that many.

◄§ TWENTY-EIGHT §►

Sunday mornings Father Himmel elevates the host and turns wafers into God, infinitely divisible, who flutters down in snowflakes into our souls, but who still tastes like the thin strips I break up for the glassed-in fish in the middle of our dining room table that endlessly circles, solemn eyes always open to any trembling in the water that might mean food.

Winter mornings it's cold in the dark at the farm; it's cold inside the high rubber boots my father wears when he hoses down stalls and hauls clattering milk cans to the deep concrete tanks where water chills them and their milk still foaming and warm from the cows. His hands are raw and red.

It's cold in the afternoons when the sky, darkening, swallows up entire houses and Mick is still out with his papers. The strap of the white canvas bag that says CITIZEN PATRIOT cuts into his shoulder. He'll walk in with his wool watchcap shoved far back on his head and there'll be tears stinging his blue eyes from the wind.

While I wait, I spill out buttons from the glass jar onto a newspaper spread out on the floor next to the stove where it's warm and I can look out into the dining room, where my mother sits near the window and makes pillows from the sacks full of feathers my father brings home from the farm where he works in the mornings. Under my cheek at night, her pillows are heavy and soft like her breasts. Feathers float upwards around her face as she sews and she blows them away with a soft sound from her mouth as she sings to herself little songs without words and her foot goes up and down on the treadle and the needle goes in and comes out of the ticking, tucking feathers inside where feathers belong.

My buttons spill out, spinning and glowing in the light from the fixture above and I sort them and pile them in heaps, emeralds and rubies from the hilts of my fathers' swords or soft opals lost from the brooches that once closed the warm cloaks of my grandmothers. The tips of my fingers are touched by their smoothness.

The blue ones I save for last; there are only three and I dig and I dig till I find them. Perfectly round with soft edges, they're the size of a copper. Their centers are streaked and darken and flash like a night sky with comets. I turn them over and over in the light from the ceiling, in the light from the stove. They're the feathers of jays, the robes of the Virgin, the eyes of my father and the spring skies of his orchard. They're blue and they burn in the palm of my hand.

God's grace, like snow and the goose feathers, drifted down around all three and, sucking the warm breath from their lungs, God gagged them, then put out their eyes with pennies so they couldn't see what He was up to and, now, while Father Himmel prays, every September, every February, God kills them again, suddenly or slowly, and seals them away side by side in their concrete tanks. Their mouths stitched shut, they will never shout Hosannah!

⊷ TWENTY-NINE ঽↄ

I read a newspaper account once that told how a Greek peasant woman had carried her sleeping infant in his cradle outside into the bright afternoon air, had left him there before the door and had gone back into the house to take up her work again. Hogs came on black tiptoes and, in the warm Greek sunshine, ate away half the child's face, including his nose, before his mother could drive them away. Since I read that article, hogs have eaten my father and mother, my brother, my friend, and, now for Christ's sake, they've eaten my dog.

My friend Jimmy lived upstairs from me for two years while I was in college. Jimmy read lots of books and clattered down the inside stairs that connected the two floors of our house. Winter afternoons he and I played chess in my room with plastic pieces and an old board Jimmy had brought from home. I chain-smoked Winstons while he tried to learn to keep his pipe lit.

Jimmy grew up in Chicago, where he went to school for twelve years with poor black kids who called him Dimmy. His parents worked hard all day, both of them, in a small art supplies store they owned. His parents were nearly cultivated and always nearly bankrupt. Jimmy's mother was overweight and loud and wretched and overbearing, but Jimmy ignored it and loved her anyway. His father scarcely spoke, being insufficiently nimble or motivated. With Jimmy's younger sister beside him on the couch every Thursday night, the father listened to Italian opera on the radio and, for once, his wife kept still.

When he was a skinny kid, Jimmy had had a touch of polio that left him slightly swaybacked, but he grew up a sunflower anyway, tall and gawky, heliotropic and openhearted, gleaming in the dingy rooms above the store; his little sister wrote him lots of letters when he came to college. On the phone once a week his mother nagged him to get his hair cut; Jimmy laughed and grew a fine black beard.

Jimmy studied literature, read the poets, memorized verses that he spouted late at night as he bounded down the sidewalk with my red setter at his side. One bitter winter night Jimmy stood me still and taught me how to stop my teeth from chattering by drawing in long deep breaths through my nose. That way you warm the air yourself before it hits your lungs. Under the streetlight in his green-and-black wool jacket, knocking one boot against the other to keep his feet warm, Jimmy rubbed my sleeves with his mittens and counted out for me how many seconds long my breaths should be; we might have been readying ourselves for childbirth.

Instead each of us married musicians who played like angels and were just as sturdy. Jimmy had two roommates and I had three; we all ate together every night downstairs in our beige kitchen at a big round wooden table. Jimmy's musician was my roommate and close friend. She was dark and uncertain with fragile features and a bottom lip that wavered in the middle of her words. Her clothes and fingernails were dingy but, with golden hoops in her ears, she played the gypsy to Jimmy's bounding heart.

Lyndon Johnson came out of the sky in a helicopter that spring to bless the seniors gathered in the football stadium. He bade them go forth boldly into the Great

Society that he'd held in trust for them while others were losing their heads. Then, surrounded by agents in raincoats, the attenuated Texan was assumed again, a hokey, latter-day Virgin.

We all got married the following July. Holding up one corner of the chupah, Jimmy stood behind the rabbi, grinned and made me laugh out loud while I struggled with the white fingers of my glove. My musician held the ring poised between his thumb and forefinger while Jimmy and I laughed. I almost dropped the daisies while my roommate tugged at my white cotton fingertips. I should have known it wouldn't work; three weeks earlier I'd wept at the conclusion of the conversion ceremony when the rabbi told me in Hebrew that my name was Ruth. The night of the wedding we drank champagne and ate corned beef and danced in circles in a friend's loft until we all fell down dizzy together in a litter heap at dawn.

That same month in the garden of her parents' house, though full of doubt, my roommate cleaned her nails, put on a veil, and married Jimmy, and I stood beside them with Ernie and the rosebushes and we signed the document that said we'd seen and heard them promise they'd never ever not love each other.

Back in Chicago, Jimmy studied medicine and my roommate played her flute. When I came to visit, Jimmy took me out one night to hear a black man sing and we drank beer, and the fire of the man singing alone in the dark on the high stool with a single light shining down on him so beautifully caught in us too. Jimmy did an internship in Harlem, where he helped organize a strike against hospital conditions.

Jimmy and my roommate came to visit soon after my

son was born. I was upstairs bathing him when they arrived. Jimmy took the stairs two at a time and helped rinse him and towel him dry while my roommate stood in the doorway and watched. Jimmy laid the baby on the diapering table, thumped his sturdy little chest, then scratched the bottom of my son's bare foot to show me his Babinski reflex. Sweet from his bath, the child laughed at Jimmy and urinated onto his jacket; Jimmy declared the child a beauty.

Jimmy and my roommate never had a child. His medicine drew him deeper into politics; she withdrew further into her misgivings. Her music faltered and her notions about their marriage grew still more tremulous; from the day she met Jimmy, she wondered whether she should marry him; as soon as she married him, she began to consider divorcing him. She never quite knew what to make of him. They separated eventually and finally divorced, like so many of the rest of us who married during that season's swim upstream.

What Jimmy saw pulled him further and further left and, for a while, he disappeared altogether. He turned up again in North Carolina, having left medicine to help organize textile workers. Jimmy's was a passionate, joyous, and tender heart. One November afternoon, not long ago, a North Carolina Klansman drew an automatic rifle from the trunk of his car, took aim, fired, and stopped the commie nigger-loving heart in its tracks.

My dog, a young brindle demon terrier, who rested his heavy rectangular head on my shoe or on the rung of my chair while I ate my meals, died a few days ago of more natural causes. When the vet thumped my dog's chest to be sure he was dead, it gave out a dismal hollow sound; we hadn't been able to save the dog either finally, though we tried hard.

⋝ THIRTY ⋜

Belly down on the grass like before on the side lawn, back near the pine trees, the wind in the leaves is in my hair and the same sun that warmed that other wind and those earlier leaves warms the soles of my feet today. A second cricket sounds as I dig down with my fingers through brown blades and green interlaced like the work of monks in a green land long ago; I dig down through small clover that my fingers bruise and the damp moss, through ants and dead leaves to the reticent black earth below, quiet, waiting to tell me. A small red spider walking on legs so fine I can't see them crosses my hand on his way and he moves across me as the warm wind does, softly, stirs me a moment as he stirs the grass for scarcely a heartbeat.

Twelve and stretched out idle with the day before me, I lay down in the light and pushed aside live grass and dead grass so I could see, but the voices were inside the house then and wandered out to me through open summer windows. They were breathing there inside, right then while a spider walked across my hand. My dad was shaving at the sink while my mother fried a chop for his lunch that sizzled through the window, and I could have walked inside and asked them right then what it meant that my brother had sent the coloring book with all the horses and the box of bright crayons on my birthday that summer from Germany, though he never wrote to them. I might have asked my mother why she sighed in the evening to herself, to the dusk, and sometimes to me, but I stayed outside as long as I could.

Then the windows were slammed down suddenly and I nailed the door shut behind me when I left that day in February with what was left of their lives in a few boxes stacked one on top of another in the back of the car.

And now sometimes on heavy staring afternoons I call some of them in out of the drizzle when they'll come, lure them in sometimes or bring them out one at a time from the boxes bound with heavy twine upstairs in the attic beneath the sloping roof and the slanting rains. I want to know and I ask them one by one over and again, but I can't hear them. Their voices have no breath, though I remember lips moving and their eyes open and blue, not dull and cold like an old grief or marred glass. Unkind, unnatural child, I prod them, unwind them, haul in the cord, whirl them around down there in the numb dusk, ask them what the black earth means to say.

My brother's colors are all gone and black leaves cover him over, shut him away from me, even though one night, one autumn, full-grown with sons of our own, both of us drunk and laughing, dumb and happy, we yelled and raced across an empty playground well past midnight and, longer-legged, he tackled me, digging his shoulder in behind my knees, and sent us sprawling, rolling in red leaves and our limbs were tangled.

A month after our mother died, a month after we buried her—a grey, bitter morning, the two of us, standing shivering close together, the wool collars of our coats turned up against the black wind that blew down the snowy hill and over the graves; he tucked my arm in against him and mindlessly patted my leather glove while warm tears for the woman who was our mother rolled down his face—a month afterwards on St. Patrick's Day he came in out of the cold to me unexpectedly at a party full of people I scarcely knew, most of them half-drunk and half-Irish, and the two of us cried alone in a room with old rosy-flowered wallpaper where the coats were piled up and Christ gazed down from the wall. Lost sheep, we wept for each other adrift, twin lambs, new orphans with tufts of grey in our hair. Then, our arms across each other's shoulders, we ranged through the house, found the keg, and sang awhile at the piano at the tops of our lungs how we loved the dear silver that shone in her hair, and later we found old men and old women and teased them and made them laugh and made them bless us.

Now soft September days come round again, when the air takes on the colors of the leaves, and the warm earth and the air glow soft with roses and gold and orange. Two years ago in my black suit, I reached through sunshine and soft air to place a deep rose on the lid of his coffin before they lowered him down through the dark to my mother and father below. Today, stretched out on my belly on tangled warm grass, I feel the sun on the soles of my bare feet, on the back of my head, and there, with the glow of that rose, in the dark behind my eyes where all their sorrow is lodged.

❧ THIRTY-ONE ❧

Like Winken, Blinken, and Nod, the three of them have sailed off in a wooden shoe and their damned ungainly deaths have sabotaged my life. In any quiet I drift until I snag like a hook on seaweed or on rock, on the old confusion of anger and longing they've left behind them.

I was confounded somehow, carelessly, not even on purpose, by someone who wasn't particularly watching what she was doing; she just lurched up against the board where I was trying to assemble the pieces of my life, so I still have to keep doing it over and over again, trying to get it right, to understand how I happened to turn out to be me, so I can be sure I'm the one who is living my life out, not someone else, and that it's my life, not stray fragments from those other lives. The mix of all of them in me leaves me tense sometimes, cancelled out, checked, stymied. Is my complaint real or just a habit?

Between my father and mother, somedays I am plagued and neutralized; choices I make often seem efforts to fend them off or to placate them. Their sniping at one another, melancholy and heedless, still goes on inside me day after day—grey days in damp, chilly rooms alone with her and she so wrapped up in her own melancholy that she could neither see nor hear me while she mended holes in other things, darned woolen socks with a black wooden egg, sat in her flowered housedresses with her flowered aprons, their pockets stuffed with kleenex—did she cry when nobody was there?

I keep trying to tell you. It was awful for her and it

frightened me, watching her. It scared me. Lots of days, she was mean and snarly and lazy and withdrawn and sighed too much for anyone trying to grow to listen to, and it infected me and that's what frightens me too, not only that she became so shriveled and withered. The more shrunken her life became, the fatter she got, the more silent, and the steadier her eating grew. Gnawing day after day like a dog at the rung of a chair, she grew more angry, sullen, sad, seeing it all amount to a house and children and your husband's steady job and a poor dumb-bunny mother who had the husband and children that God had picked out for her, and still she wasn't happy.

She didn't drive, didn't work, because my father was a man; she couldn't work anyway—what did she know?—though she loved Gaelic and sums when she was a girl in school. She did babysit when she could, anyway, some evenings, and that was all right so long as she was home before him because he didn't like to come home to an empty house, though she could sit in one all day and that was all right.

He finished work at 10:00 P.M. and pulled into the driveway at 10:30. I would already have gone out in the dark to open the garage door for him before I went to bed. There used to be two wooden doors that opened out like arms, but then he installed a metal one that he painted maroon—the new door slid up overhead when you pushed it. I was afraid someone was in there with the rakes and storm windows. The maroon was the same paint he used on the metal chairs he sat in on Sundays at the head of the garden with my Uncle Dan to watch for any rabbits and pheasants who might wander up out of the woods below our house, but they were safe because he couldn't shoot them here in town. He did warn me that he'd get his shotgun from its rack in the basement if he ever saw Santa up on our roof with his goddamned reindeer, but I knew he was kidding, though he threatened to shoot the Easter Rabbit too if he showed up. And what I wanted back then was to be a vet and to buy the state of Texas and gather all the animals, the horses, dogs, and cats, sheep and cows, pigs, even chickens some days, and keep them safe behind white fences. I thought he was kidding, but he did bring home lots of rabbits, all dead, with their heads lolling and their eyes bulging even after he or my mother skinned them and gutted them on the grey countertop and searched the naked gleaming flesh for pellets in the light from the kitchen windows.

Will it ever be nice again inside where I live? I look out through the black windows into the night outside and the snow swirls in the light from the streetlamp and my brother is still out with his sled and the snow piles up in the driveway. She pulls on her coat and boots and a wool babushka and goes out with the shovel and I hear it scraping against the concrete of the driveway as she makes a path for my father so he won't get stuck and won't try to shovel it himself, because she's afraid every winter that he'll hurt himself.

Mick ought to have done it because I'm afraid that she'll hurt Mick with her thick fist raised up over her head or me or herself and she's white when she comes inside stamping her boots and angry at Mick for not coming home. She hangs her coat to dry on the back of a chair near the stove in the middle of the kitchen, where I sit at the table again looking down at the picture I'm coloring of the pretty house with flowers in the front garden and birds. Go away to bed, she warns me and I hate her so much. She torments Mick some nights, makes him stay sitting on a chair in the kitchen until my father's car pulls in the driveway and then sometimes she sends him hurrying away to bed and he undresses shivering in the dark so my father won't know he's still up and has done something bad.

She slowed me down and flattened me out and she hurt Mick and that hurt me too because I loved him so much I bit my pillow hearing him sobbing some nights through the closet that connected our two rooms. I keep trying to find ways not to say to myself that she hated us because I know that it's bad to have been raised by someone who hates you, so I try to remember any nice thing she did or anytime I saw her that she was happy, like when she caught that big pike in Canada and how excited she was, wrapping it in a wet towel to keep it fresh, or when she was happy or laughing with other people, but I don't remember her being happy often with me or with me and Mick, though she did read me *Black Beauty* and *Heidi* and *Beautiful Joe*, about the dog a man named Jenkins abused and mutilated but who finally was adopted by a nice family that treated him right. She did do that, and sometimes she'd tell me about the little mermaid she once saw sitting out on a chunk of rock in Dingle Bay, singing to herself the way they do and combing and combing her long beautiful hair. She did do that and, when I got older and went to school, she helped me with my spelling words, but she never hugged me or looked happy to see me—never, really never—she didn't even pretend.

It mattered to her to have kids, but it didn't matter

much which ones. She was too numb, absorbed in her own grief, worn out, buried alive to love us; we were thorns in her side, where she pointed years later to show me like a child where it hurt. She took little pleasure in us and I hardly ever cried.

There was lard all over her, around her brain and her heart, and I couldn't get through it. Though she could see mermaids, she never laid eyes on me at all, and I kept thinking that maybe I could touch her, that what I did might matter to her, but it didn't, so long as I didn't pester her. I learned to be quiet, to live underground like a smart little rabbit. She probably never loved me and I break my neck still trying to find some way to love her, though she's been dead now for years and it only matters to me, but it's dumb. How could I possibly have loved her?

Everytime that I walked into the circle of her existence, I was intruding on whatever the hell she did for a living inside that head of hers. She never shared any joy she ever felt with me; she just dumped her filth and pain all over me. She taught me well the drab despair of her life and the agony of her death, so that now I need to know all this—what does it mean, after all, to be her daughter? Where have I been shut down by her—closed up like her Venetian blinds with her in that ugly house, sealed up and dreadful?

She's dead now and can't get at me anymore with her sad wretched fist of a soul, but even last night in my dream she was there, an old woman, thin and brittle, who had fallen on her back and lay there on the floor the way my dad lay that morning, and I thought she was dead, but she wasn't, though I saw that both her legs had snapped off above the knees. The lower halves were made of rusty iron and splayed out at the bottom like chicken's feet. In a voice so weak I could scarcely make out her words, she begged me to help her, to jam the narrow dry bone of her thigh back into the opening in the metal chicken legs so she might stand up again. I did it but it was awful and I was so afraid I was hurting her. The scaly skin at the joint flaked off. She was so frail.

But, that same night, I was looking for something in the basement of the house where I grew up when my mother pushed aside the old curtain that hung in the doorway of the room where the winter's potatoes and jars of tomatoes and peaches were stored. I'd thought she was dead and the house empty, but there she was with her apron and strong freckled arms. She showed me how to raise up some of the boards of the floor overhead. They opened upward like that old trapdoor off the kitchen or like the lid of a coffin. The whole weight of the house was above us.

My father dug the basement himself one summer, pushing each wheelbarrow of dirt up a wide old plank. It was always dark and musty but I liked the smell of it and sometimes we slept on an old metal bed down there in the summer to get away from the heat. You could smell the lye from the yellow cakes of laundry soap, but two of the small windows opened out onto my mother's flowerbed, so at night the crickets sang right there in the moist dirt with the snapdragons just above your head.

Could she really have been trying to help me out of there? Could she want me to do it—to unbury myself and her too somehow? Is that what all these excavations are for? I never like to believe that there's anything of her in me, but suppose there is, and suppose some of it isn't cancerous, but has to do with who she was before, and now that she's dead and doesn't have to be who she was when she grew up, maybe we could be friends and she wouldn't have to be my mother.

Before she married my father and gave birth to Mick and me, long before that, she was young and supple and loved red and ran barefoot down a windy Irish road to school where the boys had one room and the girls another. She slept in a bed snug with her five sisters, crawled out the window at night sometimes with her brothers to go dancing, all of them carrying their shoes so my grandfather wouldn't catch them. And before that even, she was a little kid, strewing grain in the morning sunlight for the geese and the chickens, searching the straw where they roosted for the eggs. And her hands were small, not fists then, and she did love babies and that house was filled with them for her to tickle and to play cat's cradle with. I've watched her with lots of babies, and with my own son, who is her grandson too, not just my father's.

That little girl with her long gathered calico skirt ran through the heather on the mountain behind their house chasing new lambs in springtime to bring them down to her father who whistled as he notched their ears with his mark. She cried, Oh, Da! my Da! one night in our kitchen and wept, sad lamb, for her father below.

That child whose blond hair fell in a long braid down her back was my mother too and, at night by the fire, she would listen to her grandmother's Gaelic, and that child loved both the fire and the warm sound of the Gaelic and she'd say words for me sometimes when I was little, though now I usually remember only the curses she taught me.

THIRTY-TWO

A few nights ago in my sleep, Mick walked in to a dim gathering where others murmured in groups or drifted one by one among white stone benches and formal terraces. I didn't know anyone until Mick walked in and sat beside me on a low couch. Drawing up his long legs and propping his elbows on his knees, full of grace and lovely angles, he began to play softly on a pipe.

As he played, his head leaned against my shoulder and I held him in the curve of my right arm. He was young, not yet fully grown, maybe nineteen, and his face, not the man's face that came later, was open and sweet like the face of the dawn and his music played over his fair skin and fine young bones like the morning itself.

One morning in grade school, Mick broke away from the nuns, swung out through a window wide open to spring, then dropped to the ground and lit out for the woods. Rolling like a colt in trillium and sorrel and violets and moss, he hid out from the priest who came looking. Clapping erasers against the brick wall of the school, I saw him and waved as he flew through the window. He laughed, scrambling to his feet, and hooted as he ran. My father beat him that night; I cried, but Mick wouldn't.

I loved him and that next summer we knocked on the screen door of an old couple, our neighbors the Teubners, to ask whether we might pick their cherries for them in return for one basket that we'd take at the end. Otherwise, Mick observed, the birds will get them all. The chubby old lady, delighted and thinking of jelly, let us in through the gate, then brought out white lard buckets with handles for us to hook on the branches.

Mick and I scrambled up into the tree and, bad crows, settled on limbs where, hidden by leaves, we ate the sweet dark cherries with both hands. We dropped a few in the buckets, but, spitting stems and pits at each other, mostly we ate until we'd eaten our fill—the juice on our chins and our fingers and faces dripped onto our legs. Cawing and sticky, we leapt down and ran out through the green gate, left the buckets still hanging for the crows and the old folks to fight over.

On a raw November afternoon my mother and I gathered dead oak leaves in a heap out by the road. Her hands on the rake were red with the cold and wisps of grey hair stuck out from beneath her scarf. Crouching down with a match cupped in her hand, she set little fires around the edges of the pile. Silent thin smoke. Orange flame, then pale ashes.

Mick lied about his homework that night to play checkers with me. When she left the kitchen, we pressed crayons against the fat belly of the stove to watch their colors run. Reds and oranges, deep purple, then black.

When I was nine, Mick woke me one night, came into my room calling my name, snapped on the lamp with its chain beside my bed, shoved me over and sat down, then read to me three or four poems by Poe. Excited, and giddy from the sounds of Poe's words, he leaned over me and whispered, Listen! Listen! and read them again. My

mind was blurry with sleep but I remember the tintin-
nabulation of all those bells and Annabel Lee and Mick's
face glowing above me, astounding us both with syllables
and sound.

In my dream last night, a friend of Mick's, who was
ambiguous and difficult to see, explained patiently, He
always loved you; it was like an explosion.

⋙ THIRTY-THREE ⋘

On the loveliest morning so far of this year's summer,
having bathed and dressed, I sit indoors in this musty
room, its windows closed against the racket and stench of
trucks and men laying down fresh asphalt on the road
outside. A brown moth, disturbed when I slammed down
the window, flutters against a dingy pane where sunlight
filters in through old sheer curtains that belonged to the
dead woman who once owned this rented house. The
curtains, this dusty stuffed chair that Gabe and my stepson
dragged in from the barn, her pink flowered wallpaper,
the rickety stand that holds my cup, and the picture of
Christ that I discovered on a shelf at the back of the closet
next to the family bible left behind by a niece or daughter-
in-law in a hurry to be gone, are all remnants of some old
woman I never saw.

That first foggy night when we arrived finally and
settled in, I carried the picture with its gold-and-black
border to the sink in the bathroom and sponged it off,
then hung it again on the small nail that had been driven
into the pink wallpaper over her bed. So now, above my
right shoulder, his woolly flock grazing in the lush grass

below, Christ sits perched on a rock ringed with small blue and larger pink flowers that, like Christ, gaze upward into the evening sky where his father sits in less humble majesty, presumably gazing downward. All around are purple and blue mountains enclosing a lake, probably Kinneret, where, equipped with a rig for hauling in those heavy nets filled with gasping and desperate fish, a boat is being rowed shoreward after the day's long labor. The sun has set already behind the mountains, but its rays light up a couple of clouds shaped vaguely like angels that float in the upper left-hand corner of the picture.

In the middle of it all, bigger than the boat, bigger even than the mountains across the lake, sits Christ on his granite boulder. The pink of the clouds kindles his fervid face and catches in the folds of his robe, its hue nearly as bright as the flowers at his feet. He sits in profile, his hair falling lightly over his shoulders, and his beard juts strangely outward from his chin as if drawn upward like the tide by the moon that must soon be rising. His hands, folded tidily like a good boy's on his knee, are large and strong-looking as if capable of much hard work, a carpenter's hands clearly or even those of a fisherman, but the features of Christ's face are delicate, wistful, not made for suffering. His hairline, at thirty-three, begins to recede; the forehead, so broad and fine, with its glowing skin drawn so lightly across the skull beneath, is ill-suited for thorns. Below his moustache, Christ's lips, pinked in by the artist, are pursed; perhaps he's whistling to himself, to his sheep, to his father. But he's all waiting, all patience, quietly certain as he gazes upward and, behind his back, the evening star rises.

The old lady in her pink room, all alone here in this

musty falling-down house, was probably reassured by his company, even rejoiced in his certainty, and surely loved the soft whistling. It's all very sweet—that's why I dug it out, sponged it off, and hung it back in its place—and the wild roses by his sandals are like those you see with their glossy green leaves on birthday cakes in bakery windows, but this won't do, of course. This Christ is the holy card Christ and he's fine for old women at night all alone in their houses; he lulls them to sleep over and over until finally one night they die, either gasping and flopping about like fish or just blinking out like the light on the nightstand or stars in the morning, but that's not what I want.

This morning, when Gabe and the children left for the ocean, I stayed behind to think about starting out again, constructing a different self from my own design, not living out the remainder of this old one I was randomly stuck with, that points me, quite unwilling sometimes, like the needle of a compass, toward people and lives I might better flee. Birth plunks us down so haphazardly alongside particular people, themselves randomly assembled, and much that we find beautiful, that tugs us, that we love, seems determined by chance; the line of a forehead etches itself into our hearts, the timbre of a voice heard long before we knew words gets buried deep and waits until one day, turning a corner maybe or sitting by an open window with our minds on sunlight or on laundry, suddenly the casual movement of an arm, a hand open and held just so, an intent look, or a single phrase uttered, a glimpse of another's heart, catches at us, stirs us, and it begins.

I loved one man so terribly and for so many years, not

only because he loved poets, but probably as well because his eyes were the same blue as my father's and, like my father, his voice was rich and deep and he smoked Camels and, walking the night streets beside me, he whistled softly under his breath. And once not long ago in the middle of a night when I'd had too much to drink and had been crying again because my brother is dead and gone for good, not at all like blue-eyed Christ with his promise to come round again, I called across the whole sleeping country to a city by that other ocean where this man with his eyes like my father's lives alone, and the phone rang but no one answered.

In the morning I wondered what it is that I need to tell him and what I think he might say to me. When he left so long ago, I soon married someone I should never have gone near mostly because he wasn't at all like him; I thought he could never scald me the way that leaving had, that he could never matter to me in the same way, and I was right, but, of course, I paid for it.

A friend explained once that it's all right, it's not really so random. She told me that each time, before we are born, our souls drift loose in the universe until we are drawn down into flesh by the particular tumult of our parents' coupling, that the matter of it, their agenda, corresponds to our own, that we belong there beside them. It's a lovely notion, so comforting in the order, the rhyme and reason, it holds out, but I wasn't convinced. It seems to me an effort after the fact to account for our having been drawn helter-skelter into the fracas of our parents' lives long before we had any say in the matter, and this morning it seems to me that it's just that din from those lives in my head that I've got to get rid of.

Particles of them are still inside there, yammering, demanding, insistent, like crazy flocks of herring gulls that flutter and whirl about, then settle, confetti-like, all over my brain until it's awash in their clamor. So I try to raise my voice, shout above it, to tell myself the story over and again so that I can hope to learn my self, how I ever came to be this particular woman with a son, a second husband now and three stepchildren, a few close friends, and all these dead people who trail clattering after me, this string of tin cans tied to a dog's tail.

For so long, I've wanted to extricate my self and my soul from all that refuse, those pieces of wreckage from my father's life and my mother's and brother's, that drift, a real hazard, across the deep in the dark. Day after day, I've tried to sort out all that debris, stack it up, order it, reassemble their lives from it so that I might separate all those pieces into me and not-me, but it's hard. You're our own flesh and blood, they murmur over and over.

Usually, I have so little to go on; like Mother Hubbard, my inventory is sparse. I've loved maybe three men. My hair has lots of grey in it; my knees creak going up stairs and ache at night after I've climbed hills or crossed the cold granite slabs here at the edge of this land. Though I love dogs, I'm uncomfortable around many people and uneasy often even when I'm alone; I have fears about a lot of things and worry too much about sickness and whether I'll ever amount to someone.

But now, this bright afternoon after my dusty morning, I understand for a moment that it's all happened again, that I've given birth too and that I've somehow nourished this child who smiles across the granite to see me climbing out here to watch with him for a whale. Grown tall, long-legged and lovely, he's like a young heron; tender-hearted, he croons to wounded gulls and feeds them bits of the lunch I've put together and carried out for him.

Then here at the edge of the incoming Fundy tide along these barnacled tops of granite boulders, I watch as he kneels in the wet and the chill and builds empires out of grey feathers, wrack, dead man's fingers, broad sleek coils of kelp, tiny limpets, abandoned periwinkles, anything he can gather, the cracked salty armor of a red horseshoe crab that, like Agamemnon the king with his carved stone lions, he sets carefully in place above the outermost gate of his doomed city. He builds even with these angry bits of lobster claw that I hold out to him, with blue gleaming mussel shells that have washed up, caught in the shreds of old rotting nets. His palaces he crowns with turrets, spiky, smelly old shells of sea urchins, she-urchins, that long ago the gulls dropped down to break open to get at the meat.

I watch closely to see how he does it, heaping up, uncoiling, balancing, arranging, as, heedless in all this deep sunlight of waves breaking at the outposts of his kingdom, my own flesh and blood, eager, absorbed in his work, he hums to himself. Often, during those long winter nights when he still swam, my young dolphin, inside me, I awoke, laughing, to be rocked in the dark by all his glad tumult.

There's a witch in the bathtub with a Band-Aid
on one breast and the wind rattles the windows
and way in the back someone dead says yes.
A tricky trollop hisses yes between kisses and
swan-feathers fly and the blood rushes and
the bullrushes assent and dive high in the air
and never come down. oh no.

Tish O'Dowd Ezekiel earned her B.A. and M.A. at the University of Michigan, where she is currently working on a doctoral dissertation on Charles Dickens as well as writing her second novel.

She and her husband, a social psychologist at the University of Michigan, have between them a wonderful daughter, three fine sons, a marvelous daughter-in-law, a number of lovely friends, an extravagantly vocal and self-dramatizing young Newfoundland, an incorrigible Scottie, and two petulant calico cats.

Floaters has been awarded two Avery Hopwood Awards in Creative Writing, two Roy W. Cowden Memorial Fellowships, and the Karl Litzenberg Award in Creative Writing.